MOONBLIND

LINDA CHANDLER MUNSON

LONGSTREET PRESS
Atlanta, Georgia

For all the women
in my life whom
I have loved

Published by LONGSTREET PRESS, INC.
A subsidiary of Cox Newspapers, Inc.
2140 Newmarket Parkway
Suite 118
Marietta, Georgia 30067

Printed in the United States of America

1st printing, 1992

Library of Congress Catalog Number 92-71786

ISBN: 1-56352-045-1

"From an Old House in America," by Adrienne Rich, was originally
published in *Poems: Selected and New, 1950-1974*, by W. W. Norton
& Company, Inc. and is reprinted here by permission.

This book was printed by R. R. Donnelley & Sons, Harrisonburg, Virginia. The text was set in Sabon.

Book design by Jill Dible.
Jacket design by Tonya Beach.

from "From an Old House in America"

If I dream of you these days
I know my dreams are mine and not of you

Yet something hangs between us
older and stranger than ourselves

like a translucent curtain, a sheet of water
a dusty window

the irreducible, incomplete connection
between the dead and living

or between man and woman in this
savagely fathered and unmothered world

—Adrienne Rich,
from *Poems: Selected and New, 1950-1974* (1975)

PROLOGUE

I fill endless pages, mother, with this writing, letters to the dead, hoping to find you. As if, somehow, in these seeking scrawls, the truth lies. Gazing back through time, I think I know now how limited the eye, how curved the vision in those mountains that you called home, the sight stopped in every direction and turned back on itself, there was an old woman who lived in a shoe. *And I know that you won't reveal yourself willingly or easily, but must be coaxed forth with signs and symbols and magic words, like a sorcerer's summons to a spirit. So under the light of a blood-bloated moon, I cast old bones, rake up buried memories, revive forgotten vows, recall broken promises, knowing I speak only haltingly in this strangely familiar tongue . . .*

WINTER EDGE

1934-35

1

She looks like a frog, like a big fat frog squatting on a log,
Annie thought, her mind moving fitful and raw behind
her straining eyes even though her body was stone still.
She was settled deep in a rocking chair in the corner of
Miss Mercer's front room, as she watched the old woman
and her daddy talking. He sat in a mahogany straight
chair, his large, thick frame spilling over the sides, and the
delicately carved chair looked as if it might break under
his weight at any minute. Miss Mercer, encased in a big
upholstered chair covered in bright red roses and blue and
yellow blooms intertwined with green vines, was listening
to him explain something as he leaned across a small
cloth-covered table, his big, motley hands gesturing
earnestly. Suddenly, she looked over and stared at Annie,
who had a frightening thought, close to panic, that the old
woman could tell what she was thinking.

The crowded room was filled with furniture of all
kinds, chairs of every description, tables stacked one on
the other in corners, a huge scarred wardrobe that almost
reached the ceiling and blocked a window, the side wall
half covered with books stacked on the floor.

Yesterday, when Annie's daddy had suggested that this
time Annie should come with him to Miss Mercer's house,
her momma had protested, saying, as she always did, that

the old woman was evil and that people who dealt with her would come to no good, but her momma, hugely pregnant, with her ankles water swollen and a constant pain shooting through her breastbone, was too sick to argue with him. Besides, regardless of what she wanted, her momma complained, he would do as he pleased anyway, so Annie might as well go ahead and go.

Her daddy had said that the old woman could help Annie's weak eyes. Annie was far-sighted, and with her large light blue eyes and dilated irises, she often seemed to be staring intently even when she wasn't. Her schoolteacher said that she needed glasses to read and was trying to get her a pair from some state organization, but her daddy didn't want to take charity from anybody, let alone the government, and said that Miss Mercer could help her.

As they walked to Miss Mercer's, the evening had turned cool and a light rain began falling. Annie had to trot to stay a step behind her daddy's hurried gait. He seemed preoccupied, striding with his head down and his arms swinging forcefully at his sides. At such a pace it didn't take long for them to cover the mile to Miss Mercer's house, and the last thing Annie saw from the front porch of Miss Mercer's when she glanced back over her shoulder was the sun dropping behind the mountains, the bluish lavender sky filling with a final explosion of orange light and the shadow of the moon already out.

Annie, for her part, had been both scared and excited at the prospect of seeing the old woman up close and visiting the dark house. Even though she regularly passed Miss Mercer's house with the other students who walked the two miles to school in the small mountain town, Annie had never seen her up close before. And, once in the house, Annie wasn't surprised to see that she was just as ugly as they all had imagined her, but Annie was surprised at how Miss Mercer was dressed in a dark silky-looking dress that draped over her squatty body with a tatted white-lace collar surrounding her nonexistent neck, and also surprised by the house filled with piles of fancy furniture and colorful rugs. Annie didn't know anyone who had rugs, or even much furniture, or who dressed up like that unless they were going to church.

The outside of Miss Mercer's house wasn't much different from Annie's own, one of ten four-room dogtrot shacks, each set on ten acres of land that used to be one farm before it was auctioned off in parcels. The only noticeable difference was that Miss Mercer's house had the front porch screened in, and she had grass instead of just dirt in the yard.

Annie's friends joked about Miss Mercer being a witch, and skittering like a flock of frightened birds, they would cross to the opposite side of the road to go past the house. Ruthie Lynn, Annie's best friend, who was kind of cowardly and who would invariably joke around when she was the most frightened, always swore that she could see Miss Mercer on the porch watching them from behind the close-wired screen or peeking out from between the heavy curtains that were always drawn over the dark windows, and she would dare the younger kids to wave to her or to make a face, *I double-dog dare you,* she would say, tossing her frizzy red hair like she'd do it herself but was giving them the chance to prove they would.

Everybody Annie knew gave something to the old woman—milk, meat, eggs—even those who didn't go to visit her for card readings and such. Annie's daddy went to the strange house every full moon and sent two chickens each week, freshly killed and cleaned. Her oldest brother, Neal, who hated the chore, used to have to take the birds over until the baby, Robbie, got old enough to do it.

Annie figured that Robbie liked to go because he didn't know any better. Born in a caul, the membrane wrapped like gauze around his large head, he had never been right in the mind, and even now, at four, he wasn't much more than a baby. Smiling his sloppy loose-mouthed grin, Robbie would take the chickens to the back door, wrapped in newspaper and still dripping, while Annie stood at the edge of the yard and waited for him. He never went inside, but he always came back with a trinket, a brightly colored bead or a small animal carved out of bone. Annie had warned him over and over against playing with anything the old woman gave him, but he wouldn't listen and had all the gifts stored in a box that he kept under his bed. In the afternoon he would take the box out and arrange the animals on the front-room floor, playing in the weak sunlight that fell through the window, moving the figures around in the dappled spots on the bleached boards.

Annie had asked him several times what the old woman looked like up close or if he could see inside the house, but he just shook his ungainly head, his eyes wandering off in different directions and said, "I dunno."

Now she sat inside the house, waiting, motionless in the rocker, the front room growing dim except for a cold circle of light cast by a milk-glass lantern sitting in the middle of the table. Her daddy and the old woman were huddled together, their heads almost touching, and Miss Mercer holding his hands, kneading and stroking them, occasionally taking her eyes away from her close inspection to look up at his face. Even though in the faint light Annie couldn't see her daddy's face, she knew the way it always looked lately, the muscles tight around his black eyes like he was struggling with disturbing thoughts too strong to dismiss.

Annie unconsciously squeezed her own hand as she watched the old woman talk to him. She couldn't make out exactly what she was saying, something about the potatoes maybe, and she guessed they were talking about the farm. Annie knew it wasn't doing well and that there never seemed to be enough money. Her daddy talked constantly about money, always money, each night at supper recounting the names of those who had been forced to sell out, or who had to go do public work to survive, telling every new loss he heard of, as he looked around sharply to see if they were wasting food, *what's wrong with the meat on that bone, girl, you too good to gnaw a bone?*

Not that they ever went hungry. Between the boys and

her daddy, they kept the kitchen and smokehouse filled with deer, possum, coon, rabbit, and the hogs that they marked by notching their ears before turning them out on the mountainside to range. But her daddy wanted property, always more property, and both Neal and Claude had quit school last year to help out with the crops they raised to sell. Now, the fall crops—collards, cabbage, carrots, onions—were all in the ground, and the hard part of keeping the insects off from July to the beginning of September was almost over as the first frost drew nearer.

Annie wished she could hear what they were saying better, but her daddy was talking in a low, deep rumble while the old woman's voice rose so high and thin that sometimes it simply disappeared into the air like smoke strung out in vapors, and her daddy, who was listening raptly, would cock his head to catch each wisp.

In her shadowy corner, Annie realized that she had been sitting so still that her leg had gone to sleep. She began to squirm in the chair and glanced at the dead fireplace, and, unaccountably, a feeling of dread filled her, and suddenly she wanted nothing more than to leave, and she hoped that her daddy would forget about her eyes, just hurry up so they could leave. Annie shivered in the evening chill growing in corners of the room. Her momma was right. The old woman was evil. Annie could smell it in the oppressive air of the house, an odor that was claustrophobic, almost strangling, as it seeped up her nostrils.

Then, afraid again that somehow the old woman could tell what she was thinking, Annie looked away from the two at the table toward the kitchen where she thought she heard noises, sounds like the weak squealing of newborn puppies or kittens, but it was difficult to see through the door in the gloom.

She was straining, trying to see, when out of the corner of her eye she saw her daddy look toward her, then turn back to the old woman and say something in a low voice, and the old woman looked over at her too, then answered him, seemed irritated, threw up her hands, and leaned back in her chair.

Annie stiffened, a sense of apprehension again filling her. She thought that now they were going to say something to her, but her daddy sat slumped over in his chair, staring at his hands, and the old woman, ignoring him, struck a match, lit a short, crumpled, rolled cigarette, and thoughtfully smoked on it, holding it like a man, lightly between her thumb and finger.

The silence was broken only by muted animal noises from the kitchen and the ticking of a big brass clock hanging over the mantel. Both her daddy and Miss Mercer seemed to have forgotten about her, and Annie felt her stomach unknotting and her pulse slowing, and in a while, when nothing more happened, she even began to feel pleased with herself again, glad that she had come to see the old woman and could now tell all her friends about Miss Mercer's froggy looks, strange ways, and cluttered house.

The more Annie thought about it, the more she couldn't wait to tell Ruthie Lynn how she had been to visit the "witch," picturing Ruthie Lynn's eager eyes growing wide, the slightly crossed one wandering closer to her nose, her freckle-splotched face glowing with excitement and her wild, frizzy red hair springing out even wilder as Annie embroidered the story. Annie could hear her now, saying, *Oooooooooh, Lordy, Lordy, Lordy!*—her favorite expression.

Then Annie's daddy said something to Miss Mercer, who nodded. He stood up and headed for the door. Alarmed, Annie jumped up and started after him.

He motioned to her. "Stay here. I'm gonna cut Miss Mercer some wood and start a fire."

Annie didn't want to stay in the house with the weird old woman, yet she couldn't disobey him, so she sat back down in the rocker, but this time she perched on the edge, flinching at the first sound of the ax, sharp as gunfire, that invaded the room through the door he had left cracked.

Sitting there alone with Miss Mercer, Annie was aware that the good feeling she had had about getting to see the old woman now drained from her, and the more she thought about it, the more she didn't really understand why she had been made to come at all. Nothing had been done to her eyes. The old woman hadn't even spoken to her. She wanted to go home, to get away from the peculiar stifling atmosphere of this strange house. Feeling the numbing cold air coming through the door sucking the color from her cheeks, Annie wrapped her arms across her chest and leaned back, making herself as small as she could. Deep into these thoughts, she didn't realize at first that Miss Mercer had called her name.

Annie stood up, hesitated, a light pounding at the base of her skull like the small, erratic throb of a frightened bird in your hand. She smoothed the skirt on her clean smock, her hands needing something to do, and then she slowly approached the old woman, whose huge wet eyes staring out of her flat face seemed to be underwater, constantly and slowly blinking.

"Yes ma'am?" Annie stopped short of the brilliantly designed rug under the table and chairs.

"Come 'ere. Come closer."

Annie took another step forward. A small step.

The old woman gave off a curious odor, a smell like deep woods, damp pines. She reached over to the table, picked up a wooden box with a large, slanted eye carved into its top, and took off the lid. Inside, there were lots of packets made out of folded white paper.

"Here." She held out a packet. "This is for your momma. She's almost ready, ain't she?"

Annie, a sensation close to fear tumbling about her heart, didn't answer.

"Well? Has she showed yet?" The old woman peered wide-eyed into Annie's face. "Speak! Has the cat got your tongue?"

Annie remembered how just yesterday her momma had pointed to a glob of blood-smeared mucus on a rag, called it a "bloody show." She said that Annie needed to know these things, that she was almost grown, said that soon now the labor would start. Annie had felt a little sick at the sight, but she knew she would have to help with the birth, and her momma had not been well since Robbie was born.

She nodded.

"She's gonna have a rough time. She's old, shouldn't even be having any babies, and this one's coming early. Your daddy said he ain't gonna use the granny woman this time. Not after that last one."

Miss Mercer thrust the packet at Annie again. "You give her this, three teaspoons when the pain gets bad. It'll relieve her. Put it in a glass of milk."

Then she pulled the packet back. "Here, I'll write it down. You *can* read, can't you?" She scrawled something on it. "And don't forget to put an ax under the bed. That'll cut the pain."

Annie nodded again and took the packet. She tried to look at what the old woman had written, but she couldn't read it that close up. The letters were just a series of feathery lines.

"You hold on to it now. Don't you tell nobody you got it, including your momma. You know, she might not want to take it. Maybe she'll think it'll hurt the baby. But it won't. So you wait. When the pain gets her, then you make her take it. You understand?"

Annie, still speechless, nodded a third time.

The old woman looked at her for a moment with a kindly expression, almost like she felt sorry for Annie, and then said, "Don't forget to clean out the baby's nose and mouth. Use your finger. Them early ones are filled with mucus. They can't breath."

Annie slipped the packet into the pocket of her smock. "Yes, ma'am, thank you."

"Hand me that deck of cards on the mantel." Miss Mercer gestured in the direction of the fireplace with one surprisingly long finger, the knuckle bent like a gnarled tree knot.

Annie walked behind the chair. The mantel was covered with all kinds of items—small statues, beads, something that looked like dried grass in large Mason jars, and smaller jars filled with different liquids and shavings.

"That's grave grass in the big jars. In the little ones, there's dried castor bean, snakeroot, Christmas rose, cat gall. You know anything about cures?"

Annie jumped at the close sound of the old woman's voice. It sounded like it was right behind her ear, but when she looked around, Miss Mercer was still in the chair, the side of her iron-gray head barely visible behind the wing of the chair.

"No ma'am," Annie said, trepidation making her voice shake. She got the deck and walked back around to the front of the chair. Standing as far away as she could, she held out the cards, and without warning, the old woman reached out, grabbed her hand in a strong grip, and pulled her next to the chair. Annie's heart, already quivering against her ribs, leaped into her throat.

The old woman smiled. The smile reminded Annie of a fish's gaped mouth when it's out of water, lying on the bank, and looking surprised at the sharpness of the sun. She let go of Annie's hand, took the deck, shuffled it, and held the cards out. "Here, girl. Pick one."

Obediently, Annie pulled a card from the deck. The old woman took the card and studied it for a moment. Annie wanted to step back, but she was too frightened to move, and before she could get up the courage, Miss Mercer grasped her hand and flipped it over. At her touch, Annie looked desperately toward the door, willing her daddy to come back in, but he didn't.

"Le Luna," the old woman whispered, nodding her head knowingly, tapping her finger on the mound across from Annie's thumb. Annie, who thought she might cry at any moment, felt a burning, tingling sensation in her palm that shot from her hand up her arm. She didn't understand what the old woman was saying. She wanted to pull away but didn't dare, felt her eyes trembling like her hands, and unconsciously bit the inside of her lip.

Miss Mercer, who seemed unaware of Annie's distress, drew her even closer, so close that Annie could see the network of spidery veins, red and blue, cutting through her bulbous brown eyes, and repeated, "The moon, girl, you got the mark of the moon, the sign of the crab that crawls from the sea."

If the old woman was going to say more, she didn't. As Annie's daddy came in with a stack of wood, she released Annie's hand. Annie retreated back to the rocking chair while her daddy built a fire. She sat perfectly still again, but now she felt even more strange, her body light as if it were filled with nothing but air.

By the time they left, Miss Mercer, with the fire blazing behind her, was snoring in her chair, her head tilted back to reveal two cavernous nostrils filled with hair.

Outside, the rain had stopped, and Annie, sucking on the salty blood from her lip, looked up at the moon, full in its autumn equinox, poised like a giant unblinking eye in the purple sky, precisely dividing the revealing light of day from the obscuring veil of night.

2

For two weeks Annie stayed out of school, afraid that five miles was too far from home to get back home in time. She hung around the house, waiting, trying to help her momma who got increasingly irritable as, bulky and shapeless under a flour-sack dress, she lumbered around the house cooking, making beds, and sweeping.

In the evening, because of the autumn chill that gathered in the house after the usual afternoon shower, her momma would pull on a sweater, and she never took it off until she got undressed for bed, not even after the stove had warmed up the kitchen, and the heat brought out bright red spots on her cheeks as she worked over the flames. Annie noticed that despite the flush in her momma's face, the rest of her skin looked cold, clammy and gray, and across her forehead, lines formed a dingy network of worry.

Her momma was forty, and this was her eighth baby, only four still living—Neal seventeen, Claude fifteen, Annie thirteen, and Robbie four. The rest were stillborn and their bodies burned out behind the house by her daddy, who said he couldn't afford to spend money on grave plots. After all, he said, dead is dead.

It was Friday night, cold weather on the way, and the air was crisp and tangy and laced with the smell of pine and smoke as Annie stood at the kitchen sink under the window. Like her momma, she was tired out with waiting and expectation. She studied the blue outline of the mountains etched sharp against a plum-colored sky as she washed up the dishes after supper until her thoughts strayed to Ruthie Lynn and what had probably been happening in school since she had been out. She was curious about a new student. He was older, almost nineteen years old, she had heard. Miss Paine introduced him as J.C. She said that he would be coming to class to learn while he built a new school, a bigger one, and that he was living in a tent out behind the school. Annie and Ruthie Lynn were too shy to ask him about where he was from or why he was still in school, being so old and all.

At recess, Ruthie Lynn had a giggling fit when he spoke to them as they walked by where he was sitting under a tree studying a book. *He's sooo good-looking, ain't he?* she had whispered to Annie. And Annie agreed, he surely was. During class, she couldn't help staring a little, noticing his dark blond hair that was combed so neat like he had just wet it, slicked it down, and pulled it back in a little ponytail, and his skin was light brown like he was in the sun a lot or maybe he had some Indian in him. She wondered if Ruthie Lynn had got up the nerve to talk to him.

Annie finished drying the dishes and hung the dishrag on the drainboard. She walked to the kitchen door to look into the front room where her momma, who hadn't come to supper and who was even more fretful than usual, lay on the couch, her hand tentatively probing at her taut belly, the nagging pains coming and going as they had for the last two weeks. All evening her momma had been on the couch, holding tobacco leaves under her nose, making herself sneeze, trying to start the labor. Her water had broken earlier that day, and she had mumbled something about a "dry birth." Then, seeing Annie's confused look, she had explained that the water helped slide the baby out. Now there would be none. Annie, looking at her now, remembered her momma's sharp words earlier when she had asked her to try to eat some supper.

Robbie was whining, standing by the couch. His nose was running from a cold, and his round, vacant baby eyes were distressed and miserable. Annie knew what he wanted. He wanted to nurse. He had still been nursing when her momma got pregnant, and for a long time he would beg, not understanding that the milk had dried up. Frustrated, his momma would finally sit down and hold him in her lap, letting him lean against her stomach and knead her doughy breasts with one chubby hand while he sucked the thumb on the other hand. Claude made fun of him, but Annie always felt sorry for Robbie, the way his little hand would clutch at her mother. Then, about a month ago, Robbie had finally quit asking. Now he had started again.

Her momma called out for Annie to get Robbie away, to do something with him. Annie got out his toys and stones and took him back to the kitchen. She sat him on the floor next to the table and began helping him to arrange them. He calmed down and began to sing some nonsensical song to the playthings.

Annie stood up and moved restlessly around the room. The kitchen was still warm from the heat of the stove, and the radio was playing "Blue Moon." The song sounded kind of draggy like the batteries were running down. Wanting to get her mind off her momma, off the labor, everything seeming a trouble to her mind, she decided to do some of her schoolwork.

She had been studying since the beginning of the school year to be in the state spelling bee. Though she had to work harder than the other students since she had trouble reading the texts, Annie was a good student, and she could spell better than anyone in the school. She had won the local competition last year for the seventh grade and knew that she could win again, maybe go all the way to the state competition this time.

As she held the tablet out at arm's length to see the words her teacher had printed in big, bold letters from the practice book given out by the National Spelling Bee Center, she thought briefly of Miss Mercer and wondered why her daddy hadn't asked the old woman about her eyes. He probably forgot, the way he seemed concerned with something else, like maybe they were disagreeing about something, and, anyway, Annie didn't want to ask him about it.

Annie was unconscious of time passing as she pronounced out loud and memorized words like *vacuum* and *Czechoslovakia*, and almost an hour had elapsed when she heard her momma call out again.

Annie went into the front room. "It's time," her momma said, pushing herself awkwardly up from the couch. Annie helped her up. "Tell your daddy. Then come in the bedroom."

Annie felt her blood quicken, kind of like the feeling she got when a storm was brewing in the mountains, a tingling in her blood. She went down the hall and out the front door to the porch where, despite the chilled evening air, her daddy and brothers had been sitting since supper. Her daddy and Claude were on the steps, both smoking cigarettes, and Neal was leaning back in the swing, staring out over the porch railing even though he couldn't see through the dark more than a few feet.

Robbie, a worried frown across his slack flat face, followed Annie out and stood next to her, holding onto her dress. At the sound of the door, Claude looked up at her, a strand of dark hair hanging long and lank over one of his eyes, and her daddy, who was talking to him, quit in mid-sentence.

Annie, avoiding Claude's eyes, spoke to her daddy. "The baby's coming," she blurted.

Her daddy stood up, stared at her for a moment, like maybe he didn't believe her, that she was mistaken.

"Momma's having the baby—" she repeated, her voice surprising her with its thin edge of anxiety, and Robbie, hearing it, begin to snivel and pull on her dress. She pushed his hand away, waiting for her daddy to say something, her mind pleading *call the granny woman, let her help Momma, go get her, please, get the granny woman* even though she didn't dare say it.

Robbie kept on pulling at her dress and calling her name. Without thinking, still staring at her daddy and waiting for him to say something, Annie slapped at his chubby hand. Surprised, he started crying in earnest, a pitiful blubbering sound, as he rubbed his hand.

Neal called Robbie over to the swing, and, grateful for the attention, Robbie scuffled over the porch boards and climbed up next to him, holding out a small carved snake for him to see. "Miss Mercer gave me," he said, sniffing the snot that had leaked down to his lip back up his nose. Neal took out a handkerchief and wiped his nose.

As Annie's daddy watched Robbie, he looked almost embarrassed. Then a distant look came over his face, his eyes becoming dense and clouded, his mind somewhere else, somewhere away from here, from them. He abruptly turned to Annie. "You know what to do," he said, and walked off toward the shed.

Claude smirked. "I guess the old man's not too happy about getting another idiot to feed." He looked at Robbie, who started to cry again and drew closer to Neal.

Annie glared at Claude. She hated him, hated his voice, husky, thick, tinged with something that reminded her of the sound of animals being slaughtered, but she knew not to say anything in reply. She had felt the back of his hand across her face several times until she had learned to avoid him and, when she couldn't keep away from him, not to cross him.

She glanced at Neal. He never stood up to Claude even though Claude was younger. Claude was his daddy's favorite, and too many times the stocky, blunt Claude had taunted or beaten Neal up just because he couldn't stand having a brother, he said, who acted like he "squatted to piss." Now Annie could tell by the way that Neal kept fidgeting, putting his hand, the skin soft and white wherever farm work had not created callouses, the fragile nails bruised and covered with white spots, up to his face, pushing at his fine blond hair, fiddling with his ears, like his fingers couldn't be still, that he just wanted her to go away, to not be bothered with anything.

Annie, angry at all of them, started to slam the door as she went back in, but thought of her momma and shut it softly. She decided to close the wood door also to keep out the chill, and her eyes were drawn to the sky where the hunter's moon had come out from behind the clouds, a new quarter moon, yellow as a cat's eye and tilted ominously on its end. *The moon, girl, you got the mark of the moon, Miss Mercer had said.*

In the bedroom, two oil lamps on the dresser threw deformed shadows on the walls, and the one small window was wet from the cold air outside. Her momma had changed into a nightgown and had propped herself up in the bed on pillows.

She looked gray to Annie, her whole face the color of ashes, and her eyes were scorched looking and bulging, like there was pressure behind them. She was trying to put a shawl on, and Annie went over and pulled it around for her, straightening it over her back so that it was smooth behind her shoulders.

"What did he say?" her momma asked between pains.

Annie, holding back the tears that threatened to erupt at any minute, felt the room breaking into pieces, everything split and webbed, held together by thin, breakable threads. "Nothing," she answered. She thought she saw a brief shadow pass over her momma's face, a quick darkening in her eyes.

"It figures. Go boil some water and put a knife in it. Get towels and rags too. And—" Her momma's voice, breathless, broke as she clutched the covers on each side.

Annie stood rooted to the spot, frightened by the way her momma looked, her face a mask of concentration.

"—go on, Annie, do what I say," she said as soon as she could talk, her voice even hoarser than before. "It looks worse than it is."

Annie went across the hall and into the kitchen and put the kettle on. She found rags and towels in the pantry and carried them back to the bedroom. Then she went back again to the kitchen when she heard the kettle boiling and poured the water in a basin, putting in a knife. She remembered how she had seen dogs, after birthing, chew the cord in two and tried to convince herself that this shouldn't be any different than that.

Nothing much happened for the next half-hour, just her momma bending forward and shoving, then leaning back, breathing heavily, her eyes mostly closed.

Annie asked several times, "What do I do, Momma?" but her momma just shook her head before leaning up again, holding onto her stomach.

Annie jumped when she motioned to the foot of the bed. "Cover the bed with some of them rags."

Making a double layer of cloth over the quilt, a multi-colored star-of-Texas design that she had helped sew on for over a year before it was done, Annie arranged a cover over the bottom half of the bed.

Then out in the kitchen, Annie was trying to decide if she should take the basin back to the room with the knife in the water, or if it was okay to take the knife out now, when she remembered the packet the old woman had given her. She went into the other bedroom where she slept, separated from her brothers by a curtain made from a sheet hanging over a string, and reached under her mattress for the folded pouch.

She went back to the bedroom to check on her momma and found her leaning back, collapsed against the headboard. Despite the chill in the room that transformed her breath into a small fog in the air, the sweat on her face gave it a ghostly sheen.

"They stopped," her momma gasped.

Annie didn't know what that meant, didn't know if she should do something, maybe try to get her daddy. She moved around to the side of the bed. Her momma was quiet now, her face limp and her closed eyelids quivering slightly. Annie touched her hand, lying open and flaccid, on the quilt. She seemed almost asleep.

"Momma?"

Her momma's eyelids opened slowly, like they were stuck, and Annie could see where small veins had broken in her eyes, threading them with lines of blood.

"It's all right. Get the stuff ready," she said. "It'll start again."

It was thirty minutes before she pulled upright again, grabbing her knees and straining weakly. Annie stood at the foot of the bed, feeling helpless. Then she remembered the medicine.

In the kitchen, Annie tried to read the directions on the packet but finally gave up. Uncertain what to do, she took the packet and the basin with the knife into the bedroom.

She was balancing the basin, trying not to spill water on herself, when she saw Claude was standing in the bedroom doorway, looking in. Annie clenched her lips and pushed past, glancing sideways at his murky-colored face. He had a strange intense look in his eyes. As she sat the basin down on the dresser, he said, "I come to see if you need anything."

Annie ignored him and put herself between him and her momma, who was straining loudly, oblivious to them or her surroundings. She had pulled her gown up around her waist and bent her knees, pulling them up and spreading them wide apart. Annie had not thought about seeing her in such an intimate way, and she flushed. Her momma continued to make loud grunting noises interspersed with long moans of exertion as she pulled on her knees.

Annie watched where she knew the baby would come out. The flesh was swollen, a large bulge getting bigger and bigger as the ring of tight membrane parted and stretched. Annie felt a weak wave of nausea moving deep in the pit of her stomach. She felt a rush of panic as she saw a thin, jagged white line appear, cutting through the ring in the center of the melon-shaped mount, and it was the sharp line that reminded her of the knife and then the medicine, and then Claude still standing behind her. She turned around, keeping her body between her momma and Claude so that he couldn't see her. She glared at him. "You know Momma doesn't want you here. Go away."

"I just come to see if you need any help." He kept trying to see past her.

Annie heard her momma's moans get louder. She wanted to turn back to her, but she wanted to make Claude leave.

She was scared of Claude, had been scared of him since last June when he had made her go with him under the porch of the house, where he had taken off her panties, messed with her, and then told her he would "get" her if she told Momma about it. She could still smell the dirt, damp and warm, that he had made her lie down in, and the thick, sweetish air trapped under the porch, making it hard to breathe, and the way he had pinched her nipples so hard that the next day they were swollen and bruised, and how he had put his hand over her mouth when she had started crying, and how he had put his finger somewhere inside her, somewhere deep and tender, and when he had finally let her go, she had felt the dirt everywhere, in her hair, on her back, between her legs and even way up inside her. Wanting to wash, she had run down to the creek. Despite the gathering dark, she had run as fast as she could, pulling at her clothes, so that by the time she got there, she was half undressed, and ripping the rest off, she ran out into the water, crying, rage filling her small heart with such a force that she held onto her chest as if she were holding it together, then, chin high, she floated out into the creek, her heated blood seeking the chill of the water, letting the anger and terror dissolve to what was now a vague sullied fear that continually haunted her like a forbidden thought hidden away in her mind. And, despite Claude's warning, she had told. She told her momma, and Annie didn't know what she had done, but it hadn't happened again, even though Annie would catch Claude sneering at her when no one was looking, like he was waiting for something, maybe a chance to get back at her.

She remembered the medicine again. "Here, can you read this packet for me? How much do I need to give Momma?"

Claude studied the packet a moment, his face becoming sly and closed. "Three tablespoons. Three tablespoons in some milk."

That didn't sound right to Annie. "Are you sure? I thought Miss Mercer said teaspoons."

Claude, irritated, shoved the packet back at her. "Three tablespoons. That's what it says. I'll go get some milk."

Annie turned back to her momma and arranged a sheet over her legs. When Claude got back with the milk, she took the glass, hesitated just a moment, thinking again, *three teaspoons i'm sure she said three teaspoons,* but her mother groaned again and Claude said, "What're you waiting for? Give it to her."

Annie mixed in the castor bean and held the glass for her mother, who still seemed to be unaware of what was going on, and she drank the milk down without a word.

"Where's Daddy?" Annie moved back to the foot of the bed, groping for some way to get him to leave.

"Gone. Down to Beech Bottom to see that nigger woman, Lacey. Neal took the idiot out to the barn." She flinched, and Claude grinned.

Her momma's voice, "Annie," almost inaudible, came to her ear, and she looked over her shoulder just in time to see the sheet was kicked off and the thin white line was splitting apart as the baby's head pushed out.

Annie rushed over and instinctively put her hand under the head. The small face pressed into her palm, and before she could think what to do, the head turned sideways as the shoulder slipped out, and then with another push from her momma, who was almost curled double as she held onto her knees and labored, the rest of the body slid smoothly from the opening in a stream of blood and fluid. Annie held a baby in her hands. Her momma collapsed back against the headboard.

The baby girl, still connected by a long thick rope of coiled, rubbery membrane, was a pale blue color and silent. Annie remembered what the Miss Mercer had told her to do. She pushed the tip of her finger in the baby's mouth, ran it around, and pulled out a plug of mucus. The baby reacted, making a small gagging noise, then a weak cry. Annie wrapped her in a towel, put her on the bed and used a rag, twisting the edge into a point, to clean out the baby's nostrils.

Annie was absorbed in what she was doing and had forgotten about Claude when she heard him say, "Christ, just what we need, another split-tail," and he walked out of the room, slamming the door.

Fresh hatred for him shot through her before her attention was drawn back to her momma, who began to stir, leaning up and pressing her stomach with her hands. She looked awful to Annie, faded and old, and her eyes were blurry, filled with water. She whispered, "Pull on the cord."

Annie did, and a gelatin-like mass slipped out onto the bed. "Feed it to the hogs," her momma said. Leaning back, she closed her eyes.

After several attempts with the knife, Annie managed to cut the slippery cord close to the baby's navel. She threw the water out of the basin onto the floor where it drained through the boards and, using her hand wrapped in a rag, she eased the afterbirth into the basin, trying not to look closely at it.

Putting the baby, who was mewing like a kitten, next to her momma in the bed, she went to the kitchen and got another basin of water, brought it back, and cleaned up. The foot of the bed was a mess, but she didn't want to disturb her momma, who was sleeping with her head fallen to one side and her chest moving slowly up and down, so she just took up the dirty rags, put clean ones under her legs and hips.

Getting a blanket from the chest in the corner of the room, Annie covered both of them up. She glanced at the basin holding the afterbirth. She couldn't do it. She just couldn't feed it to the hogs. It was then that she remembered that she had forgotten to put the ax under the bed.

Annie waited in the kitchen until past midnight for her daddy, who finally showed up drunk. He didn't even ask about her momma or the baby. Ignoring her, he grabbed some blankets to sleep in the barn. Annie was too tired by then to care.

The baby woke up only once, making soft weak noises, and Annie fixed a sugar-tit for her to suck, putting sugar and wet bread crusts in a clean cloth and tying it on one end. The baby took it and went right back to sleep. Annie's momma had not stirred since the birth. Her breathing had become loud and raspy, slicing through the cold air of the room, a sound like wind rattling tin.

Annie, lying on the floor at the foot of the bed on a pallet she had made up, jumped straight up as if she had been snatched awake by a giant invisible hand. The long night was filled with wolf howls and owl screeches that penetrated the closed-up room. She had fallen asleep about an hour earlier and had tossed fitfully, dreaming of the afterbirth in the basin. It was dissolving and turning to blood and water, a thick syrupy liquid filled with gnarled roots that looked like old deformed hands.

Disturbed by her dream, the night noises, and her momma's breathing, Annie got up, wrapped one of the blankets around her shoulders, and went to sit by the side of the bed. Her momma came awake and tried to sit up, shaking all over like she had a fever.

"Get me the slop jar." She sounded strangled and covered her mouth with one hand while she held her stomach with the other.

Reaching under the bed, Annie pulled out the jar and held it as her momma bent over, retching, though nothing came up but clear liquid. Annie set the jar down and went to the kitchen to pour some water from the pitcher. Her momma took it and drank it down in one long swallow before she turned to the sleeping baby next to her.

Annie took the glass and tried to smile, but her face felt dead and stiff. "A girl," she said, "kind of puny, but pretty."

Her momma started to say something but was seized with another spasm that made her grab her stomach and bend over, gasping.

And so it went, over and over, the rest of the night and into morning, stomach cramps, vomiting, then falling back to sleep for only a while before the spasms started again.

3

At dawn, Annie dressed and walked through the outside air, it cold and dry and the temperature below freezing, to the barn to look for her daddy. Finding him asleep in a stall, she woke him and told him what was happening, about the cramps, the vomiting, that she didn't think it had anything to do with the baby.

"Momma keeps retching," she said, "and she looks strange. Her face is all wasted and stiff, and after a spasm, her mouth draws back from her teeth, you need to come see. . . ."

Her daddy, wearing the same clothes he had slept in and smelling, to her, like a fish spoilt in the sun, turned away, didn't answer. Instead, he bent over the water pail and splashed his face. Then he rolled a cigarette, carefully filling the thin paper with the tobacco from a pouch he kept in the back pocket of his overalls and licking and sealing the cigarette with his tongue. Annie couldn't help noticing how broad and beefy his face was, fluid-filled from the liquor he drank every night, and how cruel he looked around the lips, deep lines like knife cuts on each side of his mouth. His large reddish hands shook as he rolled the cigarette.

He finally spoke. "Didn't Miss Mercer give you some medicine for her? Did you give her that, like she told you to?" he asked.

"I gave it to her last night, there isn't anymore, Momma needs something now. . . ."

Despite the cold, Annie was sweating from anxiety, and she found it difficult to breathe in the close air of the small, dark barn that had only one small window. It was little more than a shed to keep the two horses in and store tools.

Annie saw a flush come over his face, and he wiped his mouth with the back of his hand, spittle sticking in the black hairs covering the fingers. Then he hesitated and looked sharply at Annie as if he were trying to figure out what lay behind the worried frown on her small tight features, to see what she was thinking.

"She'll be all right. Just leave her alone. She's got to rest," he said, his words measured out like scarce food.

But Annie would not be put off. "No, it's more than that, just come and see her, maybe the milk was tainted, it might be a case of milk-sick, she needs a doctor, maybe the honey and brandy doctor—"

Annie was unprepared for the big square hand that leaped out and slapped her, snapping her head back until her neck cracked. Tears sprang to her eyes.

"Go on! I told you we ain't getting nobody! She'll be all right. I don't want nobody coming around here, messing in my business. Now get on inside and get breakfast going. We got work to do." He looked surprised himself at what he had done, and his hand stayed suspended in midair a moment before he clenched it in a fist and drew it back to his side.

Holding back the sobs collecting in her throat, Annie ran back to the kitchen. Numb and confused, she beat biscuit dough until her arms hurt, then fried salt pork until it was crisp, putting it on a towel to drain. She put grits on the back of the stove to boil. All the time her mind writhed with ominous feelings, thin as pins, eating at it.

Robbie woke up and came in the kitchen, whimpering for his momma. Annie said, "Momma's all right, you can see her after breakfast, get dressed and go get some eggs."

As Annie worked, she could hear her momma, still

throwing up. She went to check on her. She wanted water, more water, her mouth felt like cotton, she said through cracked lips, her voice sounding dry as dust. Annie filled a glass and wet a rag for her to hold to her mouth and took them in to her.

All day and through the night Annie tended her. The next morning, she was no better, so Annie waited until after breakfast, until her daddy and Claude had gone hunting, and Neal was off somewhere. Then she put a sweater on, wrapped her head in a scarf, knotting it under the chin, and she told Robbie to stand right by momma's bed and get her whatever she needed, not to move until she got back.

Robbie, looking wide-eyed at the baby, said, "Okay, right here." Annie checked the baby, showed Robbie how to hold the sugar-tit to her mouth, then left.

It was a mile's walk to Miss Mercer's house. She still had the ominous feelings in the back of her mind, something threatening that she didn't understand, and the sensation had grown and come together since yesterday when it was thin and scattered. Now it was like the flocks of blackbirds she could see forming patterns in the sky, dark configurations, secret winged symbols, black and fleeting against the harsh reddish orange dawn sky shading to pink over the mountains.

She drew her sweater tighter about her in the cold morning air as she knocked on Miss Mercer's door. The old woman came quickly as if she were already up and expecting someone. Annie felt an urge to run at the sight of her, but she had to see her; she had to get help.

"My momma's sick—" she glanced around unable to look the old woman directly in the eyes.

Miss Mercer interrupted her. "Come on in, girl, before you catch your death of cold."

Annie followed her into the house. They went through the front room into the kitchen where the stove was lit, warming the room, and Annie could smell the pot of coffee on the back burner. Miss Mercer sat down at the table in front of a bowl of coffee poured off to cool.

Annie started again. "My momma's sick, real sick, vomiting real bad. Two days now."

Miss Mercer watched her, sipped on the coffee, holding the bowl with both hands. "You got a baby girl, don't you?"

Annie didn't stop to think how Miss Mercer knew but pushed on, urgent. "She's real sick. I need something for her."

Pouring more milk from a pitcher into her bowl of coffee, Miss Mercer didn't say anything for a moment. Then, abruptly, she asked, "Did you give her that medicine I gave you?"

Annie nodded. "It's all gone—"

Miss Mercer squinted at her closely. "Gone? Did you give her three teaspoons?"

Annie thought that she hadn't heard Miss Mercer right at first. She shook her head. "I gave her three tablespoons, Momma's cooking spoons, just what you told me."

Miss Mercer put down her bowl. "No, I said three teaspoons, like I wrote on the package, three teaspoons."

Annie was confused, not sure what it meant, and was stammering about how she couldn't read the package, that Claude had told her it said three tablespoons.

"That was castor bean. A little kills the pain. A lot kills the patient." Miss Mercer shook her head. "You done poisoned your momma, girl."

Annie returned from Miss Mercer's house to find that her momma had finally quit vomiting, but she was lying limp and still. Her lips, flaked white, were drawn back as if she didn't have enough skin to cover her face, and her eyes were glazed over with a milky fluid. She could barely answer when Annie tried to rouse her.

Icy panic flowed along the rim of Annie's nerves. Seeing her momma, she knew it was true—what Miss Mercer had said—that her momma was dying. The awful realization hit her, cutting a pathway between her eyes like the bullets her daddy shot into the heads of hogs, splitting the muscle of her brain in two.

She needed a doctor.

Annie ran, then when she couldn't run anymore, she walked, then ran again, until she reached the doctor's cabin. She tried to tell him what had happened, frantically spilling out words all mixed in with crying.

"The medicine," she kept saying, "Miss Mercer gave it to me, I gave Momma too much, it was too much, please come help, hurry, Momma will die."

The doctor and Annie returned to find her momma prostrate, her breath nothing more than a thin raspy wheeze, and the baby, lying beside her, whined feebly as Robbie patted it and tried to get it to suck on the sugar-tit. The doctor spooned milk and brandy between her momma's lips, but she couldn't swallow and most of it ran down the front of her nightgown.

Annie's daddy and brothers came in around dark. When they saw the doctor there, Neal looked shocked and asked what was wrong. Claude, who didn't seem surprised, said it was Annie, that she was crazy, but her daddy listened calmly, his face unreadable, and Annie told him about her trip to Miss Mercer's house, how Claude had told her the packet said three tablespoons but it was supposed to be only three teaspoons, how too much was poison, how she got the doctor—

Claude's face turned livid, his eyes dense and menacing as deep night. He tried to grab her, blurted out: "I don't know what she's talking about, the little lying—"

Her daddy interrupted him. "Claude, come outside," he said and went out with Claude right behind him. Neal hung around the bedroom door for a few minutes before leaving too. Annie was disgusted with them all.

The doctor came back each day, administered brandy and honey, but it only got worse. When he couldn't get her momma to take anything in her mouth anymore, he ground up peach leaves and put them in a bag and laid the bag on her stomach. Then he roasted poke roots, ground them to a powder, and made a poultice for the bottom of her feet. Nothing helped.

Annie constantly brought cool water in and sponged her momma's face, squeezing and pressing the sponge over her lips, trying to get her to take some water. She hovered over her momma and held the baby, who fretted constantly unless it was placed at her momma's breasts, where it sucked weakly.

By the third night, Annie was exhausted. Half-asleep, she was sitting, watching, and waiting on the foot of the bed, as dark fell soundlessly in the corners of the unlit room, and she thought that she knew the precise moment her momma's soul slipped free. She thought that, released, her momma paused and touched her, a light icy brush of fingertips on her cheek.

Annie had already cried so much that she was dry, and a feeling almost like relief filled her. She walked over to the bed and used her finger to wipe off the thin line of black fluid that had run from the corner of her momma's mouth down onto her chin.

The baby barely lasted until dawn, waking only once more; refusing even the sugar-tit, it went back to sleep, its cold skin as translucent as a small fish's flesh.

Annie thought of her daddy and brothers asleep in the other bedroom, snoring, the room filled with their pungent scent, a smell like mulched earth that has been turned, and she didn't wake them, but instead, hollow-eyed and stiff, she went through the house covering up mirrors and turning pictures to the wall. Then she returned to her momma's bedroom and waited for morning.

Two women from the church came out to the house to wash the bodies. Annie wanted to help, but they made her leave the room, told her to take Robbie out, to take care of him, that she was his momma now, that he wouldn't understand what had happened, to go play with him, leave them to do their work. And Annie could see it in their eyes, in the way they looked at her and then at each other with a frightened look as if they were scared of a little girl who had done what she had done, as if they needed to get her away from her momma, like maybe she could do her some more harm. Annie, her eyes brimming with shame, took Robbie's hand and left the room.

She sat on the couch fingering the white packet in her pocket, feeling the words on it, *3 teaspoons,* while Robbie rubbed and petted his little toys as if he were memorizing the shapes. The house was empty, all the men gone, making arrangements, and it was silent, but not like an absence of sound, rather like compressed sound, like the wails Annie felt lodged in her heart, the wails of a banshee crying like a loon, wails that might burst forth at any moment if she didn't remember to close her throat, to reroute her blood away from the place where they crouched.

Distraught and distant, Annie didn't notice that Robbie got up and left the room, didn't know anything until the commotion from the bedroom reached her ears, the women's voices raised in shrill anger and Robbie's high frightened yelping, like a kicked puppy.

When she got there, she saw the women struggling with Robbie, who was yelling, "My ninny! My ninny!" Annie looked at the bed where her momma lay in her dark blue Sunday dress. The front was unbuttoned with one breast exposed, the nipple almost as white as the rest of the body.

Annie grabbed Robbie. He quit fighting and clung to her, sobbing, rolling his eyes at the panting women. "Annie, my ninny? Ninny? Annie?"

One woman flew over to the body and quickly covered the breast as if the sight of it were obscene. The other one, fuming, pulled on her own clothing to put it back in order. "Put away! That's what that child needs. To be put away somewhere. Disgraceful, just disgraceful," she spat.

Robbie howled louder as if he understood what the woman had said, and Annie picked him up and left the room. In the kitchen, she washed his face in the basin and made him a sandwich from the fried fatback left from yesterday's breakfast. "Come on, we'll go to the falls. Get your wagon, and you can pick up pine branches to bring back."

Robbie smiled and stuffed the sandwich in his mouth, but then he hesitated, frowned, looked like he might cry. "Momma?" he asked.

Annie looked away, let her eyes rove over the kitchen she had cleaned the night before. Everything was spotless and in its place, just like her momma kept it, and she just couldn't say it, saying it would make it real and release the wave of grief pushing at her control—*she could not bear it*—so she mumbled, "She's just sick. That's all. Now come on if you want to go."

The old logging road to the falls wasn't too difficult, but it was tiring. It ran two miles uphill, then across the ridge and halfway down the other side of the mountain. When Robbie got tired, Annie pulled him in the wagon, or she carried him if the way was too rough to trust the wagon to stay upright.

The narrow path that left the road going down to the falls was littered with rocks and covered in tangled overgrowth. It ended at a pool filled by the falling water under a canopy of red maples and gold birches that turned the weak autumn sunlight caught in the leafy tops into a soft yellow-green glow pooling into greenish puddles of light under the mountain laurel. Behind the falls was the entrance to a honeycomb of caverns.

The day was cold, clear, and hard, and the water felt icy to Annie's touch as she helped Robbie to fold leaf boats and float them out on the water. He hadn't mentioned their momma since they left and now seemed content as he rubbed his chubby hands together to keep them warm while launching, then sinking his boats with a long branch that he had found next to the water.

Annie's mind seemed pulled to the water, sliding along the edges of the pool where the bottom wavered clearly in the blue-green water, and then on to the center where it was so deep that the turquoise shaded to an opaque black. Annie could feel her mind slowing, taking on the calmness of the water. Here, it felt like nothing so horrible could really have happened, her momma couldn't really be gone forever, just as this place was always here, always the same, changing with the seasons, but always here. Then the sound of a red-tailed hawk, its asthmatic wheeze, made her think of the sound her momma had made right before she died, a sound like her breath was being cut off, and despite herself she started to cry silently, turning her face away from Robbie.

A noise behind her made her look around. Miss Mercer, dressed in dark shapeless garments, a hood over her head, nothing but her face and hands exposed, was making her way down the path, stepping carefully over the rocks, a croker sack hanging off her arm, while she held her skirt up with one hand and leaned on a staff with the other. Annie had the urge to run, but the only path out was the one Miss Mercer was coming down. Robbie quit playing and watched Miss Mercer with a limp smile on his face.

Miss Mercer came right over to Annie and stood searching in her sack. "Your ma's dead, nothing you can do now. Crying won't help." She glanced up sharply at Annie, then went back to searching in her sack.

Annie looked over at Robbie, afraid he had heard what she had said. Miss Mercer pulled out a milk-colored stone and, calling Robbie over, handed it to him.

"He already knows," she said to Annie.

Robbie, blinking at Miss Mercer with his blank blue eyes, took the stone, said "T'ank you," and went back to the pool.

The old woman lowered herself down onto a rock beside Annie. "Something would've happened to your ma anyway. It was bound to. No luck. She had no luck. Never had."

Annie looked down at the ground and started crying again. She didn't resist when Miss Mercer reached over and stroked her hair, drawing her hand down behind Annie's head to rub her neck. But then the old woman tightened her fingers, gripping Annie's neck.

Annie drew her head up sharply, frightened. The old woman's face was right next to hers, a web of wrinkles radiating like water from her lips.

"That's enough, girl! It's done and there's more to come. Listen to me." She released Annie's neck and sat watching Robbie for a few moments. Then she reached again into the bag, brought out a turtle shell about six inches long, and sat it on the ground.

"Look," she said, and in just a few moments Annie saw the head, then the four legs, and finally the tail emerge. The creature slowly looked around with bright red eyes, and it seemed to Annie that it paused when its searching, suspicious eyes reached her face. It looked startled and pulled back inside its shell.

"Vicious little biters," Miss Mercer said, tapping the shell, "but that's not all they do. No siree. They eat mushrooms, poison mushrooms. It don't hurt them, but the poison seeps into their flesh and builds up, and when a man eats them, he dies."

Annie instinctively drew back. Miss Mercer snickered, a rusty noise that grated in Annie's ears. "It's okay, girl, he won't hurt you. You got the mark of the moon, the power of water."

Annie was confused. She didn't know what to make of what Miss Mercer was saying. Miss Mercer picked the turtle up and dumped him back in the bag. "I'll keep him for you, feed him good, so he'll be ready if you need him."

The old woman pushed herself up. She went over to Robbie, leaned down, and whispered something in his ear. She pointed to the cavern entrance. Then she went back up the path, the bag over her shoulder, and disappeared into the woods at the top.

Annie didn't meant to stay all afternoon, but Miss Mercer had so upset her that after the old woman left, she cried herself to sleep by the pool. Having been awake for days with just snatches of sleep, she lay down on a pile of leaves and curled in a ball on the ground and slept as if she were dead, too.

The ground turning cold with the coming night woke her, and, rising, she was conscious of feeling better, as if the chill seeping through her had wrapped itself around her heart until, instead of the fragile, quivering about-to-burst organ she had carried within her for days, it was now a small, hard lump, and the rest of her body felt empty, no feeling, a void surrounding that tight small core of gravity.

Robbie was still playing quietly, rolling stones in leaves and burying the little bundles in the ground, marking the spots with twigs that he stuck upright in the dirt.

"What've you been doing? Why didn't you wake me?" Annie asked.

"Cave." Robbie pointed to the falls.

She lifted him up from the ground and brushed his clothes off. "I told you never to go in there alone. The bogeyman will get you in there."

By the time Annie got home, Robbie following along behind her with his wagon of pine boughs to add to the growing pile to put around the base of the house when cold weather set in, it was almost dark.

Inside the house, Annie, standing outside the kitchen door, saw the two women working busily. There was food everywhere, cooking in pots on the stove, already in dishes on the table. They were busily preparing for the wake tomorrow.

Annie, on impulse, went directly to her momma's bedroom, the desire to see her welling up unexpectedly and urgently, but before she could open the door, one of the women called, "Don't go in there!" and the woman came rushing over and grabbed Annie, who recoiled from her touch. "Stay out of there! And keep that boy out, too!"

Then, seeing Annie's stricken face, she softened a little. "Not yet. You can see your momma in the morning. We'll sit with her tonight."

Later that night, Annie filled a washtub with warm water in front of the stove and was bathing Robbie when she remembered that Miss Mercer had whispered something to him.

"Robbie, what did Miss Mercer say to you, today at the pool? What did she say?"

Robbie was playing with the white stone, dropping it in the water over and over. He never stopped or looked at Annie but said, "Make 'im touch Momma."

4

It was a wake just like the two Annie had attended last year, one for old Mr. Corbett and one for the little Potter girl who fell off the cliff—lots of food, people coming, milling around, going in and out of the bedroom to view the body, everyone standing around talking in low tones.

Every chair in the house was filled, and Lacey, mumbling and shaking her head while she washed dishes, had been brought in to help out in the kitchen. Annie, her eyes burning like they were filled with sand, did her best to avoid the clumps of people, but she couldn't help overhearing them talking *a better world for Evelyn the Lord praised be his name works in mysterious ways the end do you know was it hard on her horrible I heard just horrible face distorted something terrible do you know how did you hear did Evelyn know sometimes they know never said a word not a word the baby too well for the best Henry's taking it good thank the Lord the boys are almost grown what's he going to do with that child not quite right you know bad luck ever since that Miss Mercer trouble Evelyn should never have accused the old woman hexing her cows Henry should have known better should have kept giving to the old woman bad blood there—*

As Annie moved silently through the mourners, she

knew that the neighbors were all talking about her too. Everyone knew what had happened *an accident such a shame poor child living with that killing your own momma and then the baby dead too probably best something wrong in this house anybody could feel it maybe a hex bad luck comes in threes they could expect something else something else would be soon coming—*

And the women, most she knew well, others only slightly, women with hard eyes and soft voices, kept coming up to her and telling her to look to the Lord for forgiveness, to think about her momma and the baby in heaven, what a comfort it was to know the Lord had them. Annie murmured "Yes ma'am" over and over as she pulled away from one person after the other.

Robbie, scared of all the commotion, stayed right on Annie's dress tail as the women clucked their tongues and waggled their heads when they looked at him, and some of the children, many of them Annie's schoolmates, snickered behind their hands and pointed.

Even the drab, blustery morning, filled with a damp, piercing wind blowing in from the south and carrying the promise of rain, couldn't keep the men inside. Through the front-room window Annie saw them standing around the porch, looking uncomfortable in stiff shoes and ill-fitting dark suits. Her daddy had on a black hat jammed down to his bushy eyebrows and wore a black coat that looked like it had been bought for a smaller man. He moved heavy and slow among the men as he passed a Mason jar of liquor around. Annie watched him shake his head over and over. She was sure that he was talking about her, what she had done, *killed her own momma.*

Yesterday she had heard the doctor ask her daddy why he hadn't used the granny woman for the birth. He had glanced at Claude, who was listening, and then said that Evelyn didn't want the woman, that she was scared to use her after the way Robbie had come out, after she had almost died. He said that he had tried to talk to her momma but was afraid of upsetting her more so he did what she wanted. Claude's eyes had flitted around the room, coming to rest on Annie, and she had noticed the line of sweat that, despite the cold house, had gathered over his lip. Later, her daddy had told her not to talk to anyone about what had happened, that it would go better for her if she kept quiet about everything, to quit accusing Claude, that he would handle him, make it all right.

That morning, her daddy had been the first one in the bedroom where her momma was laid out with the baby beside her. Standing back away from the bed, he pulled out his handkerchief from his pocket and wiped his nose before turning away and going outside. Claude and Neal went in to view the body next. Neal's face was red and puffy, and Annie noticed the way his thin hands kept picking at his shirt collar or twirling a button, but Claude scowled and looked bored. Annie, watching from the hallway, remembered what Miss Mercer had said about making "him" touch the body. She wondered if by "him," Miss Mercer meant Claude. Frustrated, she jabbed her fist into her eyes. Everything kept going out of focus. Even the flame from the two candles at the head of her momma's bed looked strange, the edges blurred and smudged into the surrounding air.

Neal and Claude stayed only a minute. Claude went back outside, but Neal stopped and asked if she wanted him to watch Robbie for a while, see if maybe he would take a nap.

Annie nodded, and Neal took Robbie's hand, saying, "Come on, let's go see Sweetie Pie and then we'll rest for a while." Robbie went eagerly. He liked nothing better than to play with Neal's bird, who would ride on his shoulder, sit on his finger, even eat out of his mouth. For Neal, Sweetie Pie would do tricks, push acorns around with his beak, ring a small bell, or climb a little ladder that Neal had carved. Neal had found the baby bird under a bush where it had fallen out of the nest. Everyone had said it wouldn't live, but Neal had fed it small rocks with its food, like the momma does, so that the little bird could digest its food and not swell up and die. He made a bird cage when it got older and kept its wings clipped while he trained it. Neal spend a good part of most evenings with his bird, sitting at the kitchen table, patiently teaching it to perform for food, to whistle, to give him "kisses."

Later when Annie looked in the boys' room, she saw both Neal and Robbie asleep on the bed, Neal's arm thrown across Robbie, who was curled in a knot, his thumb in his mouth.

Annie went out on the porch. She saw Claude over by the outbuildings with Lacey, who had gone to get another chicken to kill. They both went in the barn.

Back in the kitchen, Annie looked at the table laden with food and thought about how her daddy wouldn't sit down to eat supper until a pot of coffee was made, how he insisted on flour-fried meat at every meal, how he would get on to her for eating one food at a time and how her momma would take up for her, "What difference does it make? It all goes down the same hole." How Claude, always on his daddy's coattails, would say something if she left anything on her plate—"Don't leave those beans. You too fancy to eat beans like the rest of us?"—and her daddy would mutter about her not knowing what it's like to be poor, to need food.

She realized now that the more was wrong on the farm, the more was wrong at supper, and she remembered her momma saying that worry can congeal in your stomach, eat at the lining, send acid up your throat, red bile, worry coursing through arteries that grow stiff. Thinking about it, Annie felt a rush of sympathy for her daddy, a sadness for his life and how little she knew of it.

As the morning wore on into afternoon, Annie knew that she needed to go in the bedroom, but the sudden urge she had felt yesterday to see her momma had been replaced with a reluctance as compelling as the urge had been, and inside her lids every time she closed them was the sight of her momma on the night she died, prostrate and dehydrated, like a husk of herself, with the fading baby lying next to her. Even worse than the way they looked was the sound and the smell. Her momma had made small sounds right to the end, rattling sounds, and when Annie would try to force water between her lips, she could smell a foul odor rising from her momma's mouth.

So it was afternoon before Annie finally took Robbie by the hand and, ignoring the murmuring that followed them, walked in next to the bed. Annie had never seen her momma in makeup, and the sight of her unnaturally red cheeks and rosy mouth made her think of the way her momma, dying, had turned the color of sour milk and the way her eyes had dimmed to the same sallow color. As Annie looked at her momma now, fixed up and dressed in her Sunday dress, she felt her heart catch, flutter, then break down, and she had to turn away. Her eyes flooded. Stumbling, her head down, pulling Robbie behind her, as she rushed out of the room, she bumped into the caskets waiting against the wall, one large and the other small.

About four o'clock Annie's daddy, along with her brothers and two other men, all of them slightly tipsy from the corn liquor they had been sipping on all day, came into the house to take the caskets to the church. The mourners moved to the side as they passed, their voices falling away from the men's path in dying whispers, scattering like leaves before wind.

Annie, watching, stood at the door as Claude took the baby from her momma's arms and put it in the small casket. The others lifted her momma awkwardly, two on each side, and Annie flinched when her momma's arm dropped and hit the edge of the casket as they placed her in the pine box.

Suddenly Robbie darted under Annie's arm and into the room. Without a sound he ran over and shoved Claude. Caught off balance, Claude fell toward the big casket, catching himself with one hand on the edge of the box, the other missing the edge and going inside the casket. When he straightened back up, his face was blotched with rage, and he grabbed Robbie by the arm and threw him against the wall. The other men, astounded, instinctively stepped back.

Annie heard herself yell, "Don't touch him! Don't *you* dare touch him!" She rushed to Robbie, who was lying in a heap on the floor. A rising tide of incredulous voices pressed behind her as people realized what was happening, indignation flowing out into the room like water spilled.

She picked Robbie up. He was quiet and smiled up at her, a strange little satisfied smile, through blood dripping from his nose.

One of the women bent over the casket to rearrange her momma. Her daddy stood to the side, his breath heavy and loud as it split the dead quiet of the room. Claude stood beside him, still livid, his face filled with blood and his eyes bulging. Annie thought that he might lunge at Robbie again. She saw her daddy put his hand on Claude's arm, give it a tug.

Then he looked over at her. "Get him out of here!" Her daddy's voice choked on the words.

"I need a rag," the woman bending over the casket said. Annie, the echo rising again in her mind, the words, *make him touch her*, walked over and looked in the casket. A thick line of blood ran from the corner of her momma's eye down her cheek where Claude's hand had hit her. Startled, Annie looked at Claude and had a flash of something like a vision. She saw the wall behind him crack and bleed, just for a moment, fresh blood flowing from a network of fissures and running down the wall.

The woman who was bent over the casket gave a sharp gasp and threw a small carved crab out of the casket onto the floor, slinging it like it was alive. Annie hugged Robbie tighter and reached down to pick it up. "It's just a toy," she mumbled, and shoved her way out of the room.

Out on the porch Annie sat with Robbie in the swing while she mopped his nose with her handkerchief. The sky, thick and boiling with dark clouds, was full of shifting shades of purple and the air filled with curious night sounds in the middle of the afternoon. She could smell the rain coming in the charged air.

At the first crack of distant thunder, Robbie pointed, holding out his chubby finger toward the woods, and Annie saw a dark figure that looked like Miss Mercer disappearing into the bushes at the edge of the road, and Annie felt something closing around her, like a web that you can't see, the way insects can't see the invisible strands that snare them until they're helpless in the sticky grasp. The door opened and the small casket was carried through feet first.

Slate-colored sheets of rain filled the sky in a sudden onslaught of thunder and lightning, but by the time the mourners had walked to the church, slowly sloshing behind the mule-drawn wagon holding the coffins, the afternoon had lengthened into a steady drizzle with the ground turning to freezing mud under heavy trees filled with water, their boughs bending under the hardening water-needles, and the air was filled with the drone of water drops.

As Annie walked behind the coffins, the sky dimmed from violet to dun, soaking colors into itself like a dirty sponge, and, despite her sweater and raincoat, she was cold. Her feet and arms and face were wet, droplets hung on her eyelashes, and the long braid down her back felt sodden.

She glanced around before going in the church door and her eye caught the shadow of a figure that she guessed was Miss Mercer again, moving among the tombstones in the cemetery next to the churchyard, and she shivered, wondering why she had never seen the old woman at a funeral before, and why she was hanging around now.

Inside the church, despite the whispering people who filled the seats, there was a stillness in the air, a gloomy inertia that hung dark as smoke in the corners of the large high-ceilinged room.

Annie walked down the aisle behind her daddy and brothers, leading Robbie by the hand. She saw Ruthie Lynn's bright red hair, but Ruthie was looking down, and it looked like she was crying. Miss Paine was right next to her, her stern profile composed and her chin lifted as if even death could not daunt her. Annie caught her eye, but she looked quickly away. Glancing around the room, Annie thought of the way the mourners all looked like black crows gathering around something dead. Annie and her family took a front pew, and sitting there exposed to them all, she felt sharp eyes penetrating the tender flesh of her back, eyes pricking her nerves, seeking marrow, and could barely keep from getting up and running.

Robbie climbed on her lap, and Annie distracted herself by straightening his shirt and licking her fingers to plaster down the cowlick that stuck up on the crown of his head. The silence of the church was sporadically broken by a muffled cough being passed around like a collection plate.

"Me cold," Robbie said.

Annie whispered, "Shhh, the rain is good. It's a sign. It means Momma and the baby are happy."

He leaned against her. Annie thought about what Miss Mercer had said, that he knew his momma was dead, but she didn't get any further in her wondering because she was interrupted by the minister, Preacher Coldren, who appeared in the pulpit.

The sermon didn't take long. He talked about the Twenty-third Psalm and how the Lord would be with the Saved, even "in the valley of the Shadow of Death," and he referred to her momma as "Sister Evelyn" and called the baby "the innocent babe" as he declared that their Sister Evelyn would be forgiven of all sins through the mercy of God and that she had gone to a better place outside this "vale of tears." The congregation listened quietly except for an occasional "Amen," or "Thank you, Lord, for Jesus." When he finished, the congregation stood up and sang "In the Sweet Bye and Bye," and Annie, who could hardly force the words over the lump in her throat, heard their voices swell on "We shall all meet together on that beautiful shore" as if they were eagerly anticipating the event.

The church was saturated with the soaring sound of the song, the slackening rain, and the occasional rumble of distant thunder, and at the end of the song, right on the part about meeting on the shore, a stream of light filled with dust came through the window next to the pews where Annie and her family stood. It streaked through the gloom and fell on Claude's face, making his features appear lifeless.

Outside, the rain had almost stopped. The pallbearers' feet, as they trudged through the mud with their burdens, made a sucking sound and then a wet plop as each foot broke away. They placed a coffin by each dug grave. The ropes to lower the coffins coiled beside them. The mourners positioned themselves around the graves, filling in behind the family and leaving a space at the head for the preacher who said a few words more to remind everyone that they were all heading for death and then stepped back for the pallbearers to lower the coffins.

Four men slid ropes under the ends of the baby's coffin and carefully lowered it into the small grave. Then they did the same with Annie's momma. The large coffin swayed unwieldy and heavy as they stationed themselves on each side of the grave and carefully lowered it, trying to keep it level, but despite their care, the coffin fell the last couple of inches and settled with a soft *plod* into the sodden ground.

The preacher intoned "ashes to ashes, dust to dust" and picked up some loose dirt by the graves and threw it in the holes. Each family member repeated the action, and then the mourners filed by sprinkling dirt in before saying a final word to the family on their way out. Annie endured the hugs of the women and the mumbling of the men by keeping her eyes on the ground and nodding her head. Robbie stood behind her. No one said anything to him.

Finally they had all passed, and Annie's daddy said, "Let's go." His voice angry as if the service had irritated him.

As Annie turned to go, Robbie pulled on her hand. "Look, Annie!" He was pointing back at the cemetery, where a field mouse, perched on the edge of her momma's grave, was looking in.

Her daddy and brothers were already gone, walking behind the mourners. When she caught up with them, people were buzzing like a drone of bees, and she distinctly heard a voice say, "Can you believe it? Not one tear. That girl didn't shed one tear." And the reply, "Makes you wonder how much of an accident it was, don't it?"

The words squeezed Annie's heart like a vise. She hadn't even thought about crying, or about *not* crying, or that anyone would be watching her to see what she did. Everything that had been shut down in her, all her senses that had concealed themselves inside her like scared living things, were released in a flood of grief. Grabbing Robbie's hand, she pushed roughly past the crowd and rushed down the road toward home.

THE APPARITION

The next weeks passed slowly for Annie. The moon that had hung heavy and low, a cold, creamy circle, a giant thumbnail of light on the night of the funeral, waned as the days passed until it was new again, the *beaver's moon* her momma always had called it.

Annie felt as if she were living inside something closed up tight, a world like an egg, where the sky curved upward into a hazy brooding horizon, and the air hung close, a strange odor, twice-breathed, sultry, although the days were cold, cloudy, with an occasional afternoon rain, and the nights even colder with light snow falling high up on the mountainsides. Lower down, the trees were shedding their leaves, but even the colors didn't look right to Annie, smears of murky red, yellow, and orange turning brown and spilling sloppily against a nebulous backdrop of weak green.

The house seemed filled with her momma's presence. Annie felt it everywhere, even in such small things as the crocheted doilies on the chairs of the front room. In the evening, while she worked in the kitchen, every pot and pan reminded her of her momma, and she couldn't shake the depression that crept through her, leaving a numbness in its wake, and it seemed an effort just to move about.

Her melancholy was laced with a mental unrest, a premonition that came from something deeper than just sorrow, a presence in the stillness of the house that made her feel the way the electrified air of a storm gathering in the mountains feels, the way a heavy sky darkens in the eye.

Her momma's bedroom, in particular, seemed alive and peculiar. Her daddy didn't sleep there anymore. Saying that Annie needed to be away from the boys, he had, surprisingly, given the room to her and even put a small pallet in it for Robbie, placing the cot next to the wall. He put another bed for himself into the sheet-partitioned room with Neal and Claude.

Annie moved her small store of clothes: two sweaters, four dresses, two blouses, and three skirts—all made by her momma from flour sacks and cotton material bought at the store in town—her underwear, socks, and shoes, along with her school notebook containing her spelling work and a comb that Neal had carved and given to her. She arranged the fold-up items in the drawers of the dresser and hung the dresses behind the door on a hook. There was a small wardrobe in the room, but her momma's clothes were still in it, and Annie couldn't bring herself to go through them yet. She also left her momma's clothes in one of the drawers, using for herself the drawers that her daddy had vacated, and she carefully placed her wooden comb on the dresser in between her momma's hairbrush and a small box containing an opal necklace, her wedding band, and what looked like a piece of bone in a handkerchief that had a very old odor.

A large wooden chest stood at the foot of the bed, filled with crocheted and handsewn items made by her momma, who had spent most evenings with her hook or needle, and the star-of-Texas quilt that her momma had used on her last night covered the foot of the bed. Feeling her heart react when she saw the quilt, Annie started to fold it and put it in the top of the closet, but when she touched the neatly stitched triangles, a strange comfort flowed through her, a warm, quiet, liquid calm spreading in her troubled breast, so instead she unfolded the quilt so that the pattern, various colors put together in a huge five-pointed star, covered the entire bed.

She covered Robbie's pallet with a small patchwork quilt from the chest, and then she helped him arrange his box of toys and other items, his crayons and such, on a small corner table that her momma had found thrown out next to the road and had sanded and painted a bright red.

Annie had been in the room only a couple of days when it happened. One afternoon when everyone but Annie was out of the house—the men out rounding up hogs off the mountain for slaughter, Lacey washing clothes in the yard, and Robbie, who was usually under Annie's feet, out on the porch stacking dried corncobs every which way. Annie thought that she would go lie on her bed and study her spelling for a while. She was to go back to school the next Monday, and she was pulled between anticipation and dread at the thought.

She saw it from the bedroom door, right in the middle of the bed, in the very center of the star, in the bright orange pointed heart of the quilt—a huge hank of hair spread fanlike and looking freshly brushed. Even though she didn't need to see the hair closer to know that it was her momma's, Annie picked it up. Long and glossy black, it was her momma's hair the way it had looked before it had gone salt-and-pepper gray, hair that had hung down to her knees, thick and wonderful, before she was made to cut it off because of the headaches, severe and debilitating, that came with her pregnancy with Robbie. At least once a week the pain would put her in bed for the day. The granny woman said that her heavy hair was adding to the problem. Annie could remember how her momma had cried, said she had always had headaches, just not this bad, and how her daddy was so angry that he had to stay out of the house while the granny woman cut the strands off right below her momma's shoulder blades. Afterward, the headaches gradually decreased in severity until they were bearable by her seventh month.

Annie looked at the long strands with the tiny waves, like ripples, her mind darting about, trying and then discarding one explanation after the other. She initially felt something almost like fright, but after a while, like the bedspread, the touch of the hair seemed to fill her with a sense of peace, a calming.

She looked around for a place to put the hair and decided on the chest. After wrapping the lock in a doily and tucking it way down in the bottom, she went out on the porch to talk to Robbie. She was going to ask him about the hair, if he knew anything, if maybe he had found it somewhere, but when she saw him, she decided not to, afraid that she might upset him, and she realized that, oddly enough, he had not asked for his momma since the funeral and Annie wondered if he really understood that she was dead, that she was never coming back.

Despite the cold day, Annie spent the rest of the afternoon on the porch steps watching him, his overalls baggy on his small body and a too-large hat perched on his head as he sang to himself over the stacks of corncobs before he moved into the yard and began sketching lines in the dirt with a stick. He seemed so intent that she finally walked out to see what he was drawing and was surprised to see shapes that seemed to have a pattern—ovals inside of ovals that looked like huge eyes, like slanted cats' eyes. When she asked him what they were, he just shrugged his shoulders and drew some more.

That night, after putting Robbie in bed, Annie put the #3 washtub in front of the stove and filled it, heating water in the kettle and adding it to cold pump water. She blocked the doors going to the hall and front room by leaning chairs against them and locked the door to the back porch, dropping the crossbar into its cradle. After she had gotten undressed, Claude came to the door one time, but she told him to go away and then ignored his calls and banging until he did.

Annie had always enjoyed bathing in the kitchen while her momma dumped kettles full of hot water in the tub for her. The room would get warm and steamy and close, and during those times her momma had seemed to her like a friend her own age. Her momma had giggled at her story about Ruthie Lynn, who, in a "girl-talk" session, had complained once that she still had almost no pubic hair, just three hairs, she had said, so Annie and her momma, laughing over the imagined sight, had started calling her "Three-hair Ruthie Lynn."

Her mind filled with memories, Annie took a long time bathing. She washed her hair, mixing an egg with the soap to scrub it and then using cold water for the last rinse to make it glossy. She washed her face with oatmeal, rubbing it hard until her skin was pink and shiny. Finally, with the tub emptied and the kitchen straightened up, she sat next to the stove to let the dying heat dry her hair.

Afterward, sitting in bed, she brushed her hair, counting the one hundred strokes under her breath while she listened to the radio that she had moved into the room from the kitchen, a music program that kept breaking up into static. Yet, despite her attempts to distract herself, she was still distressed. She was certain that the hair was her momma's. She had pondered over it all afternoon and was still thinking about it while she brushed her own hair, and then, compelled, she took the lock out of the chest and after fiddling with it for a while, she tied it with a ribbon, wrapped it back up in the doily, and put it under her pillow. She blew out the light and listened to the rest of the program in the dark.

When the radio show was over, Annie turned over on her stomach and with her hand under the pillow, her fingers just touching the lock of hair, she tried to fall asleep. It was then that she remembered where she had seen the oval shapes that Robbie had been drawing before. It was on the box in Miss Mercer's house, the small box that Miss Mercer had taken the packet of castor bean out of. She remembered it clearly. There was a large slanted eye carved right on the top.

It took a long time for Annie to fall asleep. She lay wide-eyed, and the bed sheets seemed to glow whitely in the heavy darkness while Robbie's little snore came from the corner as regular as a cricket's burr in the summer. She thought that she could hear the hogs that they had round-ed up and penned outside squealing. She imagined the shadowed lumbering shapes moving about under the full moon that was for them the herald of death.

Annie finally dropped off. At first, it was nightmares, a dream about a figure outside the window, first a shadow, then a huge black form, scratching on the pane making a horrible high screech of long nails against glass. When she woke up, she was sitting up in the bed, her eyes popped open like a doll's, staring at the empty window, and a horrible fear came over her that *he* was now under the bed. She lay back down, but she couldn't shake it off, and she kept thinking that if she let her arm fall down, off the side, *he* would grab her, wrapping his hand and fingers around her arm, the long nails overlapping and lacing together like stiff spiked webs as *he* pulled her under, and the room seemed filled with the sound of *his* breathing, a hot sound that rubbed against her skin making it feel raw and chaffed despite the cool sheets.

Annie turned on her stomach and tucked her arms under her body, lying on them, until she finally drifted off again, but it was only to more dreams, brief images, short scenarios of being chased or threatened, once through a cornfield, the sky a midnight blue that shaded to purple where a thin slice of new moon looked down like a squinted cat's eye. She knows *he* is behind her. She can hear the cornstalks rustling as *he* pushes them aside and tramples them, and she is running, thrashing her way through, unable to see anything except the tall canes like thick bars in front of her, hearing *him* coming, hidden by the silky rustling curtain. Or she is swimming in the creek, but it is different from the creek where she swims all summer. Here, there is no place to come out of the water except for a small clearing because the bank is dense and overgrown right down into the creek, and the water itself is opaque, thick, and she has the sensation of weeds, long and grasping, wrapping around and pulling at her legs. Again, it is late, the sky murky, filled with sinister clouds the same color as the water. She is naked and swimming back and forth, back and forth, in front of the clearing.

Tired, she wants to go on shore, but she knows *he* is waiting for her. She can't see *him* clearly, but *he* is there, a shadow in the overgrowth that doesn't blend with the leaf shadows, and the sound of *his* clicking nails fills the air, rising strident and piercing over the drone of the insects. She is so scared of *him* that she won't get out of the water although she can feel herself slipping down, slowing turning cold, being pulled under the water.

This time she woke up slowly, her body heavy and soggy, weighed down on the bed and her arms numb, full of prickles as she tried to move them, but when she thought about it later, she realized that she must have still been asleep and only dreamed that she woke up because she was lying in the bed, her eyes open, rubbing her arms and thinking about the dreams when a noise coming from the corner of the room where Robbie slept caught her attention. It wasn't much of a sound, just a rustle, like a soft voice murmuring, but Annie, her nerves laced with a stinging like kerosene on bare skin, jerked upright and swung her head around to look over at the corner. And she thought she saw her momma come from behind the curtain, dressed in a nightgown with the spider-web shawl over her shoulders and her hair down, long, the way it was before she cut it, falling straight down her back. Annie thought that her momma walked right by her bed, glancing at her quickly, a slight smile on her face, a conspiratorial smile, like they shared a secret. She never stopped, but walked out the bedroom door that was standing open, although Annie knew she had closed it before she had gone to bed.

Stunned, Annie didn't move for a moment. Then she leaped out of the bed and ran to Robbie's corner. When Annie pulled back the curtain, he was lying awake on his side, one hand under his cheek, not moving.

"Robbie?" Annie was surprised at how soft and calm her voice sounded compared to the pounding in her ears and the swelling of her heart pushing at her chest.

He didn't answer, didn't even look at her, just lay there.

Annie reached out and touched his cheek. It felt warm

and moist, and at her touch he closed his eyes and seemed to be asleep.

The next day was gray and cold with a brisk wind blowing down from the mountains, and Annie stayed in the house. She didn't want to see the killing. She could hear the shots, and despite her reluctance to think about it, she pictured the carcasses, slit open, strung up with a gambrel stick stuck between the exposed tendons. Her momma had always worked with her daddy and the boys during slaughtering, but Annie had stayed away since her first time, when she got sick. Her daddy had gotten mad, and Claude had laughed at her. Her momma, exasperated, had told her to go on back to the house and mix the cure.

So it became her job to mix the salt, molasses, and red and black pepper and have it ready when they brought the meat back. She would wash the meat and rub the pieces with the mixture and then they would put the meat in the smokehouse on shelves and leave it, adding more cure on the third and tenth days.

It was late afternoon when they came in with the meat from the hogs, and Annie helped Lacey rub it down for storage. When they finished with that, the men brought in the heads and put them on the table. Lacey saw Annie starting to leave the kitchen.

"Where you going, girl? You ain't sneaking out of here and leaving all this work for me to do by myself."

Annie felt a flash of anger. Her momma had never made her prepare the heads for soaking. Annie always helped afterward with making the souse, the sausage, pickling the feet, but she didn't want to do the heads.

"I'm just going to pee. Is that all right with you?"

"Don't you get smart with me. You just go on and get yourself back here quick."

Annie walked slowly to the outhouse, not knowing how to get out of helping Lacey, and she took as long as she could getting there and getting back. She had reached the kitchen door and was just going through when she saw Lacey pop something in her mouth. When Annie got to the table, she saw that Lacey had already cut the eyes out of the first head and felt like she might throw up when she realized what Lacey had put in her mouth.

Lacey stood at the stove, putting on water to boil to singe off the hair, and Annie, angry and disgusted at what she had seen, picked up a knife, cut out the rest of the eyeballs, and walked determinedly to the back door and threw them out.

It took them the better part of two hours to singe and scrape the heads and quarter them with an ax before putting them in washtubs of fresh water to soak overnight. Lacey didn't say a word to her during the entire operation.

Monday came, her first day back in school since the funeral. Annie felt uneasy, and her thoughts, when they came, were glutted in sensations, hazy ambiguous feelings.

At afternoon recess, Annie, in a sweater and knit cap, sat in the swing on the playground. The bright turquoise day was as hard as crystal and filled with the scream of birds and a strangling wind. She pushed herself back and forth as she drug the toe of her shoe in the smooth dirt of the scooped-out depression below the swing.

Annie had always liked school, but all day she had felt melancholy, hearing a warning in the beating of her heart. Everything was different now, not like before. That morning walking to school, and then all during class, her friends had looked through her like she was a ghost. Only J.C. had stopped by her desk and said he was sorry about her momma. No one else had said a word to her, not even Miss Paine, her teacher, and when Annie had asked about the spelling bee, Miss Paine had looked uncomfortable, said it was too late to prepare for it, and that she would have to drop out.

The only time she had felt good about coming back was after lunch listening to Miss Paine read. She had missed the stories read out loud to them everyday after lunch, stories about people different from the ones she

knew and places far away. She always told them to Robbie in the evening while she cleaned the kitchen, and he
even started to make up his own and tell them to her,
funny little stories about his carved animals.

She thought about the last one he had told her, about
the crab and how it had crawled into a hole thinking it
was his home, he said, but it was a strange hole, deep and
black. There wasn't room to turn around so the crab had
to keep going deeper and deeper. When Annie asked him
how the story ended, he said it hadn't yet, that the crab
was still going, still crawling down. The story had bothered Annie. It kept coming back to her, that crab forever
crawling down a hole, unable to turn back.

And now remembering the story and thinking about
going home after school, she was deep into the uneasiness
of her mind and didn't notice anything until the noise of
the playground—the yells and laughter of kids playing,
the squeak and groan of slide and merry-go-round—
imperceptibly changed to the sound of nervous laughter
and angry buzzing all mixed together, the noise coming
from a group of her classmates huddled together, whispering and looking over at her. The noise seemed to have an
actual color to Annie, a shifting of the sky between the
crowd and herself as it collected the sounds into a kind of
dirty lavender, the color of a fresh bruise.

Then a yell congealed the tension washing between her
and the group. Someone called out, "Momma-killer!" and
the others snickered and looked to see what she would do.

Annie was stunned. She felt her spine stiffen, the words
like a rod rammed down it. She forgot to push her swing
as someone else called out, "Momma-killer!" Then they
were all saying it, chanting the words in high, vicious
voices.

Annie saw Ruthie Lynn standing with the others, and
even the scabies, who wore stocking caps on their shaved
heads to keep the ringworm fungus from spreading, were
in the group when usually no one would get close to
them.

Then one scabie ran at her, and, lifting his stocking cap,

he pulled off a scab and threw it at her. Another followed and then two more, and like a game of ring-around-the-rosie, they all circled her and picked at their heads, throwing the brown crusts at her while they sang, "Momma-killer! Momma-killer!"

Annie felt something burst inside her, and a streak of pain shot along the frayed edges of her nerves. She jumped out of the swing and ran past them, wanting only to get away from them, from the words. They chased her. She saw J.C. come running across the yard, and in among the voices taunting her, she heard Ruthie Lynn's, louder than the others, and without thinking, she stopped, turned around, and swinging her pocketbook, the one her momma had made for her by crocheting a yarn cover on an oatmeal box, she struck Ruthie Lynn on the side of the head as hard as she could. The others, astounded, stopped. Annie ran inside the school, into the cloakroom, squatted in a back corner, and clutching her crushed pocketbook, she cried, her heart shattering into a million crystal pieces.

6

After the playground incident Annie didn't want to go back to school anymore, but the thought of spending all day in the house seemed even worse than what she could expect from her classmates. At least no one at school bothered her anymore since Miss Paine, having found Annie in the cloakroom, had threatened the ringleaders with expulsion.

Still, out on the playground, some of them would point and whisper, but after a while Annie didn't care. She would sit on the steps not even noticing them, lost inside herself. Several times J.C. had tried to talk to her, but filled with grief and embarrassed by the way the other students were treating her, as if she had done it on purpose, she wanted only to be left alone, to be invisible. She didn't want his pity.

Annie didn't know exactly when she started getting ill. All she knew was that it began as a tickle in the back of her throat that gradually filled with phlegm, and coughing wouldn't dislodge it. Then a popping started in her ears while a sense of fullness grew in her chest, and it all wore on her, making her always tired, weighed down with a longing to crawl into the comfort of her mother's bed, and she came to regard sleep as more desirable than waking. In two weeks' time, she was out of school, lying in bed with a constant fever and a wet, croupy cough that rose from deep down in her lungs and racked her entire body

Her father was worried. He couldn't afford to have anything else happen, no more deaths, no more talk, so he sent Robbie for Miss Mercer, who came back up the road holding the little boy's hand. Lacey took one look at the old woman as she came through the door, rolled her eyes, and refused to stay in the same room with her, telling Annie's father, "You just asking for trouble now, bringing dat witch-woman here. There ain't nothing wrong with dat girl but meanness. A switch would get her out of dat bed. Nothing but pure ole meanness."

Miss Mercer fried up onions and garlic with lard until the odor permeated the house. Scooping it all into a cloth bag, she spread the bag out on Annie's chest. With Robbie helping, she put a sheet and the star-of-Texas quilt over Annie, adding the small quilt from Robbie's bed, tucking in the edges so that no air could get under the covers. Annie groaned between the covers, sweat popping out on her face, and whenever the mixture would cool, lose its potency, Miss Mercer would have more ready and hot to take its place.

Annie stayed incoherent for two days and nights, caught in between sleeping and waking, under the swaddling heat of Miss Mercer's ministrations. She continually sought her mother in the wintery slowness of her dreams, where she climbed a mist-shrouded mountain, the icy wind blowing in a frenzy over the narrow trail and filling her chilled ears with a sound so loud it became silence, as if her ears were stopped up with water. Somehow, she knew that when she had climbed high enough, her mother would be waiting, sitting on the huge rock on top of the bluff, her skin tinged ice blue, slate eyes filled with ice slivers, and her hair coated with radiant icicles that sparkled as, whipped by the wind, they hit against one another. Each time Annie made the journey her mother tried to tell her something, but the wind snatched the words away and turned them into frosty vapors that dissipated in the air. Annie, chasing them, would feel a heavy foreboding, frigid and solid, like a sheet of ice gradually invading her body.

It took two weeks of Miss Mercer's cures to bring Annie around. Coming at dawn every day and staying until the weak winter moon came out, the old woman nursed her. She brewed sweet goldenrod and spooned the tonic between Annie's lips. She made beef tea, putting raw meat in a glass jar and capping it tight before putting the jar in water to simmer until all the juice was drawn out of the meat. Annie, after her fever had broken, didn't like the beef juice because she thought it looked like old blood, having the same brown-red color and thick aroma, but she drank whatever the old woman gave her, including the cough syrup of sugar, whiskey, and turpentine that burned her throat.

The fever left Annie so weak that there was no question of her returning to school for a while. Miss Paine began coming out once a week to give her assignments and to collect her lessons, and Annie took to spending the long winter evenings after supper sitting in the bed. She had glasses now, given to her as a gift from the ladies in the church, and she would do her lessons and then spend the rest of the evening writing in her notebook.

Annie looked older after her illness, a new maturity around her eyes, small shadows that made her formerly open and guileless eyes now appear secretive, a darker blue, and her lips no longer instantly betrayed her emotions by quivering or clenching, but remained smooth and relaxed no matter what she was feeling. She started putting her pigtails up, pinning them in circles on each side of her head, the way her momma had fixed her own hair when she went to church on Sunday.

She recorded all the strange happenings surrounding her mother's death, the castor bean, the way her mother's eye had bled when Claude touched the corpse, and all about finding the bone and hair. Writing gave her a strange sense of satisfaction, almost a physical pleasure, and she became sure that somehow she was meant to do, just as she was doing, to write it all down, and it wasn't long after she began her journal that the "little girl" dream, as she called it, came to her. After dreaming it every night for a week, she recorded it:

December 30, 1934
I am asleep and wake up. I get up and walk through the dark hallway, and the floor is sticky, like mud sucking at my bare feet. The house is silent and filled with smells like outside, the smells in the tall forests high on the mountain, where it is wet and misty and where no sunlight falls. In the kitchen I see a little girl at the sink. She is bent over the drain, and she is pulling up something long and stringy and horrible looking with her fingers. She looks up, sees me. She holds out a handful of the black strings, offers them to me, and smiles.

Annie didn't understand the dream, didn't know who the little girl was, but, strangely, the dream didn't scare her. On the contrary, Annie felt good when she thought about it, as if it spoke to her heart in a way that maybe she didn't understand but intuitively knew was important.

From the hall, standing right outside the kitchen door, Annie could see and hear them. Miss Paine was trying to get her daddy to look at the composition, holding it out to him. Annie realized that Miss Paine probably hadn't even considered that he might not be able to read. Her daddy was looking everywhere but at Miss Paine while he nodded his head at everything she said.

"I don't mean to be a bother, Mr. Williams, but I'm upset by this. It may show some kind of mental upset caused by her mother's death. I can recognize these things. You know that I was trained to be a missionary before I had to go into teaching on account of my lungs—"

Her daddy said, "No, I didn't know that."

"Well . . . yes, you see, my pastor got me this assignment, and I try to do the best I can, you know, being an outsider and all, and sometimes things are so bad, the mill accidents, moonshine fights, horrible sickness . . ." her voice ran down and she sighed . . . "but, anyway, about this paper, about Annie—"

"Annie'll be just fine, Miss Paine. Don't you worry none about it. She'll be fine." And he walked out the back door of the kitchen.

Miss Paine stood looking after him. Annie scampered back to bed.

Miss Paine came back in the bedroom. She had a strained look on her face, and after she sat down in a chair by the bed, it was a minute before she spoke.

"Annie, how are you really feeling? Is everything all right?"

Annie nodded her head. "Maybe I can come back to school soon."

Miss Paine looked uncomfortable, like she was on the verge of asking something she didn't want to, and then she held out the composition, "I'm concerned about this assignment. Can you tell me how you came to write this?"

Annie took the paper, and although she knew exactly what it said, she slowly read it through.

I think about Little Red Riding Hood that day, how her world too must have been red as she skipped through the close woods at sunset, how the redorange light must have slanted through leaves shading the green into a redviolet, and how the wolf's eyes must have been streaked raw, his nostrils flared red. I wonder how she could have missed the blood on Grandma's wall as she slipped out of her little red cape, every stitch a prick in red. I think I know how everything must have exploded red bright redblack under his tongue and teeth. I can see the room splotched with red, patches of redwhite light, and I see now that red is passed from her to me, the red bait, the red odor under the cape, the

red taste of flesh rolled on an eager tongue, the
red feel of hungry teeth.

Miss Paine had just opened her mouth to speak when
Annie said, "You said to read a fairy tale and to write
something about it, so that's what I did."

"You didn't get this from somewhere? You wrote it
yourself?"

"Yes ma'am. It just came to me." Annie didn't mention
that lots of things seemed to be coming to her lately as she
wrote in her notebook.

"Are you sure you don't have anything else to say
about this piece?"

"No ma'am . . . oh, I meant to ask how's the new
school coming?"

Miss Paine looked relieved to have the burden of the
conversation removed from her. "Good. J.C. works on it
every afternoon. He's got the foundation done and the
walls up. In fact, he lives inside there now."

"Will another teacher come here when it's finished?"

"The school board has promised one, but you know
how their promises are, just like the new school, they
promised me one for three years and nothing happened
until J.C. showed up and I got the sawmill to give us the
lumber and men to help out. Now the board acts like it
was all their doing—"

Miss Paine stopped like she realized how far she had
gone away from what she had come to talk to Annie
about. She looked at her intently. "Annie, you know I
want to help you in any way I can?"

Annie thought about how Miss Paine had been so
standoffish the day she had come back to school. "Yes
ma'am. I'm feeling better every day."

Miss Paine sighed and stood up. "Okay, I've got to go
now. I try to fix supper every night for J.C. as part of his
payment for his work. I'll be back next week."

Miss Mercer came almost every day, even after Annie
was better. Annie grew used to her and came to look for-

ward to her visits. Miss Mercer talked constantly about everything, lots about healing and medicine, and showed Annie how to put Vaseline on her eyebrows and eyelashes to make them grow and how to use buttermilk at night on her face to make it soft and white. Once she told Annie that if you wanted to see your future husband you should put a mirror where it would catch the light from the full moon and brush your hair in front of it. His image, she said, would appear over your shoulder.

Neither one mentioned Annie's momma or the castor bean, but the shadow of the deaths hung over all their visits, and Miss Mercer seemed to know that sooner or later Annie would want to talk about it. Strangely enough, it was her story of how to see your future husband that brought the subject out.

On the night of the February full moon, according to Miss Mercer's instructions, Annie put a mirror next to the window. She wasn't sure that she believed it would happen, but Miss Mercer had said it would, so she was going to try it.

The house was dark, everyone sleeping, except for Annie. When she checked on Robbie, he was turned toward the wall, the cover pulled up over his head. Her breath made puffs of cold fog in the room's quiet air, and she put the spider-web shawl over her gown to keep warm. The candle she had lit on the dresser cast a fragile, flickering circle of light against the wall and over part of the floor. As she made the preparations, she felt slightly nervous, and the air in the familiar room seemed dense. She took out the ribbon-tied lock of her mother's hair and put it on the small table where she had set up the mirror. The sight of it made her feel better.

She thought over her instructions—to keep brushing her hair; if she didn't, the image wouldn't appear, and after the image appeared, when she stopped brushing her hair, it would disappear. Miss Mercer had told her not to try to look back at the face. She must look only in the mirror, and not look right at the face in the mirror, but instead let the corner of her eye catch it. *Let the image, Miss Mercer said, reveal itself. Don't, she said, don't look at it directly, or it'll go away.*

Annie sat down in front of the moonlit mirror and began brushing her hair. She brushed absently, her mind wandering, thinking about Miss Mercer and how she had grown to like the old woman and to enjoy being with her, when she realized that her arm was getting tired and that a lot of time must have passed. The candle was dying, the flame turning a deep sulfuric blue, and the room was even colder, the air like ice.

Nothing had happened, and she was disappointed and ready to quit and had almost stopped at the end of a stroke when she thought she heard a slight breathing behind her, like a soft rhythmic split in the heavy silence of the closed-up room. Her heartbeat quickened. She had to will her head to stay still, not to look around, and she forced her arm to keep brushing. Annie locked her eyes on her own reflection, her mirrored eyes trembling in the reflection in front of her. She sat like the dead except for her arm slowly pulling the brush through her hair, cold static following its sweep, making her hair rise, sending tingles of expectancy darting to her scalp.

Then she saw a shift in the seamless dark behind her, a lighter grayness in the black. It moved in the corner of her eye over her left shoulder, a ghostly shadow, like she sometimes saw the shadow of her own eyelash if she cut her eye just right. Her heart closed like a fist, a red mass of anticipation and dread, as the form began to take shape. Slowly a profound feeling of presence invaded her, filling her as if her own flesh were folding back, opening up, a husk surrendering its soft secret core. Annie panicked, instinctively reached for her mother's hair with her free hand, and she couldn't stop her eyes from glancing toward the image. She almost cried out as the moon, caught in the mirror, chased the shadowy form from her eye.

Afterward, in bed with her hand resting on the lock of hair, she felt her body finally slowing as her heart shrunk with a feeling of loss, and when she tried to think about what had happened, to recall the image, her mind seemed scattered like Robbie's toy animals, needing to be gathered and arranged.

The next afternoon sitting at the kitchen table drinking one of the old woman's concoctions, Annie told Miss Mercer about it, that she had tried to see her future husband but had got scared, that she thought something was there, she knew it was, had felt it, in fact, had almost seen it.

Miss Mercer looked thoughtful, then stern. "It's this house. Bad blood here."

Annie was confused. "What d'you mean? I did just what you told me."

"Maybe I shouldn't of told you."

Annie was adamant. "But I know I saw something—"

"I didn't say you didn't see something. It's just a matter of *what* you saw." Miss Mercer put out her hand. "Here. Give me your hand."

Annie did, and she felt the same surge of energy that had scared her so much on that evening her father had first taken her to Miss Mercer's house.

"You see this?" Miss Mercer tapped the side of Annie's hand opposite her thumb. "This is the Mount of the Moon. Yours is high, real high. Means you're prone to imaginings, and here," she moved her finger over to a mark below her middle finger, "this is a cross. You got sight . . . if you want to use it. You can see things."

Annie looked up from her hand to Miss Mercer. "I saw my momma one night. I think it was a dream, but I saw her go right by my bed."

"Dream or no dream, it don't make no difference. Dreams tell the truth, maybe more than what you think you *really* see. But you got to be careful. When you open yourself up, you got to be strong. Anything can happen."

"How do you *see* things? What do you do?" Annie's voice was almost a whisper, as if she were afraid someone might hear.

Miss Mercer put her cup down and peered at Annie. "You got to know how to let it come to your mind. Not to think what you want to think, but to open up your mind and let the pictures come like *they* want to."

"Can you see the past, too, or do you just see the future?"

"Either one. It depends."

Miss Mercer was quiet. She seemed to be contemplating something before she leaned toward Annie, her eyes opened wide and concern on her face.

"But it's not to be done in fun. Look, here." She took Annie's hand again and pointed to the Mount of the Moon. "This mark here, this star can be bad. Delusions, depression, even madness if the rest of your hand is bad, or even worse, suicide, usually drowning." She hesitated. "Your momma, you know, had the same mark."

Annie instinctively took her hand back, felt as if her body were an instrument and the old woman's words were fingers picking at her, a song she didn't want to hear, dismal sounds from the grave. . . .

Miss Mercer went on. "Folks with that mark is drawn to water, deep water, and if they're a water sign—Pisces, Scorpio, or Cancer—it's worse. The call's in their blood. Hard to stop it."

Annie pulled herself straight, tried to snatch her mind back. "But Momma didn't kill herself. She didn't mean to die. And it wasn't in the water no how."

"There's more ways of dying than one, girl. Your momma died all right. But she died a long time ago before that last birth. Died just as sure as her body would of if she had drowned. She lived only through you kids, you and Robbie, you was her life."

Annie thought about her mother, the way she had died, her lips cracking and her skin shriveling even as she craved the water that she couldn't swallow, and Annie felt a lump in her own throat and could barely speak. "I don't know what to do anymore. I miss her so much."

Miss Mercer went to the cabinet and took out a bottle of peach brandy. She poured half a glass for herself and a small amount in Annie's cup. "Love from the grave is cold, Annie, like having ice water replace your blood, but sometimes it's what you need. It slows you down, kind of swaddles you while things have time to grow in you. It's a lot like life growing before you're born, all fluid and dark, like the womb. You got to take the dark, learn from it, if you want to see."

Annie sat for a long time, just looking down at her hands, each finger apprehensive and expectant, and she felt something sway in her, something beyond sorrow, and the words came pouring out as if they had to be released quickly before they hid back in her mind again. "That night, when Momma died, I was so afraid, upset, everything was happening so fast, she was hurting, and I wanted to give her the medicine. I asked Claude to read it for me. I thought he said three tablespoons but he says that he didn't, that he said three teaspoons, he says that. . . ." And Annie looked up, grief etched in every hollow of her small face, her eyes begging Miss Mercer to help her. "He says that I killed my own momma . . . I can't remember. . . ."

"Yes, you can. You can *see* it, Annie. Just *dwell* on it. Let the picture come into your mind. Don't try to see what you think happened. Watch the picture. Ask him the question in your mind and listen for his answer. Let him say it himself. Dwell on the picture every night when you go to bed. It might take a while, but you'll see it."

Annie's voice was barely audible as she felt her mind withdrawing, veiling itself. "But I'm scared of the pictures. I don't know if I can do it."

THE FULL CIRCLE
1879-1935

Even as a child Selah Mercer knew she was different. She lived high on the side of a mountain. The trail to the cabin rose so steeply that a horse couldn't be ridden, but had to be led. Her momma was a granny woman who could stop blood, blow out fire, and cure thrash. She was the best in the region. And her daddy, the seventh son of a seventh son, was blessed with second sight. Selah was the couple's only child.

As soon as Selah could walk, she was following behind her momma, a huge, tall woman with deep brown eyes almost hidden in the folds of fat surrounding them, gathering plants and roots. They would go out and comb the woods from the twenty-third day of the moon until the thirtieth day heralded the beginning of the Sign of Mercury. Bringing their harvest back to the cabin, they would strip off the unnecessary parts before hanging the foliage upside down to dry from a line strung in the sunniest corner of the kitchen.

Selah watched her momma pass out cures for illnesses as well as charms that would ward off evil and induce love. Before Selah even knew how to express what was meant by the concept of love, she knew how to beat periwinkle and earthworms into powder, mix in house leek, and use the mixture in meat to produce love between a man and a woman. She learned that to "nail" an enemy, you must go to a cemetery and remove nails from a coffin, saying: "Nails, I take you, so that you may serve to turn aside and cause evil to all persons whom I will. In the name of the Father, and of the Son, and of the Holy Spirit. Amen." And then you find a footprint of the person and fix the nail in the middle by hitting it with a stone while saying, "Cause evil to—the name of the person—until I remove thee."

At birthings, people got used to seeing the peculiar child, her large homely face expressionless and her protruding eyes too old for her age, as she moved about at her momma's direction, like a dwarf shadow to the granny woman.

Her momma continually instructed her in the diseases of women and babies. If a woman couldn't conceive, Selah learned to take a deer's horn, mix it with a cow's gall, and have the woman keep it on her, and she knew that the tooth of a year-old colt hung about a child's neck would enable him to teethe without pain. Barely taller than the children she doctored, she blew tobacco smoke into small hurting ears. She herself passed minnows in and out of the young mouths plagued with yellow thrush, and if that didn't work, her momma would draw it out with her breath.

She had second sight, too. But not like her daddy, who saw whole scenes in his mind. People would come to him to find lost articles or missing children, and most of the time he was right in what he saw. Unless he was reading his Bible and making notes in the margins, he would sit motionless all day, on the porch in good weather or in front of the fireplace in bad weather, with his eyes closed as if what he saw in his mind were more intriguing than what life could offer, and he never spoke unless spoken to. Then he would say only what he had to and, when he was finished, he would lapse back into silence. Selah could not remember him as anything other than an ancient, grizzled old man who, skinny and slouched over, seemed part of the front room or the porch, sitting there as weathered and beaten as the rockers he seemed rooted in.

Selah didn't have that kind of gift. But she did have pre-monitions, strong feelings, especially foreboding when something bad was going to happen, and she usually knew the people involved even if sometimes she didn't know exactly what was going to happen to them. And if she needed to see more, there was always the spell she could use, the bitter green fluid secreted by the liver of a male cat and stored in the gall bladder mixed with the fat of a white hen. She could rub the salve on her eyelids, her momma told her, and then she could see what others couldn't. She had never done it, but she knew how.

There wasn't a school in the district, but Selah was edu-cated. Her momma, who could read and write, taught her at home, using the Bible and a book called *The Key of Solomon* to teach her to read. She let Selah label the jars that held all the medicines and potions, and Selah studied the deck of tarot cards her momma kept in a carved wooden box, practicing by asking the cards questions and reading the answers. The questions, though, were never about herself. "Remember," her momma had said, "*never* read your own cards. The cards will lie to you if you do. They'll trick you!"

Her momma drilled her in the powers of planets: The influence of Saturn on business dealings, Jupiter on health and money, Mars on ruin of all kinds, the sun on power, Venus on love, Mercury on deceit, and the moon on jour-neys and visions.

The family lived on what others gave them for their ser-vices—meat, eggs, milk, produce, tobacco—and on the exchange of dry goods for the cloth that she and her momma dyed shades of red, yellow, green, and blue and took down to the store in town four times a year.

Selah wasn't prepared for her daddy and momma to die. But inside of one year they both did. Her daddy, dressed just in the yellowed longhandles that he wore to bed and under his clothes regardless of the weather, and his boots, stood up from his bowl of cornbread and but-termilk one morning and fell over on the floor, his heart stopped by the glutted fat from a lifetime of a pork-laden diet. And her momma died of emphysema, her lungs filled with mucus, coughing and choking, even as she smoked her last pipe of tobacco.

Selah was only sixteen when they died, and despite how busy she kept, fixing cures and treating people who came up the mountain, she was lonely. People who came for cures talked to her no more than was necessary. They came and went as fast as they could, nervous and uneasy while they were there, and now that her momma was dead, the pregnant women, considering her too young, had been calling on the granny woman who lived down in the town. She hadn't realized how much she had depended on her momma for company, and now six months gone by, alone, winter on the way, she was miserable and restless.

It was late October. Selah was trying to get a batch of cloth ready for the store, before it got too cold to dye in the yard. The afternoon wind whipped around her, blowing the crisp, dying leaves from the branches onto the ground. Earlier she had gathered bark from birch trees and from red-osier dogwoods and oak, and she was boiling it in a #3 galvanized tub over a fire in the yard. While the bark boiled, she built a smaller fire and burned an armful of cedar bark to make ashes, then shifted the ashes through cheesecloth and put them in the boiling dye. She put in the material to be colored.

As Selah worked, she couldn't help remembering how every time she and her momma made red dye, her momma would say, "Now, remember, the secret to the dye is not to let a man look into it. If you do, the dye will be weak and not take on the cloth." She said it every time.

A noise behind her, a steady rustling of the leaves carried on the wind, made her look around, look down through the tops of the trees lining the steep path. She caught glimpses of a man leading his horse. When he came around the last bend into the clearing, she saw he was a big man dressed all in fur, his face hidden behind a long black beard and hair that fell down to his eyes and over his shoulders. He seemed surprised to see her.

"What you need?" she asked, wiping her hands on her apron, a little irritated about being interrupted, thinking it was someone seeking a cure or a charm.

He looked amused at the abruptness of her question. "Who're you?"

Selah was confused. People who came here always knew what they wanted. This man looked mean around the eyes, kind of shadowed and shaky, like he had been drinking, and he had a rifle slung over his shoulder.

"You lost?" she ventured, backing up a little, a small flutter of fear beginning to move in the back of her mind.

"Hell, no, I ain't lost. Don't usually come up this far, but I ain't *never* lost. I'm hunting." He looked past her to the house. "You the only one here?"

Selah didn't answer.

He peered closely at her, and she instinctively backed up more. He smiled. "I reckon you are." His voice was kind of hoarse and slow. Then, as if it suddenly hit him, he said, "I know. You must be that witch-woman's girl. I knew she stayed up here somewhere. Dead, ain't they? Both of them, her and her old man?"

Selah still didn't say anything, the flutter louder now, close behind her eyes.

He tied his horse to a limb. "I don't believe in all that hocus-pocus crap myself."

Then he got a moonshine jar out of the bag slung over his horse and took a drink as he walked over to the dye pot. "What kind of infernal concoction you got going here?"

Selah ran over and put herself between him and the dye pot. "It's just dye. Don't you look at it. You'll ruin it."

He smiled again like what she had said was funny and backed away to sit on a fallen tree. He kept staring at her while he drank.

Selah didn't know what to do or how to make him leave. She had never talked to a man before, and she was agitated, her body jumpy and tingly. She felt like she had to fill the space between them with words.

"It's red dye . . . and yellow, I make a yellow dye, too.

You have to use a double handful of shredded bloodroot and a handful of wild plum. You boil them together in water." The words rushed out.

He didn't say anything, just kept looking at her, his eyes weighing, judging, like somebody considering buying a pig.

She stumbled on. "The secret to setting the dye is, to . . . to use urine on the material after it's colored. You wet it down and let it dry." She didn't even know what she was saying as she rattled on.

He squinted at her over the bottle with a kind of thwarted-up face that might have been a smile. "That ought to be something to see. You mean you just stand over it and piss on it? Hike up that skirt and piss?" He laughed at the thought.

Selah flushed, felt her face go hot with embarrassment. She stood speechless as he put the jar down, got up, and walked over, standing, leering above her.

"You're about the ugliest gal I ever seen." He kept squinting into her face, a cruel, amused smile on his lips. "Why, I bet your beaver is cuter than your face. Ain't it?"

Heat seemed to envelop her, and sweat popped out on her forehead despite the cold air. Before she could react, he grabbed her, pushed his face in hers and kissed her on the mouth. Selah had never been kissed, not even by her parents. Without realizing how she knew, she knew that they never touched each other, not even when they were alone, side by side in the bed they shared, and although her momma was affectionate toward her, it was as teacher to pupil, an affection based on sharing knowledge, not love.

This man smelled like whiskey and something else, a smell like a barnyard, thick and steamy, and he forced his hard tongue in her mouth while he kneaded her back with one hand and held her head with the other. Selah felt her balance going as if the marrow in her bones were melting.

He backed off a little, and she almost fell to the ground. "My name's Julian. What about it, gal? You want it? I bet you ain't never had it before, have you?"

Selah understood what he was talking about. She knew

from the Bible what men did to women, and she knew the place where babies came from, and now she knew without knowing that her body was soaking up what he was doing, seeping itself in the emotions rising from the touch of his lips and hands, and the fear in her mind was giving way to a yearning that seemed dangerous and familiar all at once.

"My name's Selah," she whispered.

Julian came back regularly at first, almost once a week as autumn passed into winter. He would bring meat and liquor, and she would cook for him before building up the fire and putting the bearskin rug close to it.

That first time, when he had brought her in the cabin, he had told her to take her clothes off and then he had laid her on the bed, moved over her, fierce and urgent, his hands hurting her breasts, and when he reached between her legs, spreading them and pushing himself in, she felt a path burn through her like a spark igniting a dry forest.

After the first few times, he liked to do it other ways, kneeling over her neck, his face engrossed, his slack hungry mouth working, closing and opening, as he rocked back and forth, or he would turn her over on her knees.

She couldn't get enough of him, hungered for him in a way that she knew was ugly in its savagery, and no matter what she was doing when he wasn't there, she thought about him, his wildness, what he would do to her, and her insides would contract, squeeze into tight, hard, pleasurable knots. She thought she could taste him, actually taste him, like the liquor he taught her to drink, the hot liquid filling the slick cavern of her mouth. He was a taste she could roll on her tongue, suck on, and with her mind constantly filled with Julian, her body stayed energized, her heartbeat heightened, her secret places flooded with warm, fluid emotions.

He didn't hide anything from her, told her he was married, had a cow of a wife named Frannie, he said, and four young'uns, a boy, Henry, a real "little man" who could already hunt and skin, and three girls, probably all idiots. He laughed. Anyway, he did what he wanted, no skirt was going to tie him down, and he seemed to get a pleasure out of letting people who came up the mountain to see Selah know he was there, and soon everyone, except Frannie it seemed, knew about Julian and the witch-woman's frog-faced daughter.

But Julian eventually grew tired of her. By the time winter had set in hard, he was ready to break it off. Mean and drunk when he did come, he came less and less, and when he did, he took her quickly, his motions stark and hard, and when she kept at him about coming more, staying longer, he finally blew up and said that he couldn't stand her ugly frog-face anymore. He was done with her.

Three weeks had passed since he had left for the last time when Selah made the trip down the mountain. Waiting for a full moon so that she could see the trail, she left her cabin on the night that the Oakley baby, born dead, was buried earlier in the day, and she passed down the moon-washed path like an apparition, wrapped in black, her head covered with a hood, slipping into the cemetery, becoming another shadow among the tombstones, with the small spade and crowbar tucked under her cape. The ground was still soft, making it easy to dig up the shallow-buried casket that would be reburied deeper in the spring. Lifting the box out, she put it next to the hole and pried out the nails, saying the spell under her breath. Then she reburied the coffin, spreading the snow back over the spot.

The deep night was so quiet that, except for an occasional owl hoot, her footsteps on the snow as she walked to his cabin could have been heard if there had been anyone there to hear them; and the cabin, when she slipped into the yard, stayed dark and silent while she circled the shed until she saw what she was looking for—his footprints where he had put his horse up. She fell to her knees, and driving the nail into the middle of the indentation in the snow with a stone, breathless with emotion, she chanted, "Cause evil to Julian until I remove thee," and she felt a rush of euphoria along her nerves, tracing the blue paths of her veins, similar to what she had felt with him deep inside her.

When he was just six years old, Henry Williams had saved Selah Mercer's life. He had kept her from the gallows, saved her from being hung then burned. A chubby, dirty, dark-haired, soft-voiced boy, he had spoken out against his own momma and saved Selah's life.

Everyone knew that neither one of Henry's parents—not his momma, Frannie, nor his daddy, Julian—was any good. Frannie, lazy, shiftless, and married at thirteen, despised her boring, constricted life in the pitiful shack on the mountainside. The cabin squatted on a boulder-strewn acre, with a scrawny cow, a few chickens, a scraggly garden. The cracks between the logs were chinked with clay and small stones to keep out the cold. Frannie had her hands full with four children, Henry and three younger sisters, all underfoot. Julian was gone all the time, hunting, working at his moonshine still, or down in the valley in town, womanizing. His main interests, besides hunting and moonshining, were drinking and playing his guitar. The only interest he showed in his family was occasionally to take Henry hunting with him when he wasn't going away too far or for too long.

Not long after Selah had "nailed" Julian, she answered a knock on her door to find Frannie standing there. She wanted something to stop her monthly period. She didn't want no more kids, Frannie said, her husband was no good. Feeling a wild sweet joy flashing in her when saw Frannie, Miss Mercer gave her a sack with the ashes of a great frog and told her to keep it tied close to her belly so she wouldn't bleed anymore. Wanting only to do Julian harm, she relished the dark rush of premonition she felt when her hand touched Frannie's as she was passing her the bag.

Winter set in heavy. Deep in January with the mountainsides blanketed and the streams iced over and treacherous, Julian said he was going down to the valley. Frannie told him not to go, that he had "no business in town." He pushed her away from the door, told her "*his business* weren't none of *her business*," and left. He was gone a week before he came back again, hung over, with the smell of female all over him.

The next morning Frannie showed up with the kids at a neighbor's cabin for a quilting, bragging that she had already done her laundry and scrubbed her floor before coming. A questioning glance passed among the women who knew Frannie for a indolent housewife. When the neighbors asked about Julian, she said he had gone to town a week ago and hadn't come back yet. While she talked, she picked constantly at her skirt, her eyes cast down and her voice rising high and shaky, saying that she had told him not to go, that she hoped nothing bad had happened to him because everything was all iced over, and everybody knew how dangerous it was to be traveling up and down the mountain in the heavy snow.

Knowing the trouble between the two, the neighbors became suspicious, and the next day a group of men showed up at the cabin asking if Julian had come home yet. Frannie said no, and that she was real worried, but she couldn't do nothing with all the babies to take care of, no way she could go look for him.

The men got their dogs and started a search along the trail that he would have taken back from the valley. Nothing was found. They went back to the cabin again, and as soon as the dogs got next to the pine tree by the porch, they started having a fit. The men dug as far as they could in the frozen ground under the tree, but they didn't find anything, although the dogs kept sticking their noses in the hard soil like they did when dirt is soaked with a fresh kill. Frannie, watching from the porch, abruptly turned and went inside.

After consulting among themselves, the men went in the cabin. One of them, seeing the mantel freshly scrubbed and noticing places where the wood had been whittled out, pulled up the puncheons and there he saw the drying blood. Calling the others over, he began to rake out the ashes from the fireplace.

All this time, Frannie sat on the edge of the bed, silent, her face as white as the snow that the men had tracked in on the floor, nothing but her hand moving as she pleated and unpleated her skirt. The children, all except Henry, who stood alone in the corner, were lined up beside her and the baby lay forgotten on her lap. Pieces of bone and teeth began to appear in the scattered ashes.

"Well," said the man who found the blood, "hit looks like she kilt him all right."

It was then Frannie spoke. She suddenly jumped up, slinging the baby to the bed where it wailed weakly.

"Hit weren't me," she cried. "The witch-girl did it! She did it!" She grabbed hold of one man's arm. "She came in here in the shape of a giant toad and . . . and she sat on my chest, crushing it so bad I couldn't hardly breathe or call out . . . then she changed to a bobcat . . . and she kilt him, clawed him up—" Frannie talked in fits and starts, as she grabbed one man after the other.

By the time they got her to town, the people assembled, the sheriff there, and Selah Mercer brought in to hear the charges against her, Frannie had had time to work on her story, and in the meeting house she told it clear and straight, broken only by sobs when she was overcome with emotion, embellishing it with how Miss Mercer had threatened her babies if she told and adding details like how the witch had taken Julian's blood with her, hanging the full bucket on a tree branch and flying off.

No one had ever openly accused Miss Mercer of wrongdoing or dealing with the Devil before, and many inscrutable glances were thrown over at her, standing alone as if an invisible circle surrounded her while she glared at the woman talking. Selah could feel every word drawing the noose tighter around her neck. She knew that it hadn't been that long since the trouble over on the next mountain—Tom Dula, and the witch that helped him do it, hung for murdering his girl—and many of the people standing in the room listening had seen Julian at her cabin before. They suspected what had been going on. It wouldn't take much for them to believe Frannie's story.

But then Henry, from his place in the corner of the room, spoke out, his head bowed down, his words barely audible. "Hit weren't that way. I seen it." He looked up, spoke louder. "I seen it all."

All day the snow had fallen, soft wet flakes against a gray sky, and by sundown everything was covered in white, rime hanging from the trees and all along the edge of the porch, and the shutters frosted over.

Julian had come through the door brushing the snow off his shoulders and arms. The house was dark and cold, no fire in the fireplace, no supper on the stove, the children huddled together on the bed, tired out from whining and begging for food all day. Frannie was sitting in the rocker, staring into space, her face as dead as the fire.

Julian looked around angrily.

He strode over and pulled Frannie up from the chair. "What's the matter here? Why's the fire out?"

She didn't answer. She could tell he was half drunk.

"Look here, I ain't in no mood to put up

with any foolishness."

He shoved her toward the fireplace. "Get the fire going. I had enough today." He started taking his coat off. "Them damn snoopers. Messing around with my stuff. The thread I strung through the grass around my still was broke. I had to move it, lugged it over and hid it under the bridge. Now I got to find a new place for it. Those goddamn nosy sonovabitches—"

"There ain't no wood." Frannie interrupted him, walked away a little, turned her back to him. "There ain't no supper either." She turned back around and faced him.

He glared at her for a moment, then pulled the ax from under the bed and went out. The sharp sound of splitting logs filled the room as she paced back and forth.

One of the girls started to whimper. Frannie whirled at the sound.

"Shut up! Shut up!"

She snatched up the baby and put it in the basket next to the bed. Then she herded the two girls, snatching them by the arms, up to the loft where they slept together in one bed. She told Henry to get some cold cornbread from the larder and some water and bring it up.

"Now here . . ." she told him, her hands flying around from her face to her hair to her bodice and then back into the air. She seemed to have no control over them as they skittered like a flock of frightened snow birds, aimless and panicked. ". . . you feed 'em and put 'em to bed. Keep 'em quiet. You too. You hear? I don't want to see you no more tonight."

She went back down the ladder. Sullen, she leaned against the fireplace, until a small noise caught her attention. She looked up and caught a glimpse of Henry's head looking over the loft. "You better get in that bed! You hear me, right *now!"*

Julian came in with an armload of wood and threw it down by the fireplace. He went back out again and this time came in with the ax in one hand and a squawking chicken hanging by its feet in the other. He flopped the chicken on the wood counter and chopped its head off. The body jerked wildly, its feet flopping as the blood ran onto the floor.

"Get the fire going and supper on." He pulled out the jar of moonshine from the cabinet and took it over to the bed, where he fell down, propping his feet on the footrail, and started drinking. He glared at her, his eyes blurry, red, and dangerous like an angry warthog's.

Silent, she built the fire, then went to the sink. She began plucking the chicken and throwing the feathers over her shoulder, handfuls of them. Snowy white like the flakes outside, they swirled and floated in the icy air of the room before settling on the floor. Then before he could react, she tossed the head, flinging it hard over her shoulder, its glassy eyes still open and staring. It flew across the room and hit next to the bed.

"Shit! Hey! What you think you're doing?" He leaped off the bed, ran over, and grabbed her arm, slinging her around.

"I'm fixing supper. Ain't that what you want?" She looked him full in the face. "Supper?"

He looked as if he might slap her. "Think you can sass me? Huh, do you? You stupid cunt?" Then he paused and smiled, a line of spittle stretched thinly between his chapped lips. "Supper can wait. I know what you need." He grabbed her by the hair and pulled her toward the bed.

Frannie struggled to get free. She reached

behind her, snatched the chicken body up from
the sink and swung it at him. It hit him on the
cheek, chicken blood splattering the side of his
face. Chicken feathers stirred up by the struggle
rose all around them in the disturbed air.

She cried, scratched at his face, tried to wiggle free as he groped under her skirt. He cursed
and grabbed at her. Then his hand hit the sack
tied around her waist. He looked confused.

"What's this?"

He pushed her over to the bed, knocked her
down, and slapped her face. Frannie quit fighting. He pulled her skirt up, stripped off her
drawers.

"What's this? Huh? Some kind of spell you
trying to put on me? You been to that witch?
Huh? You been talking to her?" He was hurting
her, leaning on her chest as he held her down,
twisting her hair painfully. "Speak up, bitch!"

She tried to talk, to force the words out over
the terror clogging her throat. "Hit ain't nothing to do with you! It's for me!" She struggled
to get out from under him.

"You move one more time, and you won't
never move again, you hear?" His gray face
right over hers was blotched red. His eyes, the
whites a dirty yellow color shot through with
blood, looked like they might pop out of his
skull.

Frannie made herself lay still. She couldn't
stop whining. He wrapped his hand tighter in
her hair and gave it a yank before letting go of
her and standing up.

"Now you tell me what this conjure bag is
for."

She started crying uncontrollably, sobbing,
turning her head side to side. "Hit's so I don't
get no more babies."

He looked perplexed for a moment, then

*incredulous, then he laughed. "You don't want
no more babies? Well, hell, girl, I can fix that.
You don't need no conjure bag."*

*He ripped the sack off and threw it on the
floor before turning her over on her stomach,
pulling her up on her knees, and lifting her skirt
over her head. He pressed her chest down to the
bed as he leaned on her and forced himself into
her, brutal and quick. He shoved against her
over and over.*

*Finally, he pulled away. "Jesus, that's tighter
than fucking a chicken, and," he laughed again
as if were a joke, "it don't make no babies."*

*Frannie lifted up, crawled off the bed, and
picked up her underwear as he flopped down
on the bed again.*

"Now go fix supper," he said.

*She walked stiffly over to the cooking area
and picked up the chicken. She put it in the
sink, washed it, then cleaned up the feathers,
her body doing the tasks automatically. She
never looked over at him.*

*By the time she got the chicken ready to boil,
Julian was passed out, the jar of liquor turned
over on his stomach with what was left of it
soaked into his beard and shirt.*

*If Henry had not already been awake and
watching, the commotion would have wakened
him anyway, the bellowing and the sound of
things being turned over, as his daddy, his face
split down the middle, reeled around the room,
knocking things down, trying to get to Frannie,
her face contorted in astonishment and terror
and still gripping the ax with both hands, as she
stayed just out of his reach.*

Everyone was so shocked and horrified by the boy's
words describing the killing scene, spoken in a soft
monotone, that no one was watching his momma. Fran-

nie had knocked him to the floor and was clawing at his eyes before they could react and pull her away. *Devil's spawn*, she cried, *you're just like him!*

After Henry's story, when Frannie finally confessed and told the true story herself, she said she didn't actually know when she decided to do it. In all the later tellings, she always started with, "I couldn't tell you when I made up my mind to do it. . . ." All she remembered later was that his snoring had filled the house with a hoarse rasping that grew louder and louder, an awful rhythm of wet wheezing, and the rage rising in her had felt as cold as the snow piled up against the side of the cabin. She had meant only to wake him and tell him supper was ready, but instead she put more wood on the fire and stood in front of it, her mind unable to complete even one coherent thought.

It was sometime later while she looked into the fire, feeling the heat swelling, the room getting hotter and hotter, that she felt a tide of fury rising in her and filling the frigid cavern of her chest, melting the solid knot of ice that had replaced her heart. She began to feel strangled, then something like a flash blinded her, and the next thing she knew Julian was chasing her around the room, his face split open like a dropped fruit.

When he fell, she said, he hit face down right in front of the fireplace. His hands stretched out above his head, still groping for her.

She stood over the body, looking at it. Then, without really thinking or planning anything, by pulling on his arms, she turned him over on his back and, seeing that it—she called the body "it," she said, because it wasn't Julian no more, just a body like that of a hog—was bleeding all over the floor, she got a rug and wrapped his head up. Then the thought came to her that maybe one of the children had waked up, so she stopped and climbed the ladder to the loft. Henry and the girls were in the bed and seemed to be asleep.

When she got back down to the body, she moved quickly this time, with purpose. She pulled off Julian's pants and undershorts. Then by standing between his legs, stretched out like two hairy stumps, she managed, by pulling and tugging, to drape him over a stool, getting it under his hips, and spreading out his legs in front of him. She pushed a bucket under his buttocks, right up next to the stool, and then with a knife she cut two gashes in the inside of each thigh, right up next to his testicles. The blood ran out from each hole in a steady stream—just like bleeding a hog, she had said, didn't mean no more to her than bleeding something slaughtered. In just a few minutes, the bucket was full, and the bleeding slowed to a trickle as she shoved another one in place.

She carried the buckets outside and poured the blood under the tree by the porch. Still warm, it melted the snow, but flakes were falling so fast that the crimson spot was almost covered before she got back to the door.

Inside again, she built the fire up until it filled the small shack with a feverish heat. She chopped the body into small pieces, starting with the hands. She had difficulty with the trunk, with splitting the breastbone. The big ax was awkward, so she changed to a hatchet. Then she fed the pieces into the fire. She recalled how the pieces had made the fire sizzle and pop like when meat put on to roast drips grease into the flames.

As the pieces burned, Frannie washed the sheets on the bed and scrubbed down the floor.

She still might have got off. Everyone knew how good-for-nothing Julian was—a sluggard, a liar, a drunkard, an adulterer, and she was only eighteen, and with all those babies to care for. But it was the way she had got rid of the body that the jurors dwelt on and the deliberate way she had chopped and burnt him and then said that it didn't mean nothing to her; that was what couldn't be tolerated. Frannie was hanged for her crime, and Henry, along with his three sisters, was passed to his aunt, Julian's sister, and her husband.

Within a year of the killing, Henry's small mind that had expanded beyond his young experience to hold all the violent emotions of the crime he related so thoroughly and graphically seemed to shrink into itself, wrung dry by what he had seen, and he became morose and antagonistic, wanting only to be left alone, staying in the field or out in the barn except to go in the house to eat or sleep, speaking only when he had to and never mentioning or asking about his mother. By the time he was ten, he was put out of school for his refusal to do any of the lessons and his disrespectful, almost menacing, attitude toward the teacher.

As he got older, he became even more withdrawn, and once his aunt, who had been in town, came back to find him looking at a small paper book filled with "dirty" pictures of women, and she had told his uncle, clutching the three little girls as if Henry might attempt to try out what he had seen in the pictures. She insisted that he be whipped until he repented. His aunt never got over the sight and avoided looking directly at him as if his face was repulsive.

Yet nothing moved Henry; not talking; not the prayers his aunt said daily for him, asking the Lord at the supper table to save him from his corrupt nature, her eyes rolling backward in their sockets as they sought heaven; not the whippings from his uncle, who, in the small lean-to next to the kitchen that served as his bedroom, would wait for Henry to remove his shirt and drop his pants, so as not to ruin the clothes, before he laid on the strap, working his way up and down the boy's back, buttocks, and thighs.

When Henry got old enough to move out, he did. He opened up the small cabin on the mountainside that had stood vacant since his daddy's murder and lived there alone for years, hunting, selling meat and skins, and raising hogs. Then when he was thirty years old, he went across the mountain and came back with a fifteen-year-old wife, Evelyn, part Cherokee, for whom, it was rumored, he had paid three hundred dollars. Why he went and got himself a wife is what no one could figure out, yet, unlike his daddy, he was a good provider for his new wife and later family. A hard worker, thrifty to the point of stinginess, he managed eventually, about a year after Neal was born, to buy a larger tract of land, ten acres, good bottom land.

Still, he was as reclusive as ever and stayed to himself, suspicious and alone, a bitter, harsh man with a soul as hard as flint, and when he came to Miss Mercer that autumn with Annie following along behind him, he was convinced in his narrow brutal mind that his wife—like all women, like his mother—was deceitful, dangerous, secretly hating him and plotting against him. He told Miss Mercer she was an adulteress, that Annie wasn't his child—anyone with half an eye could see that—pointing out Annie to her like he was presenting a piece of evidence, and said that it was Evelyn who was causing his run of bad luck. He explained it all to Miss Mercer as if he were unfolding an intricate scheme against himself, and Miss Mercer saw the livid red hands that clenched and unclenched as he talked, saw the knotted line on his hand reaching all the way from the Mount of the Moon to disappear abruptly at the Line of the Heart, and knew that Evelyn had become for him the embodiment of all that had gone bad in his life. *Blood will tell, it always comes out in the end*, she thought.

Miss Mercer hadn't hesitated at all when Robbie had shown up at her door, saying, "Annie sick." She had thrown on her cape and hood and, gathering up what supplies she thought she would need, had gone back with him. She still owed Henry. And to Miss Mercer, the circle that had started so long ago in the woods when Julian had come up on her dying the red cloth had continued in that meeting room where Henry had said, "Hit weren't that way. I seen it all," and had now come full around and was beginning to spiral off in a new direction.

9

Public work, her daddy called it, *I'll be away working at a sawmill, but I'll try to get home for a day whenever I can, about once a week, there ain't no choice, the farm can't support us all, you'll have to take care of the kids while I work, no choice, you can do it, school's out of the question now, no way for you to go.*

The teacher, an outsider sent in by the Board of Education, had taken him before the magistrate for keeping Evelyn out, *twelve years old, she needs to be in school, just a child.*

He had stood up in court, speaking with earnest simplicity, *six kids all under ten, wife dead, pneumonia, who's gonna keep them while I put food on the table,* he turned to the teacher, *you, ma'am, are you gonna come keep 'em for me?* She had turned away and the magistrate had dismissed the case.

It seemed to Evelyn as if she had always been surrounded by crying faces, all needing something, whining, sniffling, needing to be fed, to be washed, always needing. Day and night, they needed something, one would start, then another, then another.

Mattie, the girl next in age to Evelyn, was almost as big as Evelyn but still acted like a baby, sometimes worse than the others, refusing to help, wouldn't wash a dish or hang up a piece of clothing, knowing that Evelyn couldn't do a thing about it, couldn't make her, and the time Evelyn had got mad, livid, called her sorry and picked up the broom and hit her with it, Mattie had told her daddy when he came home, said that Evelyn beat her, and he got on to Evelyn, told her *You're supposed to be grown, not acting like a kid, how can I work if I can't depend on you to keep the kids like you should, we're family, you ought to be ashamed.*

Evelyn had protested, said how awful it was, no sleep, always something to do, no help, then she saw how he was looking at her, the disappointment in his eyes, and she had broke down and cried, after all he tried so hard, looked so tired when he came home carrying a sack of food each week, she promised him *I'll take care of every-thing, won't bother you,* and saw from the way his face relaxed, the way the wrinkles on his forehead smoothed out that she had said the right thing, said what he wanted to hear.

For the next three years, she felt as if she lived under-water, moving heavy and sluggish through days and nights that sucked at her, kept her out of breath, never any rest, until it was like she was little more than a body that washed, cleaned, scrubbed, cooked, whatever was needed, always reacting to what someone wanted, her skin stretched to a thin numbness over her skeleton, yield-ing to the pressure from others, *hold me, rock me, feed me*, and she did, refusing to stop for the headaches that came regularly, at least once a week, a throbbing ache in the bones of her face, until the pain forced her to lie down, to give in, to ignore for a short time the commo-tion of the demands, the needs that swirled around her like a storm around its quiet still vortex.

When her daddy told her *I met the man at the sawmill who sells moonshine, a good man, owns property, needs a wife, you'll like him, quiet and sober, he's offering three hundred dollars for a wife, we need money, Mattie is big enough to watch the kids now, we need the money bad, it's best for you, not a boy, but a man, a sober, hardwork-*

ing man, owns property . . . Evelyn had watched his face, felt her head start to ache, a sharp stabbing in her temple, tried to catch his eyes that constantly focused and refocused on things around the room, realized what he wanted, and said, *I'll get my things together, when's he coming for me?*

He had smiled, looked relieved, looked her in the eye *he's right outside, waiting, I'll get him in here.*

At first, Henry was good to her. Even on the first night in that strange solitary mountain cabin tucked in a cove by a stream, he had taken her so calmly, almost emotionlessly, as he crawled in the bed, opened up his long-handle underwear, lifted her nightgown and rolled on top of her—a heaviness, a prod, a sharp pain, him moving back and forth, a few hoarse grunts, and it was over. Afterward, in the moonlight that fell through the small window, feeling curious and a little scared of the big silent man, she studied his sleeping face, seeing how thick it was, like muscle, like it was made out of layers of corded muscle, coarse and impenetrable.

What she liked most was the quiet, calm air in the cabin, almost as if all the noise had been sucked out of the cabin, and outside, nothing but the sounds of the woods, birds, scampering bodies in the trees and on the ground, the hushed swish of the stream over rocks.

Here there was no one to take care of, no one demanding her attention, just Henry gone a lot, hunting, watching for his few cows and hogs that roamed free on the mountainside, brewing moonshine, coming home at sunset, eating supper, and going to bed, but usually waking up to roll on top of her later when she got in the bed. She learned that it didn't hurt as much if she relaxed and thought about something else, spreading her legs widely and wrapping her arms lightly across his hairy back. Sometimes his hands hurt her too, scraped the tender places of her body with their coarse, calloused fingers, but she never let on, and soon figured out that a little bit of grease dabbed on before she got in the bed helped. Anyway, it didn't take long, and sometimes if he was real tired, and she got in the bed real quiet, he didn't wake up at all.

If she should have been lonely during the day, or even sometimes for days at a time, she didn't feel lonely. She kept busy doing just what she wanted to do, but making sure that everything was ready for Henry when he came in, watching his eyes to gauge his reactions to what she had done, the way she made things for the cabin, a crocheted bedspread, doilies, mats for hot pots, braided rugs, the food she fixed, always hot and fresh, even vegetables from a small garden she kept herself that he was learning to like along with his meat and bread, and she was pleased that she seemed to be doing what he wanted.

Only once did she try to defy him and that was over the old woman, Miss Mercer, when she realized that Henry gave her food each week. Miss Mercer lived down in the valley, had just moved there, Henry said, from a remote cabin even higher on the mountain than they were, and she lived alone, everyone gave her something. But Evelyn didn't like it. *Food is scarce, even in good times. Why give it away? We need all we can get, we can sell any left over, we need to think about money, about never being without, bad things could happen when you're poor, need more than you got. . . .* And Henry, being at his core a stingy man—a man who didn't want to depend on anyone, a man who had spent most of his childhood as an intruder at a reluctant relative's dinner table, having to listen to his aunt's supper grace that blessed the food, her thin nostrils flaring wide over the high nasal sounds of her whining voice, as she asked the Lord to take away the taint of Henry's parents' sins from his wayward soul, asked that Jesus, in his mercy, not pass the mark from son to son, a man who had eaten daily under a disapproving uncle who counted every mouthful with an eye bleary from coveting what he didn't have and a thin mean slash of a mouth that moved constantly as if it were always devouring, a mouth that complained about every dropped crumb, every bone left with a shred of meat on it, *you eat everything on that plate, boy, you be thankful you got a place to eat, somebody to take on the burden of you children,* a man who had watched his sisters work from sunup to sundown before they could hardly walk, *idle hands are the Devil's workshop,* who had seen them grow to hate their momma, *a lazy evil murderer,* whom they could barely remember, despise a daddy, *a fornicator,* whom they couldn't remember at all—he had stopped giving.

Then the trouble with the cows happened. Before the month was out, both of the cows were giving milk streaked with blood, and the beasts would sit down and paw the ground with their front hooves while they moaned piteously. Soon afterward, the cows died, just dropped over dead. Evelyn was positive that the old woman had done something to them, maybe given them something to eat to make them sick, and she said as much to anyone who would listen until Henry, afraid that more would happen and fearful of losing his stock, had gone into a rage. They argued. He struck her. The next day the fresh bruises on her arms and cheek had blossomed like ugly fruit on her young skin, and she had panicked, then withdrawn, knew that she had to please him, figure out what he wanted and give it to him, he deserved it, he worked so hard, gave her everything, took care of her. She cried, said *whatever you want, do whatever you want, i'm sorry.* She had rubbed her arms where he had gripped them, feeling the hot places that would swell into knots in a few days.

Later, right at dusk, a purple haze lying on the mountains and the emerging moon already a shadow in the dark yellow sky, she stood on the porch and watched him burn the ears and tails of the cows that had died to remove the hex. Then, without a word, she killed two chickens and dressed them for him to take down the mountain to Miss Mercer.

Her infidelity never would have happened if it hadn't been for Henry and his potatoes. After they had moved into the valley to a good piece of land for crops, Henry got it in his head that he could grow and sell potatoes. Most people in the area didn't grow any more than they could eat, and some didn't grow anything at all, living off hogs, bread, and grease, and the money they could make on moonshining. There just wasn't any way to get produce down to market. The roads were so bad that many places were impassable on horseback or even foot. But Henry got this idea that Irish potatoes would grow good in the cool air, and even beans, he said, would grow in the mountains after they would be burned out on the flatland. So he started agitating for a road that would connect them with Raleigh where there was a state storehouse to distribute produce. He talked with other men outside the store, explained how they could do it. *Seed potatoes*, he said, *we can grow seed potatoes for the whole Southeast, and other crops, beans, corn, sweet potatoes, all we need is a road,* and his fingers would be rubbing together already counting the money he would make.

The schoolteacher wrote Raleigh and found out how to go about petitioning for a road, and after a year of letter writing to the Good Roads Commission of North Carolina, they were notified that construction would start that spring. Evelyn was proud when Henry became somewhat of a local hero, and his sordid childhood faded even further into the past as his neighbors began to see him in a new light—a shrewd, industrious farmer who, they also realized, knew how a road would expand his moonshining business too.

Spring came and the path down to the flatland, what there was of it, was already being assaulted by mountain laurel and rhododendron, tangles of white, pink, and purple blossoms, when the road-building machine and crew arrived. They set out to clear and widen a road.

Twice a week, Evelyn passed them with her two little boys, Neal and Claude, as she walked to see a neighbor who gave sewing lessons. Evelyn knew how to crochet and knit, but she knew only enough sewing to fix things, and this woman was teaching a group how to make patterns and sew clothes from them.

Coming up the path, she would always hear the deafening noise of the grader before she could see it, and Neal would start to pull back on her hand, but the baby, Claude, would always look expectant. When the crew came into sight, the operator of the grader would cut his engine until she passed, always removing his hat and saying, "Afternoon, ma'am." Evelyn got to where she looked forward to walking by there and hearing him say it. She would smile and nod back at him, careful not to meet his eyes direct, but she still made out that he was young, and dark skinned, kind of like an Indian, his shirtless chest smooth and tan, like her grandma's skin, who had been a Cherokee, and who had given her the high bone structure and the deep black hair that contrasted so highly with her kinky waves and her pale Scotch-Irish skin from her daddy's side.

Once as she was on her way back, he was down off the grader, looking at something under it. When she got opposite him, he straightened up, and seeing Neal's wide-eyed stare at the machine, he had wiped his hands on a handkerchief that he then tied around his neck and asked, "Would your little boy like to sit up on it?"

Evelyn had looked at Neal, who violently shook his head as if he couldn't speak, but Claude, holding out his arms, ran up. The man picked him up, turning to sit him in the seat, and Evelyn noticed the hard muscles in his back that knotted easily with the motion, and a birthmark right at his waist, next to the small of his back, a brown splotch shaped like a spider, or a crab, some creature with lots of legs. Claude had promptly become engrossed, trying to move every lever.

The young man turned back to Evelyn and put out his hand. "I'm Jesse. Pleased to meet you."

Evelyn shook his hand, felt uncomfortable under his expectant stare. She looked away, checking on Claude as she muttered that her name was Evelyn, then took her hand back to pat Neal, who was fretting and holding onto her skirt.

"Mighty pretty babies you got here." He smiled. He had big white teeth, almost an unnatural whiteness. "But you sure don't look old enough to have no babies."

Evelyn felt the blood rush to her cheeks. She didn't know what to say. She retorted, almost defiantly, "Well, I am. We got to go now." She snatched up Neal's hand and moved to get Claude. "Come on, let's go."

Jesse, looking slightly surprised at her abruptness, reached up and lifted Claude down, and Evelyn grabbed the little boy and hurried down the path, Claude looking back over her shoulder at Jesse and the machine.

Evelyn didn't go to the next sewing lesson. She told herself that she didn't have the time to waste, but all afternoon she moped around, working in her small garden, picking bugs off the underside of leaves and putting paper collars on cabbage to keep out cutworms, but she kept thinking about what she was missing; she liked the company of the other women, the gossip and constant chatter, though she listened more than she talked, and she fretted about the dress she was supposed to be working on. Even more disturbing, despite her determination not to think about it, were the thoughts of her meeting with Jesse that constantly forced their way into focus in her mind. His eyes intrigued her, deep set, under dark brows, eyes so black she couldn't see the irises, dense and porous as deep water.

Restless, she moved from one task to another, but her willful mind kept skittering back to him, focusing on his eyes, and then his teeth, the smooth skin of his cheek, like he never had to shave, his hand, rough and calloused but only in spots, not all over like Henry's, the play of the long, hard muscles in his back, and the birthmark, such a strange mark, almost alive in the way it moved as he did, and, thinking about it, she felt a sense of unease come over her accompanied by a light throbbing in her temples.

Jesse had watched her go by each way twice a week for a month. At first he thought that maybe it was her little brothers she had with her, but John, when Jesse asked him what he thought, had said between grunts as he sawed on a tree, "Hell no. These girls up here get married and have babies when flatland girls are still playing with dolls."

Jesse shook his head. "Maybe so." He looked at the other man and raised his eyebrows. "But that sure is a mighty fine looking momma in my book!" They had both laughed.

The next time she went by, he kept track of time, and when he thought she would be coming back, he stopped the grader and got down and pretended to be looking under it.

He didn't know quite what he was going to say, and he had been surprised at how shy, almost frightened, she was. But it hadn't put him off. Rather that skittishness, added to the wavy black hair gathered into a heavy knot at the nape of her neck and almost celibate whiteness of her cheeks that constantly flushed red, made him determined to talk to her again.

When she had scurried off, one of the men working with the clearing crew grinned and said, "Jesse, you better leave these mountain women alone. I'm telling you true. They got some mean men up here, and they don't like outsiders messing around. They'll nail your balls to a stump, boy!"

Jesse climbed back up in the grader. "Shit, for all the use I got out of them for the last month they might as well." He cranked the engine, drowning out any further comments.

It was inevitable that the brief conversations on Evelyn's way back from her sewing would lengthen out until she and Jesse were sitting in a small cove on the other side of where the clearing crew worked with saws and hatchets while the little boys played in the dense undergrowth next to the stream, cascading over rocks with a constant soft roar.

He talked openly, easily, about himself. She had guessed right about the Cherokee blood; his daddy was half-blooded. But he was younger than she had thought at first, just twenty, five years younger than she was. He asked her about herself, and she was shy about answering, not used to talking about herself, a little ashamed of her childhood. He seemed amused by her awkwardness, her hesitant stammer, nervous laugh, habit of brushing her hair back with her fingers whether or not it was in her face, her need to have it all safely tucked in the heavy bun on her neck.

Once when a slight wind blew a strand over her forehead, Jesse reached over and gently pushed it back, his hand meeting hers that was already reaching to contain the free strand, and he didn't hesitate but took her hand and brought it over to his lap. He was sitting, smoking, on the flat top of a boulder next to where she stood barely leaning on the stone as if she needed to appear always to be in the act of leaving.

"I can tell you about yourself, everything, even what you don't want me to know." He squeezed her hand, held it trapped, while he stared at her, his voice teasing. "Do you want me to?"

Evelyn's laugh was jittery. She tried to take her hand back, feeling pinpricks of excitement. Then she said something to Claude, who was getting too near the water. Jesse held on until she turned her attention back to him. She asked, her voice forced into lightness, "How can you do that?"

Jesse smiled, held her hand even tighter. "My aunt reads palms. I've watched her do it for as long as I can remember. I learned it up from her."

Evelyn didn't know what to say. Her body was acting strangely, as if a stream of feelings flowed from his hand to hers, along her veins, to her mind where she was confused, excited, a turmoil of emotions she couldn't identify flooding her.

Jesse watched her for a moment, then let go of her hand, took a deep draw off his cigarette and threw the butt down, picking up a twig off the rock that he began peeling, strip by strip.

"My aunt's known all over where I come from, and

people come to her for all kinds of things, but she won't read for just anybody. She'll glance at their hands at the door, and if she don't want to read for them, she'll tell them right there at the door to go away, that she won't read for them." He glanced up at her, saw her flushed animated face, and went on.

"Like the time with that boy. It was before I was even born. She was real young. Even then she had the gift. She got it from her momma's sister, both of them the seventh child of a seventh son. Anyway, a boy came to her wanting her to read his hand, tell him if he was lucky in love, if his girl was true to him. At that time she didn't know to turn anybody away, so she read his hand. She always said how his hands was dark red, a liver-like color with the balls on the little fingers real lined."

He held out his hand and pointed to the line making a wide circle around the base of his thumb. "This, the life line, was thick at the top and spotted with red, and the head line was all twisted like a rope across his hand. But it was when she saw the line circling the middle of his thumb that she was sure."

Jesse put his hand down. "She told him that he was bent toward evil, maybe even murder, that the circle around his thumb was a sign of hanging. He got angry, called her a liar, even hit her before charging out."

Evelyn had unconsciously moved closer to him as he told the story. Her eyes felt hot and dry and the pulse that ran from her eye to her jaw made a steady throb in her head, and when he paused, she spoke immediately, eager. "Was she right? Did he ever do anything?"

Jesse smiled, a satisfied smile, "Yeah, his name was Dula, he was the Dula boy who ended up murdering his girl. They hung him and a woman, they said she was a witch, who helped him do it."

Evelyn caught her breath. She felt a sense of threat come over her, like a half-realized form lurking in the corner of her eye, and her face broke out in a chilled sweat.

"Hey!" Jesse peered at her, the muscles around his eyes tensed, the fine lines deepened. "I didn't mean to scare you. You all right?"

Evelyn shook her head, pulled her mind back from the
cave it was staring into, looking for something, straining
to see—

"My head hurts a little. I guess I better go." She stood
up straighter, shook her shoulders slightly, as if she were
shaking off a bad dream, called the boys.

Jesse stood close to her, almost over her, so that she
could smell his breath, a warm tobacco scent that made
her dizzy, and the day seemed unnaturally bright, burning
her eyes, even though the cove they were in was shaded
with overhanging branches and vines.

He lightly touched her shoulder. "Next time I'll read
your hand for you, all right?"

She managed to look directly in his eyes. "All right,"
she said, barely loud enough for him to hear it.

Jesse put up with the ribbing of the other men, who
delighted in describing in crude, gory detail what was
going to happen to him if he kept on "messing around."
Jesse had grown up in the mountains, and he knew without being told that he was being stupid, *plumb stupid* as
his aunt who raised him would have said. *Boy, that's just
plumb stupid. Don't you got the sense you was born
with*? It was her usual comment. A bitter old maid sad-
dled with a child she didn't understand or even necessarily
like, she was confused by his needs when he was young,
maybe even a little afraid of his maleness when he got
older, and when, at sixteen, he wanted to leave, she had
no comment, just a palpable relief that floated over her
shoulder as she washed the dishes. "Do what you want,"
she said, her voice drowned out by the clanging of the
pots.

He had left home at sixteen and bummed around the
flatland and the coast, taking one job after the other. The
road work was Jesse's third job this year, but this one
looked like it would last a while, at least as long as the
weather let them work. This job, he thought, would be
different. Road building paid good and paid regular, and

he was stashing money away to leave North Carolina, somewhere away, something new, see something he hadn't seen before. Just getting out of the mountains and to the coast had been an eye-opener for him. The ocean had affected him, like something breaking loose in him, made him realize what there was to see, and now, when he got a little money in his pocket, he was going somewhere, somewhere different.

The road crew all slept in the attic of an old gristmill. It was dirty and hot, the boarded-up room holding in the sun's heat while keeping out any breeze, and the rats that shared the attic were so bold and vicious that the men had to sleep with any food they had tucked under them so the rats wouldn't get it. There was nothing to do but drink—there was plenty of moonshine to be had—talk, and play music on the guitar that John had brought with him and the old wire-stringed psaltery that they found thrown in a corner of the attic.

In the back of his mind, Jesse realized that the other men's warnings weren't all jokes, that he needed to be careful. But he didn't know what it was about the girl that attracted him so. He thought of her as a *girl*, even after he found out she was a mother and older than him, because that's what she looked like and acted like, a girl. He had been with quite a few women since he had left home, some who knew more than him, and Evelyn sure wasn't nothing more than a girl compared to them, that was plain. He was fascinated by the simple elegance of her appearance, her porcelain skin stretched thin over delicate bones, the heavy knot of hair as dark as a raven's wing on her white neck, large blue eyes that betrayed every fear, every uncertainty, and he spent many a boring evening in the attic imagining her hair loosened and her skin warm with blood, her eyes dilated and moist with excitement. He knew he could do that for her, do what apparently hadn't been done before.

She wouldn't talk about her husband, just said he was a good man, took good care of her and the kids. She did tell Jesse how her daddy had sold her for three hundred dollars and how Henry was a lot older than her. But she always ended up saying *he's a decent man, takes good care of us, works hard.*

The last time, in the cove, when he had told her about palm reading, her distress and agitation, the way she stared at him, wide-eyed and disturbed, had been, for him, like the scent of game on the air—a poignant scared odor—and he had wanted to take her right then, to feel the quivering of her breast under his hand, the panicked taste of fear on her tongue. Christ, what it must feel like to be inside that much turmoil, inside those churning raw sensations.

> *Come on, now. You promised. Come 'ere. Give me your hands.*
>
> *I changed my mind. Maybe I don't want you seeing what's in my hand.*
>
> *Then why you smiling? Give 'em here.*
>
> *You might not like what you see.*
>
> *No chance. I like everything about you. Hands and all, especially "all." What you blushing for? Huh?*
>
> *Oh, go on. Here, read 'em. If it'll make you content.*
>
> *First of all, you got to quit wiggling and pulling on your hands. I ain't going to bite you. Now, here, just let 'em lay still, nice and easy, that's right. I got to look at the whole hand first. Lots of readers just look at the palm. That's why they sometimes make mistakes. You got to look at the whole hand first . . . yours are soft. There's some hard spots, but they ain't nat-ural, your hands are natural soft—*
>
> *What's that mean?*
>
> *That means, Miss Anxious, that you are ner-vous, high-strung, that you daydream a lot, make up things you want to happen in your head. And you're sweet and kind to people . . . even if you don't like 'em.*

I don't see what—

Never mind, I'm doing the reading. You just be still. Now your fingers. See how they're shaped kind of like a cone on the end, like a sewing thimble? Means you like pretty things, you like to make pretty things. It means too that you're moody, one minute you're all right, then the next something's wrong with you.

There ain't nothing wrong with me—

Give me back your hands, I ain't finished. . . . These fingers show that you're a real woman, you like—

Go on to the lines, like you talked about in the man's hand that killed his sweetheart?

All right, settle down, your life line's here. I got to divide it by sight into years. . . .

It looks to me like that life line stops right there. Does that mean anything?

No . . . maybe . . . it all depends on other lines too. It's hard to do the years by sight. It's better to have a handprint made with smoke from a lamp and—

Does it mean I'm going to die early? Is that what it means?

Look, will you forget that line? Look here, on the heart line you got a triangle. That means you're going to have a love—

You're just making this up. Let go of me. I got to get my boys. I don't see 'em.

They're all right. You can hear them over in the vines by the water. Don't pull away. Come 'ere. . . .

They decided to meet at the entrance to the caverns by the falls. Henry was gone hunting, and Jesse got John to cover for him. *Can you leave the boys somewhere* he asked.

No, I got to take them with me. I never leave them. People would wonder why.

What she would remember most, years later, was the light in the cavern, a porous blue light that filled the huge domed cave and sank, shading to an indigo blue in the underground lake. The eerie light seemed to lay along her body like satin, and each time she entered the dim soft interior, she felt her skin peel away, leaving her exposed, blue-white bones strung together with fibers of sensation.

During that summer, the cavern interior was another world to her, and her everyday world would slip away as easily as her clothes did when Jesse took her, their bodies transforming into shadowed shapes, her skin glowing whitish blue like the milk glass vase on her mantel, and his tanned and hard skin, draped in the blue light, burnished like the love bruises she couldn't help biting into his neck as he would lay her down on the flat shelf of rock, the hard coldness penetrating the spread blanket, or standing, his shoulders leaning against the rock, lift her up wrapping her legs around his waist, her arms gripping his neck, his hands supporting her, his lips eager at her full breasts.

Sometimes they went out on the lake, a huge body of water that faded into the darkness on the other side of the cave. They took the boys and paddled out in a small boat that someone had left on the shore and then floated in the silence, even the children were quiet, awed by the primal feel of the deep water. Evelyn always thought that she could see movement beneath the opaque surface, not exactly shapes, but a change in the density of the water, and she imagined dark scales and gaping mouths, hungry maws, the activity of blind beings who lived on sensation, their souls imprisoned in the flesh, and, unaccountably, she felt her blood jell in her veins, and she drew back Neal's hand that he was dangling in the water as if he were in danger.

On shore, the boys were instructed to stay quiet, to stay hidden, and they played just inside the entrance to the cave, behind the falls, where Evelyn could check on them, but she and Jesse could be out of their sight, too. She always brought lots of food for them, sweets like vinegar pie and fruit drinks, and Jesse would bring a new toy each time for Neal, a flipperdinger or a nail puzzle. Claude was mostly content gathering sticks and rocks.

Except for the time that Henry had left for several days to hunt, and Jesse and Evelyn had met at night, the cave filled with liquid black darkness splotched with puddles of light from the lanterns. Claude woke up and got scared, cried for his momma, and Evelyn, clad in Jesse's shirt, went to him, let him nurse, but her breasts were dry, so she had to wet a rag for him to suck as she rocked him in her lap. After a long time of his fretting and fussing, she was able to lay him back down on the blanket to sleep.

Neal, standing aside, watching wide-eyed, stared at her as if trying to see something in her face. And irritated by his scrutiny, she had snapped at him *what is it? what're you looking at me for?* and he had cringed at the harshness in her voice and started to whimper.

At home, away from Jesse, away from the cavern, an unnameable fear lodged in every part of her, causing her to cry suddenly and sporadically; the sobs, gathered right under the surface of her skin, were always ready to break out, heavy and choking. At night, lying beside Henry, her fear was transformed into horrible imaginings about her sons, accidents and maimings, and during the endless nights, the room filled with the mournful whinny of screech owls, she constantly ran to their room to find them always asleep, wet hair stuck to their faces. Only toward dawn would she finally fall into a deep sleep herself, a sleep filled not with dreams but with sensations of death.

The days when she wasn't with Jesse were saturated with thoughts of him. In everything she did, in everything around her, she saw him. In the mirror when she would study her face she saw the face of a stranger, deep and incomprehensible, and her image would begin to waver and slip and Jesse's face would come into focus, for just a moment, a flash of dark eyes, lips so slick they looked almost painful, and then her own face would come back.

When Henry was home, at the supper table, the boys propped up in chairs, her mind would play tricks on her, and Henry's gesture, his lighting of a cigarette, would become Jesse's arm, the shirt sleeve rolled high and tight around his muscles, and the fingers gripping the cigarette were Jesse's, long and creased with grease from the grader. Often losing track of what she was doing or saying, she would feel the fear congeal in her stomach, eating at the lining, sending acid to burn the back of her throat.

The feel of everything—the ball of warm dough, the soft powdery backside of her baby, the clean smell of her laundry—reminded her of him, of his smooth naked body, his face, shadowed and fervent around the eyes, hanging over her own, the eyes unseeing as his face filled with pleasure. It was almost scary, the way he loved her.

10

There wasn't more than a couple of weeks of warm weather left when Henry showed up at the gristmill. It was about ten o'clock, and the night was filled with frog songs that blended with the hollow sound of moving water from the stream, and the strums of a guitar coming through the open window in the attic.

Henry yelled up at the small window. "Hey! Jesse! Jesse!"

The music stopped. In the silence, the other sounds seemed to rise louder. Then the dark shape of a head, outlined against the cloudless, light-colored violet sky appeared, looking down.

"I'm looking for Jesse. He up there?"

Another head appeared in the window beside the first. "Who're you?"

"You don't know me. I need to see you about something."

There was a hesitation. "All right. Be right down."

Henry stepped into the shadows by the door and waited. He heard the guitar start up again. When Jesse stepped through the door, Henry put his rifle in the small of his back.

"Don't make a sound. I ain't figuring on killing you, but I will if you make me." He prodded him with the barrel. "Let's go. In the woods. Over there."

Henry walked him a mile upstream to where he had left his horse. "Right here."

Jesse turned around. He tried to see through the dark, but the light from the sky was shut out by a canopy of trees. The man was in shadows. "What in hell do you think you're doing? Who are you? Some kind of crazy sonovabitch?"

Henry stepped up close to him, pushed his meaty face into Jesse's. "I'm Henry, asshole. Does that name sound like something you heard before?"

When the realization of who it was hit Jesse, his mind contracted as if a needle had been driven into the base of his skull. He felt his face flush and his mouth tighten.

"I see you do know me. I hear that me and you been sharing some property. Is that true, Jesse-boy?"

Jesse glanced at the gun in Henry's hand, weighed his chances of running. He decided he couldn't get away before he was shot.

"I guess you already know it is, or you wouldn't be sneaking around here like a weasel, would you?"

All Jesse saw was a blur before the stock of the gun hit him on the cheekbone. The ground flew up to meet him as pain exploded in his head.

"You got a smart mouth, boy. Close it."

Jesse pushed himself back up, tasting blood under his tongue where he had bitten it.

Henry moved away into the shadows and leaned on a tree.

Jesse could make out only a hulking shape in the dark. He couldn't see the rifle, but he knew Henry had it in his hands.

"Now, let's try again. I was saying it seems to me you been using my property without my permission." His voice was dead calm.

"I—"

Henry jerked up from where he leaned. "Shut up! Shut the fuck up!"

Jesse involuntarily stepped back, startled by the

viciousness of Henry's rage, a half-suffocated fury that struck out and penetrated him like fangs.

Then Henry was quiet a moment as if he were trying to gain control again. He came closer where Jesse could see him and sat down on a fallen tree trunk. "Don't worry, shitass, I told you I ain't going to kill you. You ain't worth killing."

Henry's voice was quiet again, the gun hanging loosely in his arms like he had forgotten about it. He stared at Jesse with interest like someone trying to figure out something. Jesse was spellbound by the half-closed, hooded, secretive eyes, the dark lids puffy with blood.

"You know, I don't really care. I mean, it don't mean a good goddamn to me. Not really. Christ knows that if anybody does, I know how people really are. Two-faced. Mealy-mouthed. Always out for what they can get. It don't matter who. Momma, daddy, wife . . . it don't make no never mind . . . everybody, *everybody*, is out for themself."

Henry paused and glared at Jesse. Jesse didn't return the look. He lowered his eyes, wondered if maybe Henry was just going to talk.

"You do the best you can for people, give 'em food, a roof over their head, clothes on their back, and they act like that's not enough. They always want what they ain't got."

Henry got up and walked over to Jesse. "Turn around."

Henry jerked him around, and before Jesse could resist, his hands were tied behind his back. Henry yanked him back again. Then Henry got right in his face, almost touching him. "The way I figure it is that you owe me. Right? Don't you owe me?" Henry's eyes were open wide, the black orbs full and glutted, the whites red-stringed.

Jesse wanted to say whatever he wanted to hear. "Yeah, that's right. I owe you."

Henry had his mouth right next to Jesse's face, and the overpowering pungent smell of liquor, bad teeth, and old tobacco almost made Jesse choke. His liquor-laced voice was furious now, spitting out.

"That girl didn't have a pot to piss in when I got her. I took her away from working like a nigger in that house, taking care of all those snot-nosed kids. I never gave her that dog's life that my daddy led my momma, and what do I get in return? Nothing. She just lays there, dead and cold as a goddamn fish. Sometimes so's I know I'm not fucking a goddamn corpse I try to hurt her. Anything so I know she ain't just a piece of meat thrown up in the bed. And then, she goes and gives it away to some half-assed boy, lays down and actually wants it."

The hoarse whisper shot straight to Jesse's spinal cord, sending a rush of fear up his mind that was reeling as it tried to follow Henry's abrupt mood swings.

Henry undid Jesse's belt, let his pants drop, and began to buckle the belt around his knees. Jesse, panicked, tried to wiggle away and kick with his feet, and Henry pulled a knife, stuck it by Jesse's eye, pricking the skin and drawing blood.

"Now, you want to stop that or you want to kick some more, dumbass?"

Jesse held still, the knife a blur in the bottom of his eye, his face so hot that the water running from his eyes burned like kerosene on his cheeks.

Henry pressed the knife further into the soft skin under his eye and then rubbed down the side of his face with the edge of the blade. "I wouldn't dirty my dick on you, asshole." He took the knife away and turned his back to Jesse, putting the knife back in his pocket.

Jesse exhaled, feeling relief rush through him. He wasn't prepared for the way Henry suddenly whirled around or for the impact of the big ham-shaped fist across his face, then to his stomach. Jesse fell to his knees.

Henry kicked him over and over, in the ribs, in the stomach, in the crotch. Jesse rolled over on his side, retching and bleeding from the mouth, trying to curl in a ball as Henry kept kicking him, the huge boot-clad foot coming at him from everywhere as he tried to squirm away from it.

Finally, winded, Henry backed off and sat down on the fallen tree, watching Jesse.

Jesse, lying on the ground, stayed quiet except for coughing and choking on his vomit, effectively hogtied by the rope and the belt around his knees. In between the waves of pain, he kept remembering that Henry had said, *I ain't going to kill you.*

"All those holier-than-thou hypocrites always telling me to forgive my mama, to pray for her, to live a Christian life. 'Forgive,' my old raggedy-assed aunt used to say over and over, 'forgive and turn away from evil.' Well my daddy found it nigh near impossible to turn away from an axe splitting his face in two. Momma cut and slaughtered him like a hog. And you know what, shitass, I bet he thought he knew everything about her"—Henry almost laughed, making a snorting noise—"until that ax sliced that notion right out of his head."

Then, abruptly, Henry stopped talking and sprang on him, pushed his hand flat on the ground and cut off the tip of his little finger, the knife sticking into the ground with the force of the cut. Jesse screamed, and the horse neighed.

Henry stood up. "There." He showed it to Jesse.

Jesse felt the blood streaming over his hand, another scream rising in his throat, and he choked, coughing as Henry snatched the handkerchief from around his neck.

"A present for the little woman." He folded the handkerchief and put it in his overalls. He picked up the gun and cut Jesse's hands loose. Jesse fumbled with the belt with one hand, the other hand clutched against his chest, blood soaking his shirt front. He stumbled up from the ground, his head spinning.

Henry watched him contemptuously. "Remember what I said. You don't never know them, never . . . you be gone by morning. You hear me?"

Jesse fell back to the ground. Through a crimson blur, he saw Henry mount his horse and ride off before he passed out.

11

The next afternoon Evelyn was surprised to see John, instead of Jesse, driving the grader. She had to wave him down to get him to stop and turn off the motor. *Where's Jesse?* she asked. John stared at her, looked like he was angry, and didn't answer for a moment. Then he said, *Why don't you go ask your husband?*

Evelyn felt like she had been plunged in an icy stream even though the day was hot with sunlight sharpening everything—trees, shrubs, sky—to a cutting brilliance. She tried to ask John more, but he started up the grader again and, ignoring her, went back to work.

Evelyn, dragging the startled boys behind her, ran to the gristmill, her mind filling with unspeakable fears. The old man who worked there, Uncle Newt, said that all he knew was that Jesse had left. He had seen him early that morning, packed up, and it looked like he had been hurt, his face beat up bad, a bandage over his hand.

She clutched at the old man's arm, *but where, where did he go, do you know where, please, where.* Uncle Newt looked undecided, wiped his nose with the back of his hand, looked at her, then away again, *I don't want no trouble.*

Evelyn thought her heart would burst, *Uncle Newt, please, there ain't going to be no trouble, please, please, where—*

He looked around and lowered his voice as if someone might hear him although they were the only people in the mill, *Jesse said if you came here today to tell you that you know where to come, that's all he said, that you'd know where to go.*

What Evelyn would try most to suppress in the years to come was the memory of her last trip to the cavern. The frenzied way she had run through the woods, heedless of overgrowth, charging through white oak stands, carrying Claude, almost dropping him in her haste, and pulling Neal along behind her, ignoring his protests, her mind racing ahead of her, a hazy mass of panic and fright.

At the entrance to the cave, she let go of Neal's hand, deposited Claude on the ground, *both of you stay here, Neal, you watch him, stay right here,* and rushed on in, the shift from bright light to darkness blinding her for a moment.

In the dim light it was hard for her to see anything but his outline until she was right on him. He was leaning against a shelf. His face was a mess, the nose broken, cuts all over his cheek, swellings, bruises already forming. She let out a sound like a groan or gasp and reached out to him. Their bodies touched, and he jerked back, holding onto his hand.

"What! What is it?"

Jesse grimaced, and she could see blood caked between his teeth. "Ah, hell, just my finger. The sonovabitch cut off my finger." He held his hand up. "Shit, so what? I got nine more."

Evelyn started crying. She felt sick, and when the wave of nausea peaked, her eyes went out of focus. She thought she might faint.

Jesse grabbed her. "Hey, baby, it's not as bad as it looks. Come over here, sit down. We need to talk and figure some things out."

Evelyn allowed herself to be led over to a slab of rock where she sat beside Jesse, leaned against him, and cried while he held her. She would slack up a bit, but when she would look up at him, at his ravaged face, his bandaged hand, she would start again.

"Jesus Christ, Evelyn, stop! I'll mend. Now, listen. We ain't got much time." He grabbed her face under the chin with his good hand. "Listen to me!"

Evelyn stifled her sobs, met his eyes, looked at the ravaged face, and tried to stand it, tried not to think what all this meant, for her, for her boys, for all of them.

"Is the bastard home now?"

She shook her head. "No, he didn't come in last night."

Jesse stood up, started pacing. "I want you to go home, get what you need. Leave the kids with a neighbor. Tell her you're sick or something, that Henry will pick them up. Just hurry, we got to get out of here."

For a moment Evelyn didn't comprehend the meaning of his words, *get her things, leave the kids, get out of here.* Then the impact of what he was saying sank in, and, without realizing it, she started shaking her head. Jesse kept talking, saying how they had to be careful, get away without being seen—

Evelyn interrupted him, her voice like a stranger's, high and thin. "I can't go off and leave my kids!" The statement was a surprise to her; she only realized the truth of it as she said it.

Jesse looked astonished. He stopped and stared at her, his face unreadable, and then he turned and walked off, standing with his back to her. Evelyn saw the tightness in his shoulders, little frustrated jerks, that he kept trying to shake off and the incredulous movement of his head, the black hair gathered in a short ponytail on his neck.

She went over to him, put her hand on his back, but he didn't turn around, and she could feel the knotted muscles.

"Jesse, I can't. I just can't. They're just babies—"

He didn't say anything for a moment, then sighed, turned around, put his arms around her, drew her in. "All right . . . it's all right."

He pulled away, held onto her hand. "We'll take them.

I'll get a wagon—"

Evelyn was shaking her head again, her face stricken with wanting to do what he said and knowing she couldn't.

"What is it? You don't want to stay with that crazy old man, do you?" His voice was astounded.

Evelyn felt the way she had after she lost her baby, the one conceived between Neal and Claude. She had carried it for three months before she woke up in the middle of the night with a feeling of being ripped open, everything flowing out, unable to stop the blood, the cramps, the clots, the slipping life. . . .

"I got to think of my kids. You can't take care of me and them with no job. Where're you going to go—"

Jesse gripped her arms so tightly it hurt. "Evelyn, I love you."

She crossed her hands over her stomach, thought of the periods that hadn't come for two months now, felt the weight of a growth—

A scream tore through the chamber, echoing in the high corners and bouncing off the walls. Both Evelyn and Jesse ran for the entrance. Neither boy was there. They ran outside and saw Claude sitting calmly on the ground staring at something under a bush. Neal was standing beside him, screeching, his little feet going up and down like he was running in place. Jesse was there first with Evelyn right behind him. Under the bush, disturbed by the vibrations from Neal's stomping, but not scared enough to give up his dinner, a rat snake was coiled around and feeding on a cottontail as he gave off a warning by excreting a foul-smelling liquid from the base of his tail.

Evelyn grabbed Neal by the shoulders and shook him. "Hush! Hush! It won't hurt you."

Jesse picked up Claude and held him while Evelyn quieted Neal down, finally having to slap him on the face. Neal quit jerking around and clung to her, crying, his eyes never leaving the snake's mouth working back and forth, flashes of hooked teeth, the gray-spotted skin almost indistinguishable from the ground, the rabbit half gone, a furry, bloody muddle of skin, bones, innards.

Back in the cavern, Evelyn held Claude on her lap and Neal stood as close to her as he could get, clutching onto her dress, as if he expected someone to snatch her away at any moment. He was still crying, not loud, but sniffling, occasionally pulling on Evelyn's dress. "Let's go home, Momma, let's go home?"

"I guess there ain't nothing much more to say, is there?" Jesse stood away from her, the distance between them as dense and resistant as water.

Evelyn couldn't answer. Her mind felt like the skin under a ripped-off fingernail, exposed, raw, something needing to be covered, protected from knowing that she would never see Jesse again. The thought of losing him forced itself on her, making her mind sway, go blurry, helpless with panic as the awful realization sank down into her heart.

"Evelyn, look at me. Is this it? I got to go."

She looked at him, deep into his eyes. They were shadowed, vulnerable behind clotted lashes, and moist. She had to resist, his eyes, his voice, filled with beckoning, promises. . . . Evelyn stroked the soft inside of her baby's damp thigh as she held him in her lap.

"I can't. . . ." Her mind was coming apart, spreading like water, ring upon ring of sorrow, a pounding somewhere deep in the center of her body, a feeling that was beyond emotion, like the rhythmic sound of a caged animal pacing, or beating on bars, or striking its head on a wall. "I can't."

She sat there for a long time after he left. Neal was finally quiet, sitting on the floor of the cave, and Claude was asleep in her lap. Her thoughts ranged inward like seeking eyes, looking for what had prompted her to throw away her life, looking for that deep-rooted instinct that had refused to deny her children, astonished at how the decision to stay had come to her as automatically as a lock clicking shut, and she examined all that had happened, contemplating her own heart as if it were a strange organ of some sort, and she was amazed at how, even though it was cracked, it still beat on, and she thought that she could not bear this passing, while her life remained in a place that she did not choose.

She couldn't quit looking at it, the piece of finger lying before her on a dirty, bloody, stiff handkerchief, right there, where he had dropped it when he came through the door. He had walked back out without saying anything. Occasionally, she would reach out and touch it, absently push it with her own finger in circles and then stop. . . .

Red all red everything hazed over with red like mist but red red handkerchief skin tender red inside slickred red smellred smell of slaughter thick heavy like smoke in air redsmoke pieces of animals ears heads noses hoofs like this raggedred skin shallow needs blood skin needs blood screams screams for blood screams—

The two boys played, running around the room chasing one another, but they soon got tired and hungry and begin to cry while she sat trancelike, and without looking she reached out and slapped Neal, the one closest to her, caught him on the side of the face, and Neal grabbed his cheek, yelled in surprise, then Claude began to cry even louder, scared by Neal's outburst.

—animal little animals filled with blood hungry all pieces there filled with blood rosy blood flowing ears- feethands babies need food, need to eat, food pieces of animals bloodless now bacon slabs of pig cut off offcut off knife slides through flesh so easy easy flesh divides like butter under knife peels away bleeds then blood- less—

The noise finally penetrated and she got up and lit the lamps, put wood on the fire, and went to the cupboard, fixed them each a plate with bacon and bread on it, put the plates and two glasses of milk on the table, sat the boys in chairs, and sat herself down in front of the hand- kerchief again.

—Jimmie at the sawmill lost all fingers hand just a nub said he didn't even feel it happen just saw four rub- bery looking things on the floor familiar shapes like

sausages or   like bloodless swollenslugs   saw puddle of
blood on floor   by his foot   surprised to see his hand   just
a nub   a hamshaped nub   but didn't hurt he said   didn't
hurt a bit   a curious hollow feeling all the way to the tips
of his fingers that weren't there   kind of like they'd all
gone to sleep   he watched while someone picked up the
slugs and put them in a bag and someone else wrapped up
his hand but he didn't hurt   nary a bit   don't don't think
no don't his face   blood, Jesus, the blood   face beautiful
face mustn't slip so easy to slip on blood   stickyredsyrup
her shoe slid in it   almost felldown   daddy bleeding fight-
ing shot   land fight   momma trying to patch him up   want
to help   didn't mean to fall   so much blood   pieces scat-
tered   flung around   oh Jesus, his face not his face not his
face not his face not his face not his face not his face not
his beautifulface—

Claude, stuffing the bread in his face with one hand,
reached out and touched the finger with the other, and his
mother seized his hand, gripping it and throwing it back
at him, yelling hysterically, "Don't touch him! Don't you
touch him!"

The child caught unawares choked on the bread as he
sucked in his breath and began coughing. Neal let out a
panicked wail.

The sound of her own voice brought Evelyn to some
sense of what was happening, and she thumped Claude
on the back until he quit coughing and gave him a sip of
milk. He quit shuddering, hiccuped, and began to sniffle,
and Neal, like he had been comforted too, quieted down
to an occasional sob.

It took them only a minute to finish their meal while
she stood at the window and stared out. Then she put
them both to bed and shut the door and waited for Henry
to come home.

12

Neal

Neal had been afraid all his life. All his memories were colored with fear, a terrifying, paralyzing feeling that hid in the silent spaces between his heartbeats, lay stretched along the soft sides of his ribs, beat behind the strained, insufficient skin over the hollow space at the base of his skull, residing in all those vulnerable, penetrable spots where he knew his life hung at its most perilous.

Before he was born, the fear had been outside of him, surrounding the curled core of his life, contained in the felt sound of an opposed heartbeat and carried in the steady chafing rushes of strange blood rubbing against his newly formed organs, fear trying to get inside him, inside his vital parts.

Then, after he was born, the fear moved inside him, into the hungry places of his body. Deep in the core of his eyes and crouched in the contracted muscle of his tremulous heart, it also curled in his stomach and in his bowels, gnawing at him, never letting up.

In school, he stayed miserable. He felt trapped in that one stifling room with all those loud, boisterous, emanating, threatening bodies, all fighting for space, for air, for dominance.

He hated the schoolroom itself, the way it was dark and gloomy even in the middle of the day. Old unpainted boards covered the log walls, and the ceiling was black from the smoke of leaky stovepipes suspended from the ceiling by wires. The few windows were mostly broken and covered with paper to help keep out the cold. The desks, homemade crude seats and tops, were all one size so that when he was small, his feet hung several inches from the floor, making his buttocks and legs go to sleep, and then when he got older and bigger, he had to stretch his legs out under the desk top to fit in, his feet sprawling in front of him. He was glad when his daddy said he didn't have to finish.

During his school years, the fear grew until it was both inside and outside, permeating him, his entire being, and thriving on other people's reactions to him. It was like they knew he was afraid, as if they could sense it, or somehow smell it in his sweat or on his breath, and they reacted with a natural contempt for a coward, a "yellow belly."

Neal hated the other students, all of them, especially his brother, who usually led the others in taunting him. He was especially afraid of girls. They were such messy creatures, wet, wide, open to everything, all leaks and emissions and mysteries. Besides Annie, only one girl, Ginny Long, had ever been nice to him. It was when he was in the sixth grade, but he found out why when she asked him to go into the cloakroom during recess. He had run away, and to get back at him she had told everybody that he was "queer" and that she had been trying him. She was a nasty little girl anyway, always lifting her dress to show her dirty drawers to the boys. All they had to do was ask. Her legs were covered with risings, big, runny, pus-filled sores that he saw her squeeze, then pull something out of one time that looked like a string of some sort. It made him sick just to think of it.

He was tormented every day by fears of what might happen to him at any time, whenever others turned their attention to him, and even at home at night safe in his bed, he worried. He fretted constantly about his body. His heart seemed to beat erratically, a hurried, uneven series of thumps, then nothing, until he would almost cry out from being so scared of its not starting again, and after listening to it in the dark, with his hand gripping his chest, feeling the uncertain rhythm, he was afraid to sleep, scared that he might not wake up, but might die in his sleep without knowing it.

One night in his hesitant explorations of his frightening and changing body, he found what appeared to be some kind of thread deep down on his stomach, right above his privates, and he was startled, confused, and distressed by it. He had seen Doc Moody perform an operation on a boy. The doc always did them outside under the apple tree, and anybody who had the inclination could watch as long as they didn't get too close. He had been there one time when the doc was inside a boy's belly cutting something out, and a chicken got too close, so a spectator kicked at it, but instead of running the opposite way, the chicken flapped up to the table, landed on the patient, and seemed to peer down into the hole in his belly. The doc yelled and swatted the chicken. Neal had watched the whole thing, and he had seen the doc sew the boy up with thread, stitching with a needle just like his momma did when she sewed cloth, and he was afraid that maybe he had been cut open, something taken out and then sewed up, and maybe they had given him something so that he couldn't remember, the way that boy had slept right through all that cutting and blood, and maybe, maybe there was something bad wrong with him that nobody wanted to tell him. And then, not long after he found the curious string, while he was asleep, something else happened to him. He was jerked awake, gasping, while globs of white fluid shot out of his twitching penis.

He pictured scenario after scenario of the operation he was now sure had taken place, the grisly pictures flooding his dreams, and it was, ironically enough, because of Claude that he came to realize that nothing had, after all, been done to him. Claude slept in the same bed with him and constantly flaunted his naked burly body, enjoying Neal's embarrassment. Neal couldn't help seeing that Claude was soon growing hair in the same spot or help hearing his grunts at night before he would get up and wipe himself off.

But the fear was real, the awful knowledge that he didn't think or feel like other boys, and that somehow he was repugnant to them, something to be marked and jeered at. His daddy went from looking at him with disgust when he was younger and couldn't do the things his daddy thought a boy should do, preferring to hang around the house with his momma, to not looking at him at all and talking to him only when he had to, and now Neal might as well have been invisible or dead. But Claude made up for the dismissal by constantly scorning Neal every chance he got.

Like the time Lacey had come out to the yard while Neal was cleaning out jars used for putting up food, washing them and putting them in the sun to dry. It was the year before his momma died, and Claude seemed to be at his worst that summer, always teasing Annie, asking her if she had any hair anywhere but her head yet and telling her how she could get her breasts to grow faster if she would let him rub them. Annie would get mad and refuse to answer, which didn't daunt Claude at all; then something happened, Neal didn't know what, but all of a sudden Claude stopped talking to Annie at all and left her alone, even though Neal could see the way he glowered at her, like she had done something to him.

Lacey had shown up in the yard, standing behind him, asking him what he was doing. Neal answered shortly. He didn't like Lacey. She made him more nervous than he already was around girls. It was her blackness, and the way she smelled, heavy and swampy, all the time rolling her eyes and sashaying her hips, her buttocks high and wide with her dress stretched across them and hiked up in the back. There weren't many black people around, just the two families down at Beech Bottom, and he was scared of them. They looked so different. But it was also what she did. He knew that both his daddy and Claude messed with her.

She had come up that day and was bothering him, talking about no-account things, flashing her big white teeth, her scent pungent and dense on the summer air. She got real close to him, and he could smell her breath coated with pig fat from what she had already eaten that day. *You is scared of me, ain't you, Mr. Neal, why is you scared of me . . . cause I black? huh? is you scared of black people?* Neal had stiffened, his spine snapping straight, and he involuntarily stepped away from her, his face so hot it felt painful. *Yes sir, you is scared of me cause I black . . . but I like you Mr. Neal, I sure do . . . and you know what. . . .* She moved close to him again, his back was pressed against the fence of the hog pen and he couldn't go any further . . . *I may be black* she paused, looked like she was trying to keep from laughing, *but my pussy is pink . . . pink like you face!* She exploded in giggles, and Neal heard another outburst of laughter from around the corner of the barn and saw Claude come stumbling out, holding his sides and bellowing.

Neal hated the farm, the stink, the animals, the dirt. His hands stayed filthy. No matter how he tried, how much he washed, he couldn't get the dirt and smell out from under his fingernails. He felt like he was always up to his elbows in some kind of shit, cow shit, pig shit, chicken shit. He hated it all.

More than ever he hated it with his momma gone. He missed her, the way she would get between him and his daddy or Claude, threatening Claude with a beating although she knew she couldn't carry out the threat and that her husband wouldn't. He remembered a time when he was twelve years old. She was crocheting, and he was watching her. Noticing his interest, she had asked if he wanted to try. He said yes, and she got another hook, a bigger one than the one she was using, and a ball of thread and showed him how to wrap the thread on his fingers and then how to make a chain, double back, and put double crochets in the chain. He was having a good time, enjoying working with the thread, and had the beginning of a good-sized square made when the sound of the screen door opening came into the room. His momma jumped up and snatched the hook and thread away from him just as his daddy walked in. Neal never asked to crochet again, and she never mentioned it either.

On the day of the wake, Neal found himself crying uncontrollably. It started after he viewed the body, saw her in the dress with the crocheted collar, and was reminded of the ways she had tried to help him fit in, get along. The tears had come and wouldn't stop, and, ashamed of his weakness, he had gone in the smokehouse to hide. He hadn't even got the door all the way open when he saw Claude. He was standing with his pants open, and Lacey was kneeling down in front of him, her head in his crotch. Neal would never forget Claude's face, the surprise, then the amused snarl, the smutty, sarcastic words that Claude flung at him as he held Lacey's head down with his hands, words that Neal was too shocked to comprehend, and Neal had run from the smokehouse, hating the bastard, hating them all, hating everything.

Now, with the funeral over, the house dead and quiet, he kept remembering a cave, flashes of scenes in a cave, and the bits of memory scared him, of a shadowed man, a horrible sound like a piece of big machinery, and his mother crying, a feeling of being left, of being alone, everything all mixed in his mind, rising unbidden and unexpectedly, each time more detailed and complete. . . .

A sunny walk through multicolored flowers and brilliant trees and bushes, green, pretty green, he says to his momma, and she smiles, says, God's favorite colors are green and blue— and she taps him on the nose—a bright sunny blue just like your eyes, and he is pleased at her attention, likes the feel of her hand on his skin.

A large cavern filled with dirty light bruised-looking and thick, a mist lying over the ground and a large black lake. He is out in the lake, treading water. A horrible sound is coming over the water like the sound of big machinery, of things being torn apart and uprooted. He is scared.

Then the sound of the machinery is joined by the sound of a summer squall moving in, spreading darkness, cold flashes of light tracing through the choppy air above the water like symbols of an ancient language, a pregnant charged atmosphere breaking through, swooping down, wet warm, dark, moving swiftly, filling him with more terror. The storm is only over the lake.

Next to the lake, on the shore, is a kitchen table covered with a cloth that looks like a man's handkerchief and a plate is in the center of the table. His mother is sitting at the table, crying and looking down at the plate. Behind her is a bed, a big high quilt-covered bed with a clock hanging on the rock beside it. The ticking is real loud and echoes off the walls.

A man is on the bed, lying down, just a shape, an outline, but he can tell it is a man and he knows that the man is a danger to his momma. He tries to yell at her, to warn her about the man, but he can't be heard over the sound of the storm. He sees the man go over, pick up his mother, and carry her to the bed. The man carries her strangely. Her legs are wrapped around his waist and her arms around his neck. The man lays her on the bed.

The water is swelling, lapping up to his chin, and things begin to move around his legs, long round bodies brushing his treading legs, then bumping against him. The man is doing something to his mother, he can't see very well, the man is over her, and she is clinging to him. Neal can see their shadows on the cavern wall, huge misshapen figures joined in some kind of fero-

cious dance.

Neal tries to yell again, and his voice carries on the water, Momma, home, I want to go home. The figures on the wall stop, part, and his mother's head turns toward him. He can see her face close up to him like it has been project-ed over the water, and she yells, Make him go away! make him go away!

"Mr. Grady, I need a pound of #2 nails."

"How're you doing in school, Neal?"

"I quit. Me and Claude."

"Claude and *I* . . . how's your father holding up?"

"He's all right, I guess. Nothing much bothers him."

"Are you thinking of doing public work?"

"Yes sir, probably. Claude and him can take care of the place."

"*He* and Claude . . . do you miss going to school?"

"No sir . . . well, the books maybe. I liked reading the books."

"I've got a book you would like. You can take it with you. Just return it when you're finished."

"Thank you. I appreciate it."

"By the way, you know, come to think of it, I could use someone to help me out about three days during the week, clean up, stock the shelves, odd jobs like that. You have to be able to add, subtract, and keep the books too. I'll pay a dollar a day. Are you interested?"

"Yes sir! I sure am."

"Ok, you check with your father, see what he says."

No one knew exactly where Grady had come from, and some of the older folks could remember when his dry goods store hadn't been there, but they couldn't remember just why he had come to town or from where.

Everyone knew he was an outsider and was different. He had funny habits like shaving every day, his cheeks a rosy pink and *slick as a baby's behind,* as old Mr. Potts described it. His hair too was cut off short and shaved up the back of his neck, and although the top was thin and combed across to cover what would naturally be bald, his sideburns were thick and grew down the sides of his face in shapes like pork chops. He dressed in a white shirt and dark britches every day and had a smell like some of the herbs he sold. His hands were white and soft and the fingernails stuck out a good half-inch.

The kids joked about him, calling him a pansy behind his back and mimicking his swishy walk as he moved around the store filling orders and discussing in a high, soft voice gardening and household concerns with the women who came in every month to trade their wares for dry goods.

Neal had come often, picking up lavender seeds for his mother to crush into the oil she rubbed on her temples to relieve her headaches. He liked to go to the store, its shelves neatly stacked with all manner of goods, cans, bags, and beads, candy, bolts of material, colorful blankets. Even the smell of the place excited him: herbs and the strange candles that Grady said no one ever bought, *incense* he called them. He usually had one burning in the store.

Claude

Claude had always been filled with a quiet rage, the constant emotion flowing through him, often flaring up into unexplained anger at someone or something and driving him to actions that he neither contemplated nor regretted, sometimes engulfing him in a fury that tormented him until he could find relief. Not that he realized it or wondered about it. Rather, the feeling was so familiar that he didn't distinguish it from the others that occasionally colored but never replaced it.

This passive rage had filled his small body when, as an infant, he was offered a dry breast, outraged that someone had taken what was his, and he would suck furiously, demanding that the milk come, and his mind would become clouded with a dark flood of wordless cries, like echoes in a cavern, as a band seemed to draw tighter and tighter around his skull with each pull of his working gums and tongue. All through his childhood he dreamed of taking a breast in his mouth, and pieces of the nipple would break off, turning to chunks of brown powdery material that stuck in his mouth, between his teeth, and on his tongue, and he couldn't swallow or spit the bitter chunks out, and the nipple was all ragged and half gone, but he shoved the chunks to one side of his cheek and took the rest of the nipple into his mouth.

Once, when he was three, his momma had found him dropping stray puppies into the hole in the outhouse. She had made him retrieve them, and then wash and dry them while she stood over him watching every move. He had felt he would explode with indignation as he scrubbed the excrement off and put them in the sun to dry, hating the feel of their panicked little bodies and the smell of their fear as he handled them, and he plotted how to get back at them for humiliating him, but she told him if *anything, anything at all* happened to the puppies, she would blame him, and she would take the hide off of his backside.

Neal was like a puppy, he thought, always whining, mewing, puking, and he despised the thought of being kin to him. Neal had been like a festering boil on his life for long as he could remember. Neal, always Neal, in the background, slinking around, looking scared, a wormy little bastard who wasn't worth the air he breathed. When Neal spoke, Claude would feel hatred spread through his body becoming a bad taste on his tongue, a stabbing behind his eyes, and he would find no relief until he did something to his brother, something to punish him for being alive, like the time he had Lacey tease him. Funny as hell, he thought Neal would bust a blood vessel when she had said *my pussy is pink*. His face looked like it was about to explode from the pressure of all the blood in it, the little fag.

Women, he felt, were worthy of all the contempt you could give them. Annie, the little tattletale, had told his momma about what he did under the porch, and Momma had confronted him, told him if he did it again she would tell his daddy, see that he got a whipping even if she had to do it herself. He despised her, the old hag, good for nothing but popping out babies, half of them idiots, or near-idiots. And Annie thought she was too good for all of them, that somehow she was different, not just another skirt good for nothing but fucking. She would get hers. He didn't forget. It was just a matter of time. He would show her what women were good for, what she was good for.

Like Ginny Long. She reminded him of a chicken, the way she was so scrawny and the way her head moved, bobbing back and forth, when she walked. He had been doing it to her since she was twelve. He knew that lots of other boys did too, but that just made it better, showed you how the little slut really was. Now she was saying she was knocked up and carrying on about how her daddy was going to kill her when he found out and that she was going to have to get married. He thought it was funny until he realized that she might name him, so he shoved her around, slapped her, and told her he would beat her up good if she didn't say that Buddy, the preacher's kid, was the daddy. He didn't know how it came to him to name Buddy, but once it did, he was delighted with the joke. Buddy didn't even know he had a dick, let alone know how to use it.

His daddy had asked him about the castor bean, about him saying to give his momma three tablespoons. He had said that Annie was wrong, that he didn't say no such thing, *any fool could see the packet said three teaspoons and that's what he told her, she just got it wrong, it wasn't his fault, it was hers, if she wasn't half-blind, the little whining four-eyes, she could see.* After all, he had said, what difference does it make? Now there's fewer mouths to feed and maybe that bad luck he kept complaining about would turn, *it's a long worm that doesn't turn, isn't that what you always say, well, maybe we done give this old worm a prod to turn.* And he could see in the sudden flare of complicity that lit up the dull brown of the old man's tired eyes and the way he shifted them away that he wasn't all that upset about it happening, that he had probably wanted it to, but just didn't have the guts to do it himself.

Robbie

His life had been spent underwater, blue wavery fluid that, at first, was inside him and around him, filling his body as he floated, buoyant, the same lightness inside and out, wet, weightless, warm. But then the water was only inside, only in his head and in his eyes, sometimes filling his chest too, but usually just in his head, making it heavy, full, congested. And it was hard to see through the veil of water over everything, shapes, just shapes, wavy, fluid, moving, shifting shapes that floated in and out of his vision.

It was easier to smell. Milk, his momma smelled like milk, and she was real white and soft and sweet to taste. Being with her was like floating in water again, a well of soft enclosures, between breasts, between thighs, valleys of flesh, to crawl back in, hunker down in, ringed safety, and her voice, rolling waves of rhythm, incantations, lullabies, and croons. Then she was gone. Whenever he missed her, it made him feel like he was strangling on water and he would cry.

Not like some of the others, still here. Hard, dry smells. Danger. Pull away. Sharp smells that cut into your nose, the smell of kerosene, of acrid smoke. Shapes ringed in red, fiery outlines in the water mouthing words all the time that he couldn't hear. Or black, the black shape, looming huge and hulking in his sight, thick liquid sounds coming from it and a smell like rotting vegetation, thick, sour, bad smell.

But the old woman's shape, Miss Mercer, was clear like she had some kind of invisible shell around her, the water surrounded her but didn't cover her. He could see her. She smelled like the woods and the lake at night, deep and dark, things growing under rocks and underwater. He felt good around her, not like he felt with his momma, but still safe, concealed in her circle, and he could hear her talk, a voice that would float through water, then settle like a rock, sinking right into him, and he heard.

She always gave him little things. He liked little things, smaller than him, that he could handle and carry around. He liked small places too, dark places, places that he could get into and not be seen, like the smokehouse and the shed, safe enclosures. He liked his little bed in Annie's room, tucked in the corner, covered with the blanket, small animals warm and squiggly in his arms. He liked the old woman's house, dark and warm, crowded and safe, with odors, all kinds, sweet, tangy, heavy, light, all tickling his nose, and colors floating like oil, dense in the watery air.

13

Annie stayed up most of the day now, a little weak still, but able to move around from the kitchen to the front room, out to the porch, and even to go for short walks outside with Robbie.

After spending one morning in the woods where she gathered spring beauties and fiddlefern, and where Robbie ran around trying to catch a butterfly in a field of clover covered by swarming yellow and orange puddle butterflies, they came back about two o'clock, and Annie made plates for her and Robbie from the food Lacey left on the back of the stove, some sweet potatoes and cabbage and a pot of pork stew. After they ate, she put the flowers and fern in a glass by her bed and got her work ready for Miss Paine, who usually came to see her on Monday afternoons.

Annie managed to get a short nap in before voices at the front door woke her. Lacey was saying, "She's back there somewhere, probably piled up in the bed." She sounded surly, mad as usual when anybody showed up that she might have to wait on, and then Annie heard Miss Paine's polite answering murmur. Miss Paine was still talking as she came down the hall, and when she walked into the room, Annie couldn't believe her eyes. Ruthie Lynn. Ruthie Lynn was trailing behind her, looking kind of sheep-faced, and clutching something in her hands.

"How're you feeling today, Annie?" Miss Paine asked, her voice strained and her back still ramrod stiff from Lacey's rude reception although she should have been used to it, and she was flushed from the walk from town.

Annie could barely speak from the shock of seeing Ruthie Lynn. "Fine, ma'am." She tried to see around Miss Paine to where Ruthie Lynn stood half-hidden.

Miss Paine stepped to the side. "I brought Ruthie Lynn with me. She's been wanting to come see you."

Ruthie Lynn's face looked about the same color as her red hair. "Hey, Annie. Bet you're surprised to see me." She gave an uncertain smile. Annie looked at her suspiciously but couldn't help being glad to see her even as she remembered how hurt she had been.

"Yeah, I am."

Miss Paine looked from one to the other as if deciding what to do next. "Well, I'm going to go to the kitchen and brew up some of that delicious tea that Miss—what's her name, Annie, the woman who's been taking care of you?"

"Miss Mercer. She'll be over after supper."

"—the tea that Miss Mercer brings here, while you girls talk." She left the room.

Ruthie Lynn moved a little toward the bed, gave a small, thin laugh. "I can't believe that you really get to see Miss Mercer. Ain't she scary?" She seemed excited by the thought of the old woman despite her unease with Annie.

"Well, she *is* kind of strange, but she's real nice to me." She noticed that Ruthie Lynn was gripping a pocketbook just like the one she had hit her with that day on the playground, an oatmeal box with a crocheted cover. Annie had tried to straighten hers out, but it was crushed too bad, so she had poked holes in it and given it to Robbie to collect bugs in.

Ruthie Lynn saw her looking at the pocketbook. She held it out. "I made it myself," she said. "Here, it's for you." The box was covered with blue crocheted shells.

Pleased, but still confused about how she felt, Annie

took the pocketbook. It even had a piece of paisley cloth sewed under the crocheted handle to keep the yarn from stretching. "What's in it? It feels heavy."

Ruthie Lynn smiled. "Why don't you look and see?"

Annie opened the top. The pocketbook was stuffed with fudge wrapped up in a checkered cloth.

"I hope you can eat it. I mean, you know, since you been sickly and all."

Annie pulled out a piece, took a taste. It was just right, hard, but not too hard, and just sweet enough. "This is really good. Did you make it yourself?"

"Yeah, you know how I have to do all the cooking. Momma's so fat she hates to move around. She tells me how to fix things while she sits at the table and shucks peas or peels potatoes, anything just so she's sitting down. She must weigh about three hundred pounds now."

Annie laughed despite herself, picturing Ruthie Lynn's momma who *was* the biggest woman she knew and, to hear some tell it, also the laziest woman in the region, but who had managed to produce nine kids to do her work for her even though her husband, a bandy-legged man with flaming red hair, wasn't any higher than a wagon wheel and skinny to boot.

"Shame on you, Ruthie Lynn. She don't . . . not three hundred pounds!"

Ruthie Lynn looked serious for a moment. "You're right. She don't weigh three hundred pounds. That was last week. Now she weighs 350 pounds!"

Annie smiled and munched on the fudge, not knowing what more to say, and in the awkward silence that followed she held out the pocketbook for Ruthie Lynn to get a piece.

Ruthie Lynn took one but didn't eat it. She fidgeted for a moment then blurted out, "Annie, I'm sorry for what I did. I don't know why I acted so mean and hateful. I been wanting to tell you for a long time, but I was *sooo* ashamed and afraid that you hated me so bad you'd never talk to me again, and then you got sick and left school and—"

Seeing Ruthie Lynn's face, all screwed up like she might cry at any minute, Annie thought she might cry herself. She had believed that it didn't matter to her anymore, what happened, the way she felt betrayed and rejected, but the pain came flooding back. She looked at Ruthie Lynn, the freckled skin flushed with the effort of admitting to being wrong, her quick eyes hopeful and pleading.

"It's all right. I know you didn't mean it. Here, come sit over here on the bed and tell me about everything going on at school." Annie smoothed her a place to sit.

Ruthie Lynn practically jumped across the space between them and plopped down on the bed, reaching out to hug Annie. "*Ooooh,* Annie, thank you. I'm never going to do nothing like that again. Never."

Annie hugged her back. "Now, about school. What's going on, anything?"

Ruthie Lynn glanced toward the door, then back at Annie, her eyes filled to bursting with something to tell.

"We got to watch out for Miss Paine. She don't know that anybody knows this."

Annie immediately joined in, feeling like there had never been anything wrong between them. "Why don't you take her my work? She usually grades it out in the kitchen before she leaves so she can help me if I need it. And bring back the tea. That way she won't have any reason to come in for a while . . . oh, here, take her some fudge too."

Ruthie Lynn grabbed the papers and fudge and ran out. She came back with two cups, one in each hand, and pushed the door half-closed with her foot. Getting settled on the bed, she started right in. "It's Ginny Long. You know how awful she is," Ruthie Lynn made a face, "well, she kept getting sick at school last week, throwing up and having to run outside. It would go on all morning long. She looked green, I mean, *green,* like a tree frog!"

Annie didn't like the Long girl. She was nasty, always hanging around boys, saying dirty things to get their attention, and she had pulled a cruel joke on Neal, asking him to go in the cloak room with her when she knew he wouldn't, and then she told everybody about it.

Ruthie Lynn looked toward the door again. "Well, the other day, she was real sick and had run outside two or three times, and Miss Paine asked her to stay in when she let the rest of us go outside for recess. Well, you know how Pattie is, she was going to find out what it was or die trying. So she didn't go out, but hid in the cloak room and heard every word."

Ruthie Lynn told Annie that Ginny was pregnant, that when Miss Paine had confronted her she had started crying, and when she finally admitted it, she virtually worked herself into a conniption, saying her daddy would kill her when he found out. Miss Paine tried to calm her down and kept insisting that she say who it belonged to. Ginny wouldn't tell for a while, then finally she broke down.

Here's the best part, Pattie said that Ginny kept saying that it was most likely—now get *this*—most likely Buddy's! *Buddy Coldren!* Can you believe it?"

"No! The preacher's kid?"

"Pattie said she would of give anything to see Miss Paine's face when Ginny named Buddy. You know how her face works up and down like she's got ants under her cheeks when she gets upset, and how she snorts through her nose."

Annie had eaten two pieces of fudge without even knowing it. "What're they going to do? Is Ginny still in school?"

"Yeah. But get this, she said they been doing it regular. And guess where?"

"Where?"

"Under the church. In the basement. Right under where his daddy carries on every Sunday about *sinnnning* and *luuusting.*" She could hardly contain herself as she drew the words out the way Preacher Coldren did, and her voice rose so high it cracked on the word *lusting.*

Annie got another piece of fudge. "Shhhhh, Miss Paine'll hear you."

They were both silent as they contemplated the enormity of this revelation.

Annie broke the silence, handing Ruthie Lynn the pocketbook. "Here, put this somewhere out of my reach before *I* weigh three hundred pounds!"

Ruthie Lynn got one more piece before putting the box on the dresser. "You know how Buddy always sits up front in church, all spic and clean, right up front, and nobody can holler 'Amen' louder than him."

Annie grinned. "He was probably all worked up thinking about what had gone on under his feet and he was saying 'Amen' to that."

Ruthie Lynn didn't get to put in her two-cents' worth on Buddy's probable excited state because Miss Paine came through the door. Ruthie Lynn quickly swallowed whatever she was going to say.

"Annie, this math is all correct. I'm going to take your composition with me." Miss Paine stopped by the bed. "Did you two have a nice visit?"

"Yes, ma'am." Ruthie Lynn's mouth was working strangely as she tried to chew her fudge, not to laugh, and to talk all at the same time.

Annie tried to cover for her. "I can come back to school next week. Miss Mercer says I'm all right now, and that I'll quit being so tired soon."

Miss Paine patted her hand. "Good. I'll be glad to see you back in class again." She turned to Ruthie Lynn, who had managed to swallow her fudge and compose her face. "Come on, Ruthie Lynn, we need to go now." She strode out like she was leading a procession.

Ruthie Lynn stopped by the bed, bent over, and whispered to Annie. "Oh yeah, I been saving the best for last. That fellow, J.C. He's been asking me about you, all about your folks, and when you was coming back to school and all, and I asked him why he wanted to know, and Annie, he looked like I had caught him with his pants down, the way he turned kind of red and said, 'No reason, it's just Annie seems real smart in school and nice too, like a real nice girl . . .' anyways, I'll tell you about it later. I got to go now before Miss Paine has a hissy fit. Bye."

At supper Lacey kept up a clatter of background noise and comments. "It ain't enough that I gots to put up with that old witch-woman coming here, and that skinny schoolteacher, but now she's bringing that little frizzy-headed loud-mouthed gal with her."

Annie felt a stab of anger toward Lacey, who seemed to like nothing better than to stay on her all the time. "Ruthie Lynn didn't bother you. She came to see me."

Lacey hung the pots she had just washed on the wall, banging each one against it. "If you's so sick, too sick to help out around the house, you is too sick for company, especially *that* company."

Earlier that day, when Annie had got back from the woods with Robbie, Lacey had been washing clothes in the yard and Annie had offered to help. "You just go on in the house," she had said, "get back in the bed and work on being sick so you don't have to do nothing." Annie had held back what she wanted to say and walked on to the house hearing Lacey behind her. "Just pure-tee meanness, that's what's wrong with you."

Neal, who hadn't touched a bite on his plate, suddenly broke in. "Grady's offered me a job. Two days a week. A quarter a day. I'd have to stay one night. Doing stock and cleaning—"

Lacey hooted. "That sissy-man. His fingernails is longer than a woman's who don't do nothing but lay around and let some man take care of her. You want to work for him—"

Claude leaned back in his chair, his eyes going from Annie to Neal, then resting on Robbie, who was spooning rice and gravy in his mouth. He looked at Lacey and smiled. "Now ain't that two peas in a pod, Neal and Grady? I wonder if they'll get married and have kids, maybe another little Robbie?"

Lacey laughed, a gushy liquid laugh, and Neal, looking even more disturbed than usual, flushed.

Claude, on a roll now, turned his attention to Annie. "And we need to keep an eye on Miss Priss here. I was at the store today getting some nails and that fellow, the blond one that's building the new school, comes up to me and asks me about Annie, how's she doing and when's she coming back to school. I told him it weren't none of his goddamn business." Claude grinned. "You should have seen his face."

Annie had heard enough and was half out of her seat.

"Shut up, Claude. Annie, sit back down and finish eating your meal. Don't waste good food." Her daddy turned to Neal. "A quarter a day. That's as good as you'd get to do public work."

"Yes, sir." Neal stared down at his plate like it would walk off if he took his eyes off it.

Claude, pouting at being told to shut up, motioned to Lacey to bring him some more coffee and she scurried over and filled his cup. Annie saw Claude squeeze Lacey's rump as she stood next to him. Then Claude smirked over at Annie and sniffed his hand, challenging her with his eyes to say something.

Robbie knocked over the bowl he was eating from and dropped his spoon and specks of gravy-covered rice flew in Claude's face. Claude jumped up. "Jesus Christ, do we have to let that little idiot eat at the table!" He wiped his face with his hand.

Robbie, scared by the anger in Claude's voice, started to cry. Lacey picked up the spoon. "There he goes, now he's gonna blubber all night, nothing'll shut him up."

Annie took the spoon from her and wiped it off, held it out to Robbie. "Here, Robbie. Quit crying. Lacey'll get you some more rice." She looked defiantly at Lacey, who shuffled over to the stove and fixed Robbie another bowl.

Annie's father stood up. "Claude, come on out on the porch. We got some talking to do."

Annie didn't offer to help with the kitchen. Instead she lifted Robbie out of the chair, wiped his mouth on a rag, and said, "Come on, let's go wash up before Miss Mercer gets here."

Miss Mercer showed up right at dark, coming into the bedroom, a dark moving bundle of clothes, wrapped from head to foot in black.

"Did that girl come see you today, the one with the big scar on her wrist?"

Annie had stopped being surprised at what the old woman said, and it didn't even occur to her to wonder how she knew Ruthie Lynn had come over, or how she knew about the scar on Ruthie Lynn's wrist from a bad cut on chicken wire when she was small.

"Yes ma'am."

"Good. I know you like her. Here, I got some strength restorer for you. You need to drink it every day." She pulled out some tree bark from the sack that was constantly with her and showed it to Annie. "It's wild cherry. I'll fix you some now."

Robbie trailed after Miss Mercer to the kitchen, saying something about the butterflies in the field. Annie could hear Miss Mercer mumbling a reply, but couldn't hear what she said.

She had to drink every drop of the restorer under Miss Mercer's watchful eyes. When Annie was finished, she said, "I think I should go back to school now."

Miss Mercer nodded. "Best that you do. Get out of this house." Her tone implied that the subject was decided and closed.

Miss Mercer looked around, studying the room although she had been in it many times before. "You like it here . . . in your momma's room?"

Annie wasn't quite sure how to answer, but she didn't have to because Miss Mercer walked over to the dresser, opened the box that held her mother's few pieces of jewelry and the handkerchief. She picked up the handkerchief, and Annie felt her heart jump, a little startled jump. She drew her breath in and held it.

"What do you make of this?" she asked Annie, holding out the handkerchief as if it were open and they were looking at the curious bone contents.

Annie was glad for the distraction of Robbie climbing up on the bed to sit at the foot where he liked to draw and color in the book Annie had made for him.

"Well?" Miss Mercer came back to the bed, still holding the handkerchief out to her.

"I don't know . . . it's a bone of some kind, I guess."

"I know what it is," said Miss Mercer, "and I know about the hair, too."

She told Annie what everybody in the area knew, or at least what they suspected, about Evelyn, something going on with her and the road worker Jesse, about how Henry had run him off, about how sick her momma had been for a long time after that, quiet and off to herself.

Then she told her what only she knew, about the summer meetings at the cave, the cut-off finger, Jesse's wanting her momma to go off with him, how Evelyn had gone back to the cave the next morning, left her boys still sleeping, and slipped out before the light of dawn had split open the night sky. . . .

Miss Mercer pulled the bone out of the handkerchief and handed it to her. "I think she would have drowned herself in that underground lake if it hadn't been for you."

The bone felt heavy to Annie, weighed down with old memories and spilled blood, and it lay in her hand like some kind of beckoning to the past. Her mind was filled with a jumble of questions, but "Me?" was all she could say.

"Yeah, you girl, *you*, curled in a hard little knot of new life, you kept her from dying."

Annie's felt a mix of emotions—sadness at her momma's loss, anger at those who had done it to her, love for her momma's bravery, a yearning to see her again—all tumbling around her heart like the cascading of a waterfall.

"How do you know all this?" Her voice, rising from somewhere deep inside, was unfamiliar to her own ear.

"Cause I seen it. You can too, you can see it, if you want to." Miss Mercer turned away.

Annie couldn't sleep. She heard over and over Miss Mercer's words, *you can too, you can see it*. She had been trying to do what Miss Mercer said, to be able to see things, and she had tried to see that night with Claude, but nothing had come to her no matter how hard she tried. Yet she felt a fierce tugging, a force pulling her, a deep desire to know about her momma, how she had been, so she decided to try.

Annie got up and got the piece of bone and the lock of hair. She got back in the bed and focused her mind, lying there in the cold dark, moonlight filling the room until everything looked almost silvery. She looked at her momma's face in her mind, studied it, let it come to her

. . .

> *she is feeling her way through dark woods, her mind lost in a morass of pain, a constant pounding behind her eyes, and her body is burning, a hot liquid flowing along her nerves, she goes into a cave, dead calmness coming over her as soon as she steps into the huge atrium and smells the stale water of the dead lake, the hollow sound of contained air plugging her ears, by the light of a single lantern, she wraps a piece of her hair that she cuts with a knife from over the nape of her neck with a piece of bone in a handkerchief that she takes from her pocket. Finding a niche in the cave wall, she stuffs the wrapped bundle in and seals it with dirt and small rocks taking comfort somehow from the ritual. And then she walks over to the lake, pushes off in the boat, and floats for hours, the light extinguished, the darkness thick as swaddled cotton around her. . . .*

Annie came awake with a start, sat bolt upright in the bed. The room was flooded with light. It was morning, and she could hear activity outside her door. Robbie's bed was empty, the covers thrown on the floor. She looked frantically around, confused until she saw the hair and bone next to her hand and it all came back to her—the cave, her momma, the dream.

14

After five days of light rain and dropping temperatures, Friday turned dry and mild, so Annie decided that the next morning she would take Robbie and go to the cemetery. She had dug up a small magnolia tree in the woods that she wanted to plant on her momma's grave before she had to go back to school.

Saturday morning, it was dark outside and the house still sleeping when she dressed Robbie in a long-sleeved shirt and overalls, rolling them up above his ankle-high shoes and, over his wiggling protest, making him put on a sweater, saying, "Shhh, you'll wake up everybody. You can take if off when the sun comes out. Go on out and get your wagon."

She pulled on a sweater too, a creamy off-white wool that slipped over her head and hung halfway down her legs over a long blue-flowered cotton skirt. Her momma had knitted the sweater just last year, making it big and roomy the way Annie liked, and she had sewed the skirt on her fingers, using four squares of material from flour sacks, sewing them together and gathering the skirt at the top, then adding a waistband and button. She could make a skirt in just a couple of hours. Annie laced on her shoes and brushed her hair behind her ears, braiding it in a long plait down her back.

The moon was still a dim shadow in the morning sky as she got some work gloves out of the shed along with a spade and put them in Robbie's wagon. She and Robbie carried the tree out from the cellar and put it in the wagon too. Then she tied the tree and tools down, leaving room for Robbie to sit if he got tired of walking.

Although the last part of the path to the church was steep and narrow, the first part was easy with the road cleared and flat, so Annie let Robbie pull the wagon while she followed along behind, walking slowly with her arms crossed over her chest against the chill. The sun was starting to come up, turning the lower lip of the slate sky into streaks of pink and turquoise shot through with light, and the road was draped with a gauzy white mist swirling around her legs.

She had not been back to the cemetery since the funeral, and despite her desire to go today, she found that her mood kept shifting like colors caught in a puddle of water, wavering between a need to see her momma's grave and a sense of dread that would suddenly fill her. Unbeckoned images kept flitting in her mind, memories of the birth, the wake, the church, the service, all saturated with a blue haze of grief, and the more Annie tried to push the pictures away, the more she felt a deep sadness that seemed to have no core but to permeate her body. She kept thinking that maybe, after all, she was making a mistake going up there, opening it all up again, as foolish as intentionally striking over and over a bruise that is still full of blood.

Annie was deep in thought and didn't notice that Robbie was out of sight, already around a turn, until she lifted her head from looking at the ground. Determined to go on, she quickened her step.

When Annie came around the cliff, she saw Robbie stopped in front of the new school talking to J.C. She hadn't thought about running into J.C., although she knew that she had to pass the school to get to the cemetery path, and at the sight of his tall, slim body leaning carelessly against a stack of lumber, a cup in one hand, a cigarette in the other, she felt a moment of panic at having to talk to him, and she had to force herself to return the casual wave he gave her when she walked toward him. She set her face into a small smile. The sun had come up higher now, and Annie felt suddenly hot with her sweater on.

Robbie called to her, "Hurry, Annie, hurry!" He started up the road.

"Hey, Annie. I ain't seen you in a while." J.C. smiled at her and took a sip from his cup. "Where you going with that tree?"

"To the cemetery. It's for my momma's grave." As soon as the words were out of her mouth, she regretted them. Now he would remember what had been said about her and about her momma's death. To cover her trepidation, she abruptly turned and called to Robbie. "Robbie, wait a minute. Wait for me."

Robbie wasn't much farther than he had been before because the road was slanted up, and his face was red with the effort of pulling the wagon. Giving up, he sat down and began to draw in the dirt.

J.C. didn't seem to notice her discomfort. He motioned toward Robbie. "He's a sweet kid. He just told me how he was going to the 'resting place,' where his momma was."

Annie looked at the ground *coffins one after the other an endless chain of coffins sinking into the ground a huge hungry hole cold wet dirt falling like rain on top of them disappearing down the hole* and said distractedly, her voice barely audible, "That's what he calls it. I don't know where he got it from."

She looked back up at J.C. He had an intent look on his face as he watched her, and her mind felt turned inside out, as if his eyes were moving over her thoughts. . . . She tried to shake off the feeling. "We got to go. It's a ways up there."

She made to move away. J.C. straightened up, threw his cigarette down, and ground it out with his heel.

"How about if I go along to help you?" He smiled, and Annie felt it again, that sense of intimacy moving like choppy water between them, like he knew exactly what she was thinking.

She made herself smile. "Sure, why not?"

"Wait here." Setting the cup down on the stack of lumber, he went in the school.

Despite her shyness, Annie couldn't help noticing how good he looked. He never wore overalls like the other men and boys, but dressed in dungarees and flannel shirts. This morning he had on a brown-and-green checkered shirt, with his hair pulled back in a short ponytail, and she liked the way he always looked fresh-washed, like he had just stepped out of a tub.

He came back with some tools, wire, burlap bags, and a bucket and called to Robbie to pull the wagon back, but Robbie couldn't get it turned around. Annie went and got it, bringing Robbie back with her.

"I already got a spade," she said, brushing the dirt off Robbie's hands where he had been drawing in the road.

J.C. fit the tools in the wagon. "You don't know much about planting trees, do you?" He sounded teasing.

"I know you got to dig a hole." She couldn't help smiling as she opened her eyes wide and put her hands on her hips.

He laughed, and the sound made her feel good. "Well, yeah, that's right, you *do* have to dig a hole. But you got to plant it right and prop it up. I'll show you. Come on." He took up the wagon handle. Then stopped.

"Does a branch from the river run by close to the cemetery?"

Annie nodded. "About a quarter-mile behind the church."

"Good."

When they turned off the road onto the path, J.C. went first with the wagon and Annie walked behind him, holding Robbie's hand.

"Are you tired?" she asked Robbie after a half-mile of walking uphill.

Robbie nodded his head.

"J.C., let's stop at the river and rest a few minutes."

The bank exposed from the winter's low water was covered with a flock of blackbirds foraging in the mud. The birds took to wing at their approach, several giving an alarm in a high whistle, their wing beats filling the air with a loud swoosh, the sound wind makes blowing through a pass. They landed in the trees, covering the branches like clusters of dark fruit and protesting the interruption of their feeding with a deafening chorus of high, slurred *teer-ers*. Robbie, delighted with the noisy show, let go of Annie's hand and ran to the edge of the bank.

Annie and J.C. sat on fallen limbs to keep off the dew-wet ground while Robbie gathered pebbles and twigs and put them in his pockets. J.C. asked Annie when she was coming back to school, and she remembered what Ruthie Lynn had said, that J.C. had asked about her, and was pleased, but then she remembered Claude's account of his encounter with J.C. and the memory embarrassed her.

"Next week. Probably Monday." She felt at a loss for words and covered it up by retying her shoe.

J.C. seemed to sense that she didn't want to talk about school and absorbed himself in rolling a cigarette for a moment. Then he asked, "What kind of tree are we planting?"

Annie was relieved to get on another subject. "It's called a Star Magnolia. It's really more like a large bush. It has big, pretty white flowers and smells sweet. I thought I could put it there to be kind of like a marker since there's not one."

"When'd you dig it up?"

"Last week. But I kept it in the cellar and put wet sacks over the roots."

He stood, took her hand, and pulled her up. "Ok. Let's get going."

The church rose up before Annie, coming out of the morning mist that was still not quite burned off, and the sight stirred her, creating a churning feeling in her stomach. The building, set in the middle of a cleared acre, loomed over the fenced-in cemetery off to one side, where graves extended around to the back of the church, and on the other side there were tables made from sawhorses and plywood and an open shelter for church gatherings.

"Here it is," she said, stopping in front of the steps *the rain falling all around her on her hair her face her eyelashes everything under water cold wet wind people staring wet needles in her back blackbirds whispering rustling behind her* as if he couldn't see the church for himself. The words were more for herself than him, to confirm that she had actually come back.

"Here it is," she said again.

Even Robbie stood like a small statue staring at the church his eyes unblinking, a studied concentration on his face replacing the blandness usually there. J.C. stood to the side, saying nothing.

Finally Robbie broke the silence. "Me help?"

"Sure." J.C. picked up the wagon handle and followed Robbie over to the gate leading into the cemetery. Annie trailed behind.

Most of the graves were marked with small crosses or low tombstones, and some looked tended, but most weren't. Robbie pulled J.C. by the hand until they were in the far corner at the back of the cemetery, where he pointed to a grave. "Momma," he said, "resting here."

Seeing the earth, the finality of the dirt, Annie was swamped with a quiet rage, a palpable bitterness that sank into her heart like lead, making her think that she couldn't take another step *blood running from her eye blood flowing down the pale skin over the rouged cheek black fluid running from her mouth* when Robbie ran back to her and wanted to be picked up. Holding his small body made her feel better, and she hugged him tight. He gave her a goofy smile and said, "Plant tree, now?"

J.C. got the spade out of the wagon. "Pick a spot."

Annie put Robbie down and walked carefully around the graves, avoiding stepping on them. "Right here between them," she said, "so that I can always tell where they are."

J.C. shoved the spade in where she indicated. "While I

dig, you and Robbie cut off any broken branches and trim the roots. Just make sure you don't cut the tap root, the big one."

Annie pulled off her sweater and Robbie's and set to work with the shears J.C. had brought, Robbie pointing out the broken places and Annie snipping them. When they finished, J.C. was still digging.

"That hole looks big enough to live in," she said, wiping the dirt from her hands on the burlap sacks in the wagon.

J.C. quit digging and put the spade down. "It's got to be. So the tree can *live* in it."

"Very funny."

"No, really, the dirt has to be loose so the tree can put down roots or it won't take. It'll die."

Annie could tell from the shadow that passed over his face that he was conscious of saying "die," and she tried to ignore the twinge she felt. She said, "Well, let's put it in."

She held the small tree up while J.C. arranged the roots in the hole as carefully as a woman arranges her hair for an important occasion. Then he told her to hold it still while he filled the bucket, and seeing Robbie watching, he said, "You too, Robbie, you help Annie hold it so it stays straight." Robbie scampered over to grab a branch on the side. Annie liked the way J.C. included Robbie even though they didn't need any help.

J.C. came back with a bucketful of water and refilled the hole by alternating the water with the dirt and packing it down each time. Then he stomped on the soil around the base of the trunk.

Annie stepped back to look at it. "Is it done now?"

"Not quite yet." He wrapped up the trunk in the burlap bags he had brought, tying them on with some of the rubber strips. "This'll keep the weather from getting to it and keep rabbits and mice off of it until it gets stronger."

Getting wire and stakes and pieces of rubber, he staked the tree, pulling taut the wires attached to the rubber rings he had put around the branches. "Now it's done." He gave a final twist to the wire he was working with.

He went over and stood next to her. "Kind of pitiful looking, ain't it, all bare and chopped up like that."

Annie stared at the tree. "It won't be when it blooms. It'll be beautiful. Momma used to pick the blossoms and put them in a vase on the kitchen table, a carnival vase with all different colors, and the flowers were snowy white. . . ."

It was so strange, the dream that she had the night before she went out into the woods for the tree *her momma young beautiful long hair loose, a white room large windows, sunlight falling like yellow rain, a tangle of green plants lush leaves slick as membrane some veined pink and purple, i wish i could grow plants like that annie says, she answers you can, annie asks do they need water, she points to the full shining stalks and says never—*

Annie felt tears spring to her eyes along with the understanding that she would always carry her momma's death with her, clutching the memory under her heart like an ugly baby, ignoring the stares and whispers of others, holding firmly to the small misshapen body like you would hold onto love, and, giving in to the sadness, somehow she found herself in J.C.'s arms, her face hidden in his shoulder while she cried.

When she had quit shaking, her sobs easing, he put his hand under her chin and lifted her face. "No matter what happened, Annie, no matter what anybody says, it wasn't your fault. You *couldn't* hurt nobody." And then he let go of her.

She wiped her eyes. "Come on, Robbie's run off down to the branch."

They found Robbie lying stomach down on the bank staring at a brown wedge-shaped head about twenty feet out in the water. The head kept popping up and down in different places, moving farther out and diving at their approach.

J.C. squatted down beside him. "It's an otter. You must be near his den and he wants to get in. They usually go in underwater, but with the branch so low, the entrance is probably out of the water. You want to look for it?"

Annie wasn't used to anyone actually talking to Robbie like he could understand what they were saying except for her and Miss Mercer. Miss Mercer would chatter to him the whole time she was at the house as Robbie followed her around. It reminded Annie of a cowbird following a cow, the way Robbie was always right next to her.

Anyone else, if they didn't ignore him, which was usually the case, talked about him as if he weren't there. One of the worst was Lacey, who had called him "dat little idiot" until one day Annie, fed up with it, slammed down the pot she was drying and told her never to say that again. Lacey had looked surprised at the tone in Annie's voice and had mumbled something about her being "sassy," but Lacey had quit calling him that, at least in Annie's hearing, and now referred to him as "dat little boy" with as much contempt as she could load into the words. When Annie thought about it, she realized that Lacey treated her differently since Miss Mercer had been taking care of her, and she suspected it had to do with Lacey's being afraid of the old woman.

At J.C.'s question, Robbie popped up, nodding his head so vigorously that it looked like it might fly off, and Annie had to smile at the sight.

"Look around for holes up here on the bank top. He always has a back door so that he doesn't get trapped. Then we'll know where to look for the front door." J.C. started scanning the ground.

Robbie motioned to Annie, his small hand making a grabbing motion. "Help look, Annie, back door," and he got down on his hands and knees and began crawling around.

In just a few moments, he let out a whoop. He had found two holes about a foot apart.

J.C. walked a straight line from the holes to the riverbank. He stepped down in the dried mud and looked carefully at the rocks. "Here it is, under these rocks."

Robbie scrambled down next to him and then went over and stuck his hand in the hole.

"Careful, there might be one already in there," J.C. said, and Robbie snatched his hand back like he'd already been bitten.

J.C. pulled him away. "Come on, the otter can't come home until we leave."

Robbie looked doubtful about leaving until Annie mentioned breakfast. He climbed up the bank, stopping to look at the holes on the top again. "Back door," he said, almost thoughtfully, before following them back to the path.

"Why don't you and Robbie come in? I'll make some coffee." J.C. was unloading his stuff from the wagon.

Annie thought for a moment. If she stayed away for about another hour everyone would be gone at the house, out of the kitchen, and she and Robbie could have a quiet breakfast without having to put up with the usual snideness from Claude, the sarcasm from Lacey, and the discomfort of her daddy, who seemed to want only to be alone these days, to be out of the house, and who talked to no one except Claude unless he *had* to say something to her or Neal. Neal looked more and more miserable at home and got quieter and quieter until he was little more than a shadow, perking up only on the days he went to help Grady out at the store.

"Sure, why not?"

Inside, the school was still a skeleton of a building, the rooms sectioned off and the windows in but no walls around the classrooms yet except for a cloak room closed in across the back. A loft ran halfway across the top with two windows cut in each side. Sun was coming through the east windows, and the uprights striped the floor and walls with dark rectangles. The corners, though, were steeped in shadow. To Annie, the room looked like a giant spider web with dark streaks reaching out in every direction.

Annie sat down on a blanket spread on the floor and watched J.C. wash up in a basin, then stoke up the fire in the stove and put a kettle on to boil. He got out three cups and a tin of sugar. Robbie immediately spied a box of nails and started making patterns with them on the floor.

"I don't have any milk. Is that okay?" J.C. asked.

"Sure. Do you cook here?"

"No, not much. I eat every night with Miss Paine. It's part of my pay." The water started to boil, and he dumped some coffee in the pot.

Annie was amused at his disregard for measuring. "How do you know how much coffee to put in like that?"

J.C. grinned back. "I don't. It's never quite right, but it's always hot. . . . You know, that's what Miss Paine is sometimes, *a pain*. I mean, she's nice and all, but she's got this idea that I ought to be a preacher, and she's always at me about it, not direct, but all the time hinting."

"Why does she think you should be a preacher?" Annie was surprised.

"I guess 'cause it was a preacher that told me about this school. But I don't have no idea of being any such thing. She keeps trying to get me to go to church with her. You know, she wanted to be a missionary herself, go overseas, but she told me she couldn't. They wouldn't let her because of a spot on her lungs, so she figured working in the mountains would be doing the Lord's work as much as being a missionary to the heathens. She says she likes teaching, but she gets discouraged sometimes by the way folks think of her as an outsider, and by things like having no roads. She says she can't get used to the way there ain't no real doctors, and all the accidents and sickness—men cut practically in half by sawmill accidents, snake bites, typhoid fever, fights over moonshine runs. You should hear her go on."

J.C. took the pot off the stove and set it aside to let the grounds settle. He sat down beside her on the blanket.

Annie smiled. "She talks a lot, don't she?"

"She sure does. She talks from the time I get there to the time I leave. But she's good to me. She helps me with reading and writing, even lets me go through her books and take any that I want."

"What about you? Where're you from?" Annie fiddled

with her skirt, avoiding looking directly at him now that he was so close.

"I'm from Virginia. I got nine brothers and three sisters. I'm the oldest. I met the same pastor that got Miss Paine the teacher's job here. He was on a circuit ride, and he told me how she would let me go to school if I came over here and helped her out with some carpentry. I could read a little, but nobody in my family has any learning. They live off moonshining. I don't want no part of that."

J.C. shook his head and changed the subject. "Miss Paine says that sometimes at the church here they snake-handle. Is it true?"

"Yeah, Preacher Coldren does, and some of the old women and men, Miss Paine too. Have you ever seen it? It's kind of crazy . . . scary too, I think."

"No, I never seen nothing like that. But I'd like to."

When he poured the coffee, he filled Robbie's only half full and added water to it. Looking in a tin, he brought out some bread and took a piece over to Robbie with a cup of coffee. Robbie said, "T'ank you," settled down flat on the floor on his stomach, and began to eat and drink.

The coffee was rich and hot and sweet, and it tasted wonderful to Annie. J.C. positioned the pot on the side of the stove to keep it from boiling again and pulled up an old school desk that Miss Paine had brought over for him to use and sat down facing Annie.

Annie was conscious of the rich smell of newness from the piles of sawdust and split lumber and cans of paint. The air was alive with dust caught in the sunlight and a feeling of activity in the tools placed around the walls.

Robbie, stuffing the last of the bread in his mouth, ran over and asked to go outside. She looked at J.C. "Is there anything he can get hurt on?"

"No, I don't think so. All my tools are in here. He'll be all right."

After Robbie left, she stood up and walked around, looking at things and touching them while J.C. watched her. The morning flooded back on her, and the memory of how it had felt next to J.C., how good his arms had felt, the way he had said, *you couldn't hurt nobody,* as if he had no doubt of it, swamped her, and she was overcome with an urge to tell him, to tell him everything, about the castor bean, about how she thought Claude had said three tablespoons but he said he hadn't, how he had called her a little blind liar, and said she had better leave him alone about it quit poking at it just shut up, how she had told her daddy Claude said three tablespoons and how her daddy had turned away, mumbled, *what's done is done, just forget it.* She had gone over it again and again in her mind, dwelled on it, tried to see it, she asks, *three teaspoons,* he says, *no, three tablespoons,* each time she asks, and he says the same thing, *three tablespoons, tablespoons, three tablespoons* always she hears him say *three tablespoons. . . .*

"Hey, you're going to rub the wood off that window sill, and I got a hunch you ain't seeing nothing out that window." J.C. was standing behind her.

Annie pulled herself back, her last thought of how guilt could be a lot like the dark sunspots that now filled her eyes, evaporating as she turned back toward J.C. as the thought was replaced with a consciousness of being alone in the room with him. A little uneasy, she tried to think of something to say.

"There's a visiting preacher from Tennessee coming to the church tomorrow night. I hear he's a snake-handler. You want to go?" She didn't believe she had said that. She never went to those meetings anymore. She had gone with her momma occasionally only because her momma wanted her company.

"You bet I do. I guess I might as well see what's in store for me as a preacher." He smiled and drained the last of his coffee. Annie couldn't help but smile back with the thought of how J.C. could never look like old prune-faced Preacher Coldren with his wild gray hair flying in waves back from his shriveled-up skin.

Robbie came through the door with a black three-legged puppy at his heels. "Look, Annie, name's Jo-Jo." He placed his hand on its head, and the dog whimpered a little, licking the side of Robbie's leg.

Annie glanced at J.C.

"I saw a man throw her in the creek with a stone tied to her. I guess it was because she's crippled. Looks like she had some kind of bad accident. Anyway, the water was clear, and I could see her trying to swim up, and the rope holding her back while she floated like a fish hooked on the end of a line. I got her out. I been feeding her until I figure out what to do with her. She's scared of people and stays mostly under the building. She won't come out for nothing but food and then only after you leave it."

"Jo-Jo likes me." Robbie squatted down, wrapping his arms around the puppy.

Annie was shaking her head. "Robbie, you know there's no way Daddy's going to let you have that puppy—" but when she saw his face start to crumble as he held the puppy so tight that its eyes seemed to bulge, she hesitated, looked at J.C., who shrugged, and she relented. "Okay, we'll try to keep her, but no promises—"

Robbie jumped up before she could finish.

"Come on, Jo-Jo. Ride in wagon." He was out the door with the puppy right behind him, using her one front leg like a peg leg, keeping it stiff in the center of her chest and hopping on it.

J.C. walked Annie outside. "She looks like some kind of Labrador. They usually make good dogs."

Annie couldn't help but worry a little. "It's not that. It's whether or not Daddy will let her stay. He doesn't believe in pets, thinks everything has to pull its own weight, be used for something. I don't know . . . I'll try anyway."

Robbie was already on the road, pulling the wagon, the puppy piled comfortably on his sweater in the back, and she ran to catch up with him.

"Don't forget about tomorrow night," J.C. called to her. "I'll meet you at the start of the path to the church."

Annie had already forgotten her hasty suggestion in her worry about the puppy, but even in the midst of her apprehension, she couldn't repress a flash of glee at the thought of telling Ruthie Lynn about meeting up with J.C.

15

That Sunday, Annie waited on the porch to catch Neal when he came home from Grady's. She wanted to talk with him before the others came in. It was late afternoon, sunny and breezy, the air filled with querulous sparrow trills as little brown birds flitted in and out of the trees and hedges. She saw him walking up the road, his head down, watching his feet as if he were scared of stepping on something.

Neal seemed surprised when he came up on the porch and saw her sitting in the swing.

"Can I talk to you a minute?" she asked.

He sat down beside her. Robbie came through the screen door, letting it slam behind him. Neal flinched at the sound.

"Don't slam the door," Annie said automatically.

Robbie never glanced their way. With a pork chop in each grimy hand, he went down the steps toward the shed, his overalls scroungy in the seat where he had been playing in the dirt earlier.

Annie smiled at the sight of him, his little flat face intent on his task. "I bet I know who the other pork chop is for. That dog is going to weigh a ton if she eats everything he gives her."

Neal didn't reply. His eyes were dull as burned-out

coals, and they moved languidly from one object to another.

Watching him, Annie felt a rush of pity for him. She knew how miserable he was at home, how he hated coming back to the house after being at Grady's. She could see it in his body and face, the way he moved around slow like an old man instead of a boy, the way he drew further and further inside himself, rarely speaking to anybody. His nose was always in a book that Grady had given him. The thought came to her that he might not help her. His heart was so closed that he didn't seem to care about anything or anybody.

She put her hand on his arm to get his attention. "Neal, can you do something for me?"

Neal's pale face flushed like she had embarrassed him by touching him, and she could feel him withdraw, a slight tensing of the muscles, through his thin cotton shirt, like a puppy that's scared of being petted, but is too frightened to bite.

"What?" he asked tentatively.

"I want to go to church tonight, but I don't want to take Robbie. Will you watch him for me, put him to bed and all? I don't want Lacey to mess with him. And watch the dog. Keep her away from Daddy and Claude."

"You're going to church?" Neal's voice rose a little on the question, and he seemed really to listen for the first time.

Annie thought for a moment about whether she should tell him, then decided to go ahead. "I'm going with a boy from school. The one building the new school. J.C. He wants to go."

Neal, his brow pinched, looked directly at her for the first time. "Does Daddy know where you're going?"

"No. And I don't want him to. Claude neither. Nobody. I want you to say I'm at Miss Mercer's, that she asked me to come over. You can say you don't know why. I'll think of something later."

Robbie had come up on the porch with Jo-Jo right behind him, and was listening to them. "Annie, me go?"

He climbed in her lap, greasy hands, dirty pants, and all.

Neal absently petted Jo-Jo, who kept her head pushed up right next to Robbie, as if it were attached to his leg.

Annie spoke very gravely to Robbie while she wiped at his hands and face with her handkerchief. "Jo-Jo can't go. So who's going to watch her if you go?"

Annie had let Robbie play with Jo-Jo all day yesterday and then kept her in the shed out of everybody's way during the afternoon and evening. Her daddy knew about the dog. He asked Annie about it when he got home yesterday. She had said that Robbie had found it in the woods and that it had followed them home. Maybe, she suggested, it would make a good barn dog, kill rats and stuff. He had only nodded noncommittally and so far had ignored the dog.

"You need to stay here and take care of Jo-Jo," Annie said.

If Robbie could have looked calculating, he would have, his features drawn up into a mask of concentration. He asked, "Jo-Jo sleep with me?"

Before Annie could protest, Neal spoke up. "Sure, we'll put her in your room after everybody goes to bed, and she can sleep with you. Okay?"

His deal made, Robbie nodded and gave Neal a loose, sloppy grin. "Okay."

He screwed up his face again. "Pretty Boy? Me play with Pretty Boy?"

"You bet. I taught him some new tricks."

Annie smiled at Neal. "Thanks."

"Sure thing, Sister."

She hadn't heard him use that term since her momma died, *Sister,* and the sound of it made her feel not as alone as she usually felt.

Annie and J.C. could see specks of light from the church lanterns flickering through the trees. As they walked, the sky darkened to deep blue and yellow gauze, and pale stars came out to sit on the edges of the purple mountains to the west.

They stopped in the shadow of a large pine on the fringe of the churchyard. Despite the chilly night air, the clearing was filled. Men and older boys, all dressed in overalls or white shirts and galloused pants, stood around talking in small groups. They saw clusters of women, like flocks of birds in dark dresses and small patterned frocks made from flour and feed sacks or cloth bought at the dry goods store, swoop through the yard going directly into the lit-up church, children in tow.

J.C. wanted to know if so many people usually came to the meetings, and Annie told him no, that people had probably heard about the visiting minister, a Reverend Beasley, who had just gotten out of jail for snake-handling in Durham. A lot of them, probably the ones standing around the rim of the yard, were there just to see what would happen. Others—Annie pointed them out—weren't local. They most likely came with the Reverend from Durham.

"But you can tell who the elders are—they call themselves 'saints'"—she said, "because they keep together and kiss one another. The men kiss the men, and the women kiss the women."

J.C. had barely got a shocked "What?" out of his mouth when one middle-aged, balding man walked up to a male newcomer and, giving him a vigorous hug, kissed him full on the mouth.

"See. There." Annie nodded toward them with her head. "Those are two of the saints. He's giving the other man a holy kiss. That's what they call it."

J.C. grimaced. "You'd *have* to be a saint to kiss those ugly old men."

Annie couldn't help wondering if coming was a good idea. She remembered how it was here that she had seen a side of her mother that had frightened her, a scary, frenzied, secret self that normally hid behind soft bleached aprons and stoic silence. And it wasn't just her momma who changed. The services would transform familiar, ordinary people, people she saw every day, into creatures as fascinating and horrifying as the beautiful patterned scales of the serpents they caressed—

She was drawn out of her thoughts by the sight of Miss Paine coming up the path. She walked by without seeing them, stepping out like she was late, her face reddened from the climb and her whole body, striding along, moving at odd angles, the joints loose. She strode through the churchyard and went directly inside without turning her head.

"Boy, she looks all worked up, don't she?" J.C. whispered as she passed.

Next Preacher Coldren came up with a man dressed in a suit. Annie figured that he had to be the visiting minister. They stopped right in front of Annie and J.C. and exchanged kisses with other saints who, seeing the ministers, stopped their visiting to greet them.

Annie was surprised at how young the Reverend Beasley was. He had dark hair combed back from a high forehead and a smooth, unlined face that glowed in the night. He had the most intense brown eyes she had ever seen. They reflected light like glass as he talked to the men, yet when he turned his gaze on her, they looked black and glutted, and she had a peculiar feeling of being absorbed by them. He had barely looked at her before he continued on, scanning the crowd, his eyes sliding from one face to another, focusing and refocusing. Then he looked out beyond the faces into the dense woods, a kind of dreamy look on his face.

To Annie, when she had been caught momentarily in his vision, he seemed to radiate something insidious, a nebulous sense of threat flowing outward from him in oily ripples, and she felt a moment of trepidation.

J.C. said, "You're shaking. Are you cold? Here, take this jacket." He slipped out of his coat and put it over her shoulders. Annie drew it around her.

In a few minutes the two preachers, arm in arm, went into the church and everyone else followed. Annie and J.C. were the last ones through the door. A man shaped like a bull, whom Annie didn't recognize, all head and shoulders with no hips, shut the door behind them.

The room was packed. Extra benches had been placed along the walls and children sat scattered on the floor. Annie and J.C. took a vacant spot on a side wall, down close to the front. They had to stand, but they had a good view of the pulpit and the platform. There was a white cloth-covered table and, beside it, on the floor, a large wooden box.

Annie whispered in J.C.'s ear. "On the table up there, that's poison in the jar and the lamp is for them to put their hands in the fire. The snakes are in the box."

The crowd's expectancy beat like a common body pulse, a shared heartbeat, passed from person to person as they got settled, the saints in front and the others around them and in back. Most clutched their Bibles like weapons.

Placed in sconces, lanterns threw long shadows over the floors that climbed the walls and bent up onto the ceiling, randomly turning faces into dingy shades of yellow as the illumination caught a cheekbone or expanse of forehead and making the room seem crowded with unseen presences, ghostly images slipping around among the living.

Annie saw the Reverend Beasley stand up from the front row. He had taken off his jacket and turned up his shirt sleeves at the cuffs. He had opened his collar in contrast to the other stiffly suited men. A guitar was slung from a wide strap hanging over his shoulder and swung around so that it rested against his back, as if he had shoved it out of his way. He had a broad chest and thin waist, and overall, he had a lean, stark, wild look about him, and the thought came to Annie that he was actually good-looking in a dark kind of way.

He didn't go up to the pulpit but instead slowly walked up and down the platform with his head hanging as if he were alone and contemplating something terribly important. Then suddenly he stopped pacing and brought his guitar around in front of him and started strumming chords, tentatively at first, but then picking up the tempo as he tuned in on a song, and then he walked over to a man in the front row who also had a guitar. That man joined in, the duo increasing in animation. The other man, responding to the music, smiled a wide grin revealing several missing teeth. Then a woman, one who had helped to lay out Annie's momma's body, jumped up and joined in, holding up a tambourine over her head and shaking it. Some of the members began to clap and sing. The song rose to a high pitch swelling through the room. On the last chord, the minister shouted, "Thanks be to JEEE-sus! Yes! Yeees! I love you, Lord!" and was answered in kind by the congregation.

The minister, as elated now as he had been pensive before, hopped back up on the platform, slinging his guitar around on his back again. This time he went up to the pulpit where he stood a moment scrutinizing the crowd. A nervous shift rolled up and down the aisles in the wake of his probing eyes. Finally he pointed to a hawk-faced man several rows back. "Brother, would you read from God's word for us. Mark 16:17–18."

The man, obviously pleased to be singled out, opened his Bible and stood up. He cleared his throat, and in a high nasal twang, his voice quavering with emotion, he read:

> *And these signs shall follow them that believe. In my name shall they cast out devils; they shall speak with new tongues; they shall take up serpents; and if they drink any deadly thing, it shall not hurt them; they shall lay hands on the sick, and they shall recover.*

He sat down.

The minister stood with his head bowed during the reading. In the silence that followed, broken only by a baby's whimper, he slowly lifted his head and stared out over the congregation, and although he didn't move his eyes this time, the skin tightened on the back of Annie's neck, and she felt her backbone stiffen.

"And these signs shall follow them that believe." He repeated the words with awe in his voice as if he were hearing them for the first time, his mind seeming to circle the words, savoring them, memorizing them. The magnetic sound of his voice was still hanging in the air when suddenly he slammed his fist down on the pulpit and shouted, "And *I* believe, brethren, *I BEEElieve!*"

The congregation came to life like an animal cut loose, shaking itself all over to verify its freedom, and responded with a chorus of "Amen!," "Glory be to God!," and one young woman, rocking back and forth, a baby sitting in her lap, wailed, "Oh, Jesus, Jesus, Jesus Jeeesus. . . ."

Annie, who flinched at his outburst, felt the room closing in, curving around her like a smooth, seamless sphere. The air seemed to move in rhythmic heaves in waves of emotion. Suddenly she was hot, burning up, the intense air clogging her throat like smoke. She pulled off J.C.'s coat and handed it back to him. She shifted her position so that she was partially behind his shoulder.

When the congregation calmed down, the minister told them that he'd just got out of jail, "incarcerated like the first Christians," he said, "for following the law of God." But nothing could stop him, he said. He jabbed his finger at them. "No sir, Brothers and Sisters," his allegiance was not to Caesar but to Almighty God who had called him and gave him the Power.

Annie was used to the singsong cadence of Preacher Coldren's voice, but Beasley's was even more so, rising at times strident as a blackbird's screech with pitches made in a high whine of excitement, then dropping unexpectedly to a low monotone, the pauses and cadence erratic and abrupt. The congregation hung on every word, and the pregnant silence when he finished his story hung like a visible haze, punctuated by sporadic exclamations: "Praise the Lord" and "Yeees, Jeeesus."

Beasley became thoughtful again, his eyes turned inward, releasing the congregation for a moment. Then he asked the toothless man to play something. "Anything, brother, play something for the Lord." The man played "Rock of Ages" and sang the words in a thin, high hillbilly voice.

A girl whom Annie recognized from school got out of her seat and walked down to the platform. She fell on her knees, lifted her arms, and prayed out loud. The preacher intoned, "Oh yes, yeees, Jesus loves you, young Sister. He loves you. Pray to him! Pray any way you want! Talk to the Lord!"

Soon about thirty people, mostly women and a few men, were down in front kneeling and praying out loud while the preacher played and sang a song about how happy they would all be in heaven. . . . *When we allll get to heeeaven, what a day of rejoicing that will be. When we alll see Jeeesus, we'll sing and shout the victory!*

A woman standing next to the guitarist started to jerk, her head and body shaking ferociously all over. Two women behind her shouted and clapped and stomped their oxford-shod feet.

The preacher quit playing. He broke into tongues, speaking in a monotone of nonsense syllables that rolled from his mouth like high water as the Spirit began to flow through the crowd. A group of women and men began to dance wildly on the platform in a kind of deranged jitter-bug, sporadically kicking the wooden box of snakes while twirling around backward, their arms flopping in front of them and their heads lolling back and forth. Then children moved out into the aisles dancing and clapping happily to the music.

Annie was silent, but the same spooked feeling she'd always had when she came with her momma forced its way into her mind as she watched the service. She looked up at J.C., who was absorbed in the goings-on.

"Pretty strange, huh?" She had to speak up to be heard over the commotion. In contrast, her voice sounded thin and sharp, like twigs snapping under your feet.

He nodded, not taking his eyes off the hysterical activity on the floor. "Look, that's Miss Paine. Over there." He pointed to the side of the platform, to where, turned away from them, Miss Paine was caught in a spasm, shaking so savagely that it looked like she might break into small pieces.

Annie remembered how shocked she had been the first time she had seen her momma get the spirit *the way you lost control, Momma, spewed out gibberish like it had been hidden away behind your heart or maybe wrung out of a second strange heart that only you knew about* and unconsciously she rubbed the mark on her hand, feeling it more in her mind than in the tips of her fingers *a star Miss Mercer calls it and she says you have one too and she talks about being crazy, about being mad, about being alive while you're dead and dead when you're alive* then she slipped her hand in her pocket.

After the frenzy peaked, the preacher went up to the pulpit again. This time, he told a story about a congregation that collected food for a family that was hard-up, and when they carried it over, the woman, he said, had gone through the offerings and complained that there wasn't nothing sweet to eat. "She never said 'thank you,' not once." He shook his head, dismayed at the thought of the woman's ingratitude.

Then abruptly he asked, "Do *you*, brethren, forget to thank the Lord? Do *you* let a day pass without thanking *Him* for giving you salvation?" He jumped up in the air like he had been prodded from behind. "Thank you, Lord, for JEEsus! Thank you!" His voice broke with emotion.

The crowd, already at a fever pitch, responded with loud, ardent cries of "Thank you, Lord," and one man, a weaselly-looking fellow, leaped up and began testifying how he had gone to a service of Reverend Beasley's in Tennessee because he had throat cancer, and the preacher had prayed over him, and, Praise the Lord, the cancer had gone away. He couldn't even talk before. Anyone who didn't believe him could ask his brother, who was with him right now. He couldn't even say *one word* before, but now he was healed, and he wanted to say "Thank you, Reverend Beasley! Thank you!"

"Hallelujah!" Beasley shouted, throwing his arms into the air over his head. "Thank the Lord, Brother, *He* did it. I'm just the instrument of his goodness. Faith, you got to have faith!"

Several others testified as to how the Lord had helped them. The congregation got more and more vocal and worked up with each telling. The preacher paced. He couldn't stand still.

"Oh, the spirit is moving tonight. It's *mooooving.*" He turned and shouted out at them. "Do you feel it? Do you feel the power?" He ran down to the table and slapped it flat-handed. "Do *you* feel the spirit?"

In response, the congregation went wild. Some dancing, some talking in tongues, some singing and clapping. Then Annie saw Ginny Long making her way down to where the preacher was praying with his arms outstretched while his body trembled and tears rolled down his cheeks. Ginny stood before him and started to quiver. Then her spine began snapping from side to side. She dropped to the floor, her arms still flailing and her pelvis contorted up off the floor.

J.C. took an audible breath. "Jesus, look at that! That's Ginny! Is she dying?"

No one around noticed Ginny as they all responded to the spirit in a variety of ways, except for the preacher. He bent down and put one hand on her head and the other on her raised pubic region. He pressed down hard and cried, "Praise be to God!" and Ginny collapsed and lay still.

Soon more girls had dropped down in convulsions in front of him, and he was going down the row, placing his hands on them and shouting before they, too, would pass out.

Chanting hymns, several of the saints removed the top to the wooden box. A communal moan of anticipation passed over the crowd. The preacher, gleeful, yelled, "We got snakes right here, *right here*, brought in by sinner-men, right up here. If you want to handle, come on down. If not, step back, step back. Make room for the Lord's work."

But before the shift could take place, an impatient saint was already taking out a large timber rattlesnake, holding it in the middle, his arms stretched stiffly out in front of him while he danced in jerky circles. There was some confusion as those wanting to move back pushed through the tightening crowd.

Annie and J.C. were shoved even more against the wall. The two wood stoves in the room combined with the press of people and activity had driven the temperature up until the air was steamy with heat and excitement, and Annie, already agitated by the service, found it difficult to breathe.

Preacher Coldren, singing and stomping in a circle, draped a long copperhead over his shoulders, the snake's angular head weaving right at his temples, and several other men passed a clump of smaller snakes from one eager hand to the other. Miss Paine was sitting down with a rattlesnake hanging over her shoulder, his head down her back and his rattle hanging between her breasts as she cooed and swayed, her eyes closed and a smile on her face. Two sisters stood behind her, stroking and petting the snake. The Reverend Beasley placed a snake around his head like a crown where it clung for a moment before falling to the floor. He snatched it up and put it back on his head. Everyone seemed happy. They were having a good time.

"How long does this go on?" J.C., incredulous and seeming a little uneasy, asked.

Annie, pressed against the wall, crossed her arms over her chest. She watched, entranced, seeing them all *melting, merging, turning one into the other, a large writhing mass of shimmering scaly flesh,* and felt something squeezing her mind wrapping it in coils, swallowing it.

"Annie? How long does this go on?" J.C. asked again.

"Long as anybody wants it to."

J.C. peered down at her. "Hey, you want to leave?"

Annie straightened up, openly anxious. "If you've seen enough—"

J.C. grabbed her arm. "Sure, let's go. I seen plenty." He threaded their way through the spellbound crowd.

Outside, despite the mournful whinny of an owl nearby and the circling of a nighthawk, the air seemed stagnant in comparison to the frenzied quickening going on inside the church. Annie welcomed the calm. She felt the sweat that had popped out on her face drying in the night air, and her blood slowed.

J.C. put his arm around her shoulders and pulled her a little toward him as they walked away from the church. "Thanks for bringing me. You didn't seem to like it much."

Annie gave a weak smile, lowered her head, and shook it at her own vulnerability to the way emotions seemed to seize her, her mind snatched from her. "I guess not *i think about it all the time, Momma, i imagine how the colors must have been that summer, blackberries ripe on the balds, orchids and asters, laurel everywhere, fireflies in the valleys* let's get away from here."

"You want to check on our tree? Maybe give it some water while we're here."

Annie looked up. "That's a good idea."

They turned back and went around to the cemetery.

J.C. checked the supports on the tree and looked at the branches in the weak light coming from the church windows. "Looks good. Let's find something to carry water in."

Under the steps behind the church, Annie found a bucket and J.C. went around the front and got one of the lanterns hanging by the door. He led the way to the stream, holding the lantern in one hand and Annie's hand in the other. Annie carried the bucket. The woods closed in behind them; muffled by the shut door, the heated noise of the ceremony blended into the noises of night insects.

At the stream, J.C. put the lantern up on a rock and watched while Annie dipped the bucket. "I sure could use a swallow of that," he said.

When she handed him the bucket, he said, "I need something to wash the taste of that service out of my mouth." He drank by dipping his hand in and cupping handfuls of water.

"Want some?" He put his full hand out to Annie, who guided it to her mouth and drank thirstily.

J.C. leaned against the rock while she filled the bucket again. He seemed to be in no hurry to leave. The sound of the water, full and flowing, was fused with the chant of the rising wind blowing through the trees.

"It's a real nice night." J.C. rolled and lit a cigarette.

Annie stood awkwardly between the stream and path as if poised for flight.

J.C. peered at her over his cigarette. "You ain't scared of me, are you?" He smiled like the idea of anyone being scared of him was amusing.

"No, I ain't scared of you. Why should I be?" Annie relaxed a little.

He shrugged his shoulders. "I don't know. But you look all bowed up over there, like a cornered cat, so I just wondered."

Annie smiled, realizing how she must look to him. "Well, I ain't!" She tried to sound emphatic.

"Then come on over here and let's visit a while."

Annie went over and he helped her up on a rock across from where he was leaning. She arranged her skirt and got comfortable. "Ok, so let's visit."

J.C. was looking at her, letting his eyes move over her like he was measuring her, a hazy smile on his face. The silence grew, and Annie was just about to ask him what he was looking at when he said, "You sure are pretty," like he was reaffirming an earlier opinion.

Annie gave a little nervous laugh and pushed distract-edly at a strand of hair that had come out of her braid and hung down beside her face *the night you died momma your beautiful hair all chopped off and gray you just slipped away and i wouldn't even have noticed if fluid, black like ink, hadn't run from your mouth making a dark jagged line down your chin* trying to tuck it in.

"I mean it. You know, like your eyes. They're a color like the sky is in the middle of a hot summer, a kind of green-blue color," he paused, "clear, like colored glass. Those kind of eyes look right into a man, see everything."

Not knowing what to say or do, Annie did neither, just fidgeted, and J.C., still watching her closely, seemed to realize that he'd made her uncomfortable.

"So, why, Miss Fidget, is it you get so upset about all that snake-handling stuff. Are you that scared of snakes?"

"Naturally, I don't *like* snakes. But that's not all of it. It just don't seem right. I don't see how doing that stuff makes you a better person."

"It probably don't. Do any of your people handle?"

"Momma—well, not really, I mean I never saw her handle snakes, but she did speak in tongues sometimes. I only saw her do that twice. I didn't go regularly. I don't know. It just all bothers me. I guess I don't know exactly why. Lots of things bother me, I guess."

Annie seemed to spend most of her days lately with the figure of her momma right behind her eye, and since Miss Mercer had started telling her about her momma's life and everything, she would find herself constantly staring at her hand *endless hours staring at my hand, so much like yours, the skin translucent like the flesh of a newborn, maybe the key to all this, to you, is somehow contained in my body's secret symbols and signs, where Miss Mercer says no shape, no spot, no line is accidental, and, it's true, in my thin white nails i see the streams where you met him, flowing mirrors filled with sharp sunlight, and in my raised bruised veins i see jagged mountains splitting that unconcerned Carolina sky* and looking at herself in the mirror as if her face belonged to a stranger and she had to memorize the features so that she could recognize it again.

"Why do you think she did it?"

"I don't really know . . . but I know she wasn't like Miss Paine and some of them others, always preaching and telling you what the Lord wants you to do. She never even mentioned religion much, hardly at all. She was a real quiet person, easy to get along with, always working at something, busy, real busy and quiet *I believe, Momma, that for you, in that place, nothing was soft, no mountain mist, no tender cloud, no delicate foliage, it seems to me, relieved the harshness of your life* maybe it, the church and all, was a way to make up for something she didn't have in her life—"

A picture of the frenzied snake-handlers pushed its way into her mind and she thought she saw herself in the press of bodies, a figure like herself, and she was overwhelmed with a raw discomfiture, like a speck stuck on your eyelid.

She jumped down off the rock. "I don't want to talk about it anymore."

J.C. looked a little surprised at her brusqueness, but stood up, tossed his dead cigarette. "All right."

He had picked up the bucket to leave when suddenly Annie thrust her hand out at him.

"Look, see here, I've got this mark. Just like my momma had. It's kind of a bad luck mark *the mark on the heel of my hand, a star, although it looks more like a creature to me, Momma, some kind of creature that crawls, see how it crouches on the mount of the moon, see the darkness, the danger, the terror, the forbidden love, look, see the line running from the moon creature to the line of the head, see the madness, a mind lost in swamps, see the living death* that's what Miss Mercer told me, a bad mark—"

Annie felt her skin turn inside out, each nerve lying exposed and weeping for him to see. She hadn't meant to burst out like that. It had all just spilled out, and she felt the chagrin leap into her face.

J.C. put the bucket down, reached out and took her hand, looking at it. Every movement of his eyes flowed heavy over her vulnerable veins and arteries. He put his arms around her, drew her to him. "Annie, people make their own luck. A mark on your hand can't hurt you if you don't let it."

His breath curled warm in her ear and on her neck, and when he kissed her on the cheek, she lifted her face a little. It seemed natural for him to do it again and again, soft, hesitant kisses, and when she drew back and looked him full in the face, everything about her lying open, disclosed, guileless, it was inevitable that he cover her lips with his.

16

When Annie came in from the church service, it was late, the moon barely visible, a round haze behind smears of dark clouds streaked across the sullen sky like smudges from a dirty thumb. And as soon as she stepped through the door, Claude came from the kitchen into the front room, stuffing a piece of cornbread in his mouth.

"Where you been so late? Everybody's already in bed. Don't try to tell me you been over at that old woman's house all this time."

Annie ignored him. She took off her sweater and hung it on the pegs next to the door. When she tried to go around Claude, he blocked her way and reached out and grabbed her arm with his hand, squeezing it tight.

She pulled back, but he clutched her even tighter.

"Let go of me!"

Claude snatched her close, putting his face right next to hers. She could see a crusty spot, over his nose, with a drop of fresh blood on it between his eyebrows where he had been picking at a bump. She looked back defiantly into the dingy whites of his eyes where the brown irises were dilated like the wary eyes of animals, shrewd and unblinking. She could barely breathe, his pungent breath, coated with corn liquor, filled her nostrils, and his hand felt greasy and grainy from the butter on the cornbread.

"You going to make me? Huh? Huh?" He squeezed her arm more, his fingers digging in.

Annie clenched her teeth. She looked away, tried to hold still, but she flinched when she saw their locked shadows pinned to the wall in a circle of light from the lantern.

He gave her another jerk. "Or maybe that hotshot fellow that brought you home, that shitass carpenter, is going to make me. You think I didn't see him? The way he was hanging all over you."

Annie tried to relax her body; she tried not to pull against him, not to make it worse. Making herself look at him, she composed her face into a blank and kept her voice low and steady. "I got to get in bed. I got school tomorrow." She glanced toward the hall, hoping that her daddy or Neal would hear the commotion and come in.

Claude, following her gaze, abruptly released her arm, letting his hand brush against her breast. Annie recoiled, and he smiled, an ugly pleasure spreading over his murky face.

"I was just worried about you, that's all. You never know what might happen to a little girl like you out there in those woods all alone." She could see that he was enjoying himself, his smile wide and false. He whined, mocking her. "The bogeyman might get you. You wouldn't want that to happen now, would you, little girl?"

"I can take care of myself." Annie raised her voice despite herself, yet a thin edge of apprehension lay along the edge of her mind *his face floating over her, intent and engrossed in what he was doing, almost vulnerable in its concentration, pinching her breasts over and over and over* and a feeling of guilt came over her, dark and dank, with its core in the spot where his hand had touched her breast, like the white cord in a festering boil.

Defiantly, Annie stared back at him. She despised the color of his eyes. They were the color of earth, a worm bed of dirt, damp summer worm-laden dirt *dirt everywhere, in her hair, on her back, under her dress, inside her, black, gritty, wormy* and, despite her resolve to be brave, she unconsciously crossed her arms over her breasts and drew back.

"So where you really been? Off with that asshole somewhere?

Annie glared at him, hugged herself tighter, squirmed *his fingers in her, putting dirt in her, burying her* pushed a strand of hair back from her face.

"See, the cat's got your little pink tongue already. Or maybe that asshole's got it. Is that where it is? You been putting it in his mouth maybe, and he bit it off? Here, let me look. Open up." He stuck his own tongue out and wiggled it at her while he reached out his big square hand for her chin.

Without thinking, instinctively reacting to his shadow-pocked face and the thick yellow-coated tongue lolling at her, Annie knocked his hand away from her. She pushed past him and ran down the hall to her room.

Once inside, she snapped the small wooden latch into place and leaned against the door. Her whole body beat like one giant panicked pulse, and for a moment, she didn't hear anything but the pounding inside her until his voice hissed through the door.

"Go ahead, you little slut, run. Lock the door. You won't always have someplace to run. Or a door to lock."

Later, in bed, curled deep under the quilt, Annie dreamed an awful dream, a dream about a deep night that was filled with an overpowering smell of rot and mournful animal wails, bleeding moons, and legged water creatures. She tossed and turned, hearing Miss Mercer's comments about *seeing, seeing tragedy in a comment, horror in the flicker of an eye,* and she tried to draw her mind away, but the unsleeping dream squatted tenaciously behind her heart, kept rising to rest again and again on the rim of her eyelids. . . .

> *the moon, full and cold, dripping blood, hanging in a motionless sky over a dark sea while hidden animals howl, she watches from the front porch of an unlit house as something*

awful slithers up from the water onto the sand
and crawls toward the house. . . .

Annie jerked awake each time, then fell into an exhausted sleep again. Finally, right at dawn, as she lay dreading the dream, knowing she would fall asleep again, her mind drifted to earlier that night, to J.C., and her body filled slowly with a sensation of his presence, liquid and warm, and she heard a soft fluttering like night moths behind her ear. The last thing she remembered was images flooding her mind the way light from a rising moon illuminates a dark landscape *her momma and a man, two merging figures of pale creamy shifting reflections, low-flying pearly-colored night birds, an albino snake shedding its skin. . . .*

The next morning Claude passed her door several times, looking in, grinning and flashing his dingy teeth until she pushed the door to. She didn't go in the kitchen for breakfast. The thought of facing him caused an agitation in the pit of her stomach like nausea. She told Lacey that she wasn't hungry, that she wasn't going to school because she was sick.

After breakfast she thought they had all gone out, but then she heard Claude's voice, raised, "Come on, Lacey, there ain't nobody here . . . she don't matter, let her hear it, so what . . . forget the kid, he don't know what he sees . . . right here, bend over . . ." and then Lacey's syrupy giggle and the other sounds, the squeaking of the table rocking, Claude's husky grunts.

That afternoon her daddy wanted to know why she didn't go to school. She said she was sick, couldn't go, that she didn't even feel like getting up to come in the kitchen for supper. He grunted, said he was fed up with everybody being sick all the time, if it wasn't one thing, it was another. He would send for Miss Mercer. Annie protested, said she didn't need anybody, just some rest. But, irritated at her, he sent Neal anyway.

Later that evening Miss Mercer showed up. She stood

at the foot of the bed, staring at Annie, who looked dark and fevered around the eyes, her skin wan with a bilious cast. When she asked what was wrong, Annie just shook her head and looked down at her hands picking at the quilt.

"I just don't feel too good," she said. "I don't think I can go back to school for a while."

Miss Mercer fussed and fretted as she straightened the covers and fished for the cause of Annie's relapse. She got nowhere. Annie said only that she hadn't slept good, that she had had bad dreams. Miss Mercer drew her mouth into a small knowing knot at the revelation and went in the kitchen and brought back a cup of lime tea.

"Here, you drink this." She watched until Annie downed it all.

Then she poked around in the sack she always had with her and brought out some small tins. Choosing two of them, she mixed some of the leaves together and tied them in a piece of cloth. "Keep this in your hand tonight. In the morning you and the boy come over to my house. Early. Don't mess around. Come right after breakfast."

Annie looked at the tied-up cloth. "What is it?"

"It's nettle and nosebleed."

"What's it for?"

"Sometimes you ask too many questions."

And before Annie could ask more, Miss Mercer was bundled up in her dark swaddling garments and going out the door.

"You won't dream any. You'll get some sleep. It takes away vision." The words floated back over the old woman's shoulder.

Robbie, who had been playing on the floor with Jo-Jo, followed her out. When he came back he had a trinket in his hand. Annie was already beginning to drift off.

"Robbie, it's time for bed." Her tongue felt thick and her words sounded too slow.

The last thing she remembered was Robbie pulling off his own clothes as she tried to get up to help him.

The next morning Annie told Lacey to go ahead and feed Robbie, that she was staying in bed again, and Lacey went off with Robbie trailing reluctantly behind her as she muttered about lazy-butt girls who weren't worth two cents.

Soon as everyone was out of the house, Annie got up and got dressed, helping Robbie with his overalls. He filled the pockets with his toy animals, and then they walked with Jo-Jo over to Miss Mercer's.

The sun was out and the day was unseasonably warm with a bright yellowish glow spread over the sky and flowing down through the trees. Just the warmth made Annie feel better although she kept an eye out for Claude. Despite herself, she was scared that he would catch her alone and make good his threat. Miss Mercer opened the door as they came in the yard.

The house was the same as Annie remembered except maybe more crowded with furniture and items of every sort. She wondered again where Miss Mercer got them all, but she didn't think she should ask. Robbie settled down right away just like he belonged there, clearing himself a spot on the front-room rug and taking his animals out from his pocket.

"Did you eat yet?" Miss Mercer looked at Annie like she would know if she didn't tell the truth.

"No ma'am."

Miss Mercer put on some grits to boil, fried up some sausage and eggs, then made gravy from the grease and milk, and put it over a biscuit that she got out of a tin. "Here, now you start off by eating. You're as skinny as a bedrail."

Annie didn't realize how hungry she was until she bit into the fat sausage. She had skipped meals yesterday and this morning to avoid Claude, and the food tasted good. Robbie, who'd already had breakfast, put down his share just as if he hadn't eaten earlier.

Miss Mercer, who finished her bowl of eggs, grits, and sausage first, puttered around the kitchen. Jo-Jo came scratching at the back door, sniffing, and Miss Mercer let her in and gave her a piece of sausage. Robbie pushed the

last piece of his biscuit in his mouth and then crawled
back into the front room on all fours, pushing a toy cow,
with the dog trotting right behind him.

Miss Mercer said, "Let's fix a few things for supper
before we get out of the kitchen. Get it all done at once."

They put dried peaches and pears in a big pot on the
stove to steam the fruit in water and sugar. When the fruit
was plumped up, she said, they would make dumpling
dough to drop into the hot boiling juice. The fruity smell
floated through the kitchen combining with the scent of
herbs drying from lines strung kitty-cornered next to a big
pie safe.

"Dried's not as good as fresh, but it's better than nothing when you just got to have something sweet." Miss
Mercer put a top on the boiling fruit.

After that, Annie shelled peas while Miss Mercer cut up
two cleaned chickens, putting the pieces in a bowl to cook
later. Then Miss Mercer fried fatback in a deep heavy pot
until it was crisp and all the grease cooked out. She added
the peas, two pig's feet, and water, chopped an onion and
threw it in, then sprinkled the water with black pepper
until the surface was covered.

"It's the onion that makes the difference," she said,
"gives it the flavor. And you don't need nary a drop of
salt. Plenty of salt in that pig already."

It was almost noon by the time they finished in the
kitchen. Miss Mercer talked constantly, directing Annie in
what to do, how to do it, and why to do it a certain way.

"Let's rest a while." She wiped her hands on the bib
apron that covered her dark dress. Then, taking it off, she
moved into the front room where Robbie was still playing. Unlike the kitchen that was filled with plenty of sunshine coming through a back window, the front room was
dark, the curtains drawn and one of the windows completely covered by the large wardrobe. Annie thought
about how she used to pass this house every day with her
friends and how they had wondered about the dark windows and joked about the witch that lived inside. It
seemed so long ago, yet it was only months.

"Look here." Miss Mercer lit a lantern and carried it over to a large table covered with folded clothes, boxes, and bags of all sorts.

Annie followed her. Miss Mercer unfolded a piece of cloth. It was an orange color, but not like a pumpkin, not a bright orange. It was deep, like the sky is sometimes at sunset, a liquid, pervious reddish orange, shaded and muted.

"I got this color by dying it red first, then dying it yellow. It took three times in the yellow to get it right. Boy, I thought I wasn't never going to get it the way I wanted it."

"It sure is pretty." Annie reached out and stroked the material. She liked the feel of the cloth, smooth and cool.

"It's your color, ain't it? It'd go good with all that brown hair you got." The old woman spoke, not looking at her, but fussing with the cloth, folding and unfolding it. "It'd make a real pretty jumper, maybe with a waist that buttons on the side and a real full skirt."

Annie couldn't believe her ears. Miss Mercer sounded as if she were going to give her the material.

"You could sew it up real nice, yes sir, a side-buttoned jumper." She suddenly looked right at her. "You want to do that?"

Annie took the cloth the old woman handed her and stroked it like you would pet a small animal. She wanted nothing more than to make a dress out of it.

"Yes ma'am, I do. But I don't know if I can sew a dress. I know how to do a skirt. Momma showed me, but she never showed me how to do a dress."

Miss Mercer was already on the other side of the room moving several chairs out of a corner. Annie put the cloth down and went over to help her.

Behind the chairs was a strange-looking machine.

"Ever seen one of these?" Miss Mercer asked.

"No ma'am."

"Well, it's a sewing machine. See that treadle down there. You just rock it back and forth, and this needle goes up and down, and you sew. Easy as falling off a log."

Annie was examining the curious machine when Miss

Mercer stuck a chair behind her. "Here, sit down. Give it a try." And she handed her a scrap of cloth.

Annie folded it to make two layers and looked at Miss Mercer.

"Go ahead. Put it under the needle."

Annie did, and Miss Mercer reached around and pushed a lever to put the presser foot down. "Now treadle."

Annie rocked the treadle, and the needle moved up and down, the foot feeding the cloth through and out the back. Miss Mercer picked it up and broke the threads.

She held out the material to Annie. "Now ain't that as pretty of a stitch as you ever seen?" Annie saw that the stitches were small, even, and straight as an arrow.

"You can make your dress on that machine. Makes 'em faster than you can spit in a fire. I'll show you how to do the pattern." She turned and headed out of the room. "But, first, come in the kitchen."

By now Annie had quit being surprised at what the old woman said or did and obediently got up and followed her, giving the cloth a stroke as she went by. She was already feeling better, just imagining herself in the orange jumper. She had a white blouse that she could wear under it.

Miss Mercer had apparently decided that Annie's hair needed some attention. She had Annie sit on a kitchen chair on top of a thick book to make her higher. Then she took Annie's hair down, brushing it out until it lay straight and untangled down her back. Picking up and twisting a section until Annie flinched, she ran a lit candle up and down the length of the twist.

"This gets rid of split hairs. You just singe 'em off."

Annie tried not to think about what would happen if her hair caught on fire, but Miss Mercer seemed to be perfectly comfortable with the smell of scorched hair that tinged the air. She did Annie's entire head, twisting and singeing.

"I got some rain water caught in a tub out back. Let's wash it and rinse it in some lemon juice. That'll make it nice and shiny."

While Robbie and Jo-Jo ran around the yard, Annie bent over the washtub while Miss Mercer scrubbed her hair with soap two times, rinsing it in between the first and second soaping and for what seemed like forever after the second one. Then the old woman mixed lemon juice and cool water and poured it over Annie's hair before wrapping it in a towel.

Back inside, Miss Mercer had Annie sit in the kitchen chair again and she rolled Annie's wet hair in rags by tying the rag onto the hair right at the scalp, then twisting the hair around the length of the rag before looping it up and tying the end of the rag to the top, the whole time telling Annie precisely how to do it herself.

"Girl, you're going to have a head of curls," she said and she laughed, revealing several missing bottom teeth that Annie had never noticed before. "You go sit out here in the sun and watch Robbie while your hair dries some. I'm going to go fry up that chicken and put the dumplings in the fruit so we got something to eat when we get hungry."

Annie liked sitting out in the sunny yard and the way her hair felt so clean and fresh, and she was excited at the prospect of making the dress on the sewing machine. She was throwing sticks for Jo-Jo to retrieve when Miss Mercer came back out.

"Let's go see about that pattern now. After all, you need a new dress to go with all them curls you're going to have, don't you know." And she chuckled again.

They laid the material out on the cleared table, and Annie cut the skirt the way her momma had showed her, a long strip for the waistband and two large squares for the skirt. Then Miss Mercer brought in some paper and smoothed it out on the table.

"We need two pieces for the bodice. One for the front and one for the back. You can sew them at the shoulder and sides. And you need some bias strips to bind the edges with." She peered at Annie. "You see what I mean?"

Annie nodded. "Yes, but doesn't the bottom of the bodice have to fit in the waist?"

"Right, but the shoulders got to fit too. So you got to use darts."

The old woman showed her how to measure herself with a string and then how to draw a pattern on the paper to cut the cloth by. They had it all measured and cut out when Robbie came in. "Annie, me hungry."

Miss Mercer motioned to him. "Go get you a piece of chicken. It's fried up on the back of the stove."

They sewed until late afternoon, finishing everything but the hem.

Miss Mercer held the dress up to view it. "You can do the hem on your fingers tonight and it'll be ready for school tomorrow."

Annie saw Miss Mercer cut her eyes toward her when she said "school tomorrow," as if judging her reaction. Annie smiled. "I'll stop by in the morning on the way and let you see it on."

Miss Mercer smiled back and folded the dress up, putting it on the table. "Now, let's see about them curls. Your hair ought to be dry now."

Annie sat down and Miss Mercer took out the rags one by one, drawing her fingers through the strands of hair as she untied them. Then when they were all out, she carefully parted Annie's hair in the middle and combed it back from her face and down her back.

"Go look," she said.

Annie went over to the large mirror above the fireplace mantel. Her hair fell in waves and loose curls all the way to her waist and shined like the sun was trapped in it.

"Looks good, don't it?" The old woman sounded pleased with herself.

"I love it!" Annie tossed her head and watched the curls swing from side to side.

It was getting dark outside by the time they finished up the chicken and ate cobbler, washing it down with milk-laced coffee.

Miss Mercer finished washing the last dish and handed it to Annie to dry. "Does your daddy know where you're at so he won't worry?"

"I told Lacey this morning where I was going. She'll tell him." She hadn't really told anybody, but she doubted if they would care as long as she got home before too late. The thought of going home depressed Annie, and she wasn't anxious to leave.

Afterward, in the front room with Miss Mercer deep in her stuffed chair smoking a rolled cigarette, seemingly oblivious to everything, Annie rocked in the wooden rocker. Robbie, almost asleep, was curled up in her lap. Jo-Jo was spread out on her back with her legs dropped open lying in front of the fire. Time seemed almost suspended to Annie, and she thought of the first evening she had come here and sat in this very chair, scared and anxious, all her attention focused only on herself and how she felt, no idea of what was going to happen. . . then the thought of her momma brought back all that she had been able to forget during the day, all that had happened—with J.C., with Claude, the dreams.

As if she sensed the disturbance in Annie, Miss Mercer roused herself. "So you went to that snake-handling service the other night." It was more of a statement than a question.

Annie nodded her head although she didn't know if Miss Mercer could see her across the dim room. It didn't matter because the old woman didn't wait for a response, but went on almost like she was talking to herself.

"I never took much to them kind of things. Not even to churchgoing. Not that I don't believe in God, you know. I believe, sure enough, there's a higher power, but I don't see what shouting, and singing, and messing with snakes has got to do with it. My daddy used to say that religion's in your heart."

Annie thought back to the frenzy of the church service and how it always upset her to see it. It sure took faith to pick up those snakes, but it seemed almost evil in a way.

Miss Mercer's voice broke in on her thoughts. "Lots of things are shown by a man's heart. You know, it's funny how many ways you talk about the heart, a person has a *good* heart or a *bad* heart, or you ask, *can you find it in your heart*, or you say you're *heartbroke*, you know, there's hundreds of them sayings about the heart. That's how you know that what counts is your heart. It don't make no difference whether you call it 'heart,' or 'soul,' or 'spirit.' It's six of one and a half-dozen of the other. Take for example, your granddaddy Julian—"

Annie stopped rocking, the never-spoken name jolting her mind. She leaned toward Miss Mercer; she didn't want to miss a word.

"That man just had a *bad* heart, no two ways about it. He was a mean, cruel, evil man. Anybody can tell you that. But your Daddy now, he's different. He's a cold, cruel man in lots of ways, but he's not evil. He's just self-ish, looks out for himself, and he's set in his ways. That don't say he don't mean well most times, but it does tell you he can do wrong when he thinks he needs to."

Annie thought about what Miss Mercer had said. Her feelings toward her daddy were confused and disturbing to her. She couldn't keep herself from saying, "He didn't love Momma."

Miss Mercer lit up another cigarette and took a long draw. "Well, I guess he loved her about as much as he could love anybody . . . which isn't much. Whenever I used to look at his hands or read his cards, it used to scare me a little. He has bad signs, you know, livid hands, a twisted line of head, the signs of a murderer. But I was wrong. He ain't no murderer. He may have the leanings, but he ain't got the heart for it. No sir—" she leaned for-ward, jabbed her cigarette at Annie—"it's Claude. He's the one. He's Julian's grandchild in every way. That boy is evil."

Annie's heart, like a large ear, drank in the old woman's words, then spilled them out to flow along her arteries, and she felt a familiar fear spreading through her.

Miss Mercer sat back again. "I feel it when I get around him. That boy knows I can feel it. That's why he stays away from me. Evil to the core. No two ways about it."

Annie, shaken by her words, got up, carried Robbie to

the couch, and laid him down. Then she went over to Miss Mercer and sat down on the rug next to her chair.

"I've been having some bad dreams. . . ."

The words gushed out of Annie like a released dam, one spilling over the other—about the moon dream the other night, about the times she tried to see what happened the night of her mother's death, what had happened with Claude when she got home from church, his threat— and just saying all of it, having Miss Mercer listen and nod her head every so often, made it all seem better, washed away the panic that had engulfed Annie every time she tried to think about it, especially about Claude. As she talked she felt her worry being replaced with anger, an outrage that he could treat her any way he wanted, the suspicion that his meanness had probably caused her momma's death, a cold quiet fury like a block of ice filling her body.

Miss Mercer listened, then stubbed out her cigarette. "You say every time you see yourself ask him, you see him say the same thing, to give her three tablespoons?"

"Yes ma'am, every time."

"Then you can rest your mind, girl. If that's what you see, that's what happened. I told you, you got the gift."

Miss Mercer got up. "Come on, now. I need to walk you and the boy home. Tomorrow's another day."

Later that night, sitting on the bed while she hemmed her dress, Annie thought about what Miss Mercer had said on the way home—that a heart is like a house filled with rooms of all kinds. Some, Miss Mercer said, are familiar, bright sunny rooms that anybody can go into, rooms for family and friends, but others are private rooms, just for yourself, and there are locked rooms too, rooms that even you don't go into because you're afraid to, rooms so dark that the air is like a piece of stretched skin that doesn't want to let you in. But, she said, you have to explore *all* the rooms, learn about yourself, know the dark rooms as well as the light rooms. Then nobody could hurt you. Nobody.

17

Annie went back to school the next day. Dressed in her new jumper, her long hair pulled back into a low, curly ponytail, and her glasses tucked into her sweater pocket, she had stopped by Miss Mercer's house, so she got to school a little late, right as class was starting. She took her usual seat close to the back of the room, intently aware of J.C. watching her from two rows over.

Miss Paine gave the older students a description writing assignment in their English book while she worked with the lower grades. The students sat in a circle on the floor and gave the answers to math problems that Miss Paine flashed at them on big cards.

Annie slipped on her glasses as Ruthie Lynn leaned over and whispered, "Annie, you look great! Where you been? I thought you were coming back Monday."

Cutting her eyes over to Miss Paine, Annie saw that she was glancing irritably in their direction. "I'll tell you at recess."

Annie opened her *Enlarged Practice Book in English Composition*. The assignment was farther into the book than Annie had worked by herself. She browsed quickly through the lessons she had missed. Then on page thirty-seven, she read:

Opposite page 32 is a picture of an old house. Notice the trees, the shadows, the roadway—a score of things to stir the emotions. You cannot help thinking of how much has taken place in this ancient dwelling, of the good times and the sorrowful times it knew. Write a forty-line description of the outside of the house and of how you imagine the inside of the house to be. Personify the dwelling, if you wish.

Annie studied the picture. It was a house like she had never seen in real life, big and white, two-story, with a yard filled with flowers, bushes, and a big front porch with rocking chairs on it. She let her mind roam around the old house, looking at the yard, smelling the flowers. Then she imagined herself inside, walking all through the rooms, peeking in the closets, looking behind doors, checking her reflection in the distorted old mirrors. A feeling of nervous anticipation like she got exploring in the woods came over her, and she dipped her pen, opened her composition book, and began writing.

> *Once upon a time, a little girl lived in a big house that had mirrors in place of windows and all the stairs went sideways instead of up and down. The rooms weren't squares but circles and not all the doors led somewhere but many opened up to nothing at all.*
>
> *Outside was a yard filled with trees, shrubbery, and flowers. All the paths in the yard forked every few feet until the forks were forking. The yard was endless and the little girl thought that it probably stretched to the sea where the water, she had heard, was an endless lake that forked off in all directions.*
>
> *The little girl's days were filled with the chore of finding her way from room to room and finding the right door to the yard so that she could pick some flowers, but she never got any*

*satisfaction from finding her way because all
the paths would all change and the next day she
would have to hunt for the right way all over
again.*

*Sometimes she thought she saw something
move in the yard, quick glimpses of shapes
caught in the corner of her eye, but if she tried
to look directly at the shapes, they disappeared.
She tried not to think about them, but she knew
they were always around, hiding over in the
corners of her eyes.*

*The little girl lived in the house so long that
her mind became a web of questions, making
even the smallest choice become impossible.
Then one day she thought she heard a baby crying but whenever she tried hard to listen, it
stopped. She wanted desperately to find the
baby. I won't listen, she thought, instead I'll
look for the sound. So putting cotton in her
ears, she began to see her way to the sound, following the thin whine floating on the air of the
house, a mournful blue tone in the gray air—*

"Class, recess time. Fifteen minutes. If you want water,
get it now." Miss Paine was standing in front of the room
again.

Ruthie Lynn latched onto Annie's arm as they walked
outside. "Well, what's going on? How did you get your
hair like that? Is that a new dress? Did you see how fat
Ginny Long is—"

While Ruthie Lynn prattled on and on, Annie spread
her sweater on a grassy spot, carefully sitting on it and
tucking her new dress under her so that it didn't touch the
ground. Looking around she saw J.C. standing on the
other side of the yard. She couldn't see his eyes, but his
head was turned her way, and she couldn't help thinking
he was looking at her, the force of his stare making her
body react with a light, warm pulsing and a flash of memory of him holding her, the taste of him on her tongue. . . .

". . . everybody knows about it now, but Buddy's deny-
ing it. He says it ain't so. I heard his daddy's fit to be tied,
practically crazy. . . . Annie, are you listening to me?"

Annie stood up. "Not right now. I got to talk to J.C."

She crossed the yard under his gaze and, nervous, could
barely make her lips form a small smile. "Did you get
over seeing that church service?"

"I *did,* did you?" J.C. looked at her searchingly. "I
thought you said you were coming back to school Monday."

Miss Paine rang the little hand bell that she used to call
them in, and Annie, not knowing quite how to answer his
question, said, "I guess we better go in," and turned to
go.

J.C. grabbed her arm and turned her back around. "I'm
walking you home. Wait for me when we get out." Seeing
her pull back, he let go. "Please?" He smiled.

The desire Annie felt to talk to him, to touch him,
invaded her eyes and revealed itself openly. She didn't
care, and smiled back. "I'll wait."

On the way home that afternoon, Annie lost her shyness, felt like she had always walked with J.C. at her side,
his hand resting lightly around her waist, teasing her
about her essay. Miss Paine had gone down the aisle having students read their papers. Afterward, she would tell
them precisely and in detail what was wrong with their
expression. She had asked Annie to read hers aloud and
then become flustered, not knowing what to say in
response to Annie's story.

"I liked to of died when she finally choked out, 'Uh . . .
uh, that's very interesting.' She looked like she'd swallowed a fish bone and needed a good chunk of bread to
knock it out." J.C. laughed out loud.

"Well, at least it got her off the essay track. She
couldn't wait to go on to math after that." Annie had
enjoyed reading her paper and thought that it was actually pretty good.

"It *was* a little weird . . . but good. Did you just make it up, just like that, on the spot?"

"Yeah, I like to make up stories. I write some of them down in a book I keep. It's something I started doing when I had to stay in bed so long."

As if by a prearranged signal, they stopped at the edge of the woods before the clearing leading to Annie's house, putting their books on a rock and drawing back into the shadows of the overhanging branches. J.C. took her in his arms.

"So why didn't you come to school Monday? Because of me?"

Annie settled in, felt the long, hard length of him, the close warmth of his skin, heard the quiet fall of his words, and a rush of longing made her breath come rapid and skimpy as a small child's. "No . . . no, just some trouble at home, that's all. It's all over now."

And, later, when Annie crossed the clearing alone, having convinced J.C. it would be better for her if he left her there, she thought she could not bear the passing over to the place she called home, the house rising before her like bad dreams rise in a sleeper's eye, unbidden, uncontrolled, and the pleasant, soft, ripe yearning that had filled her in the clearing drained out of her, leaving behind a hollow feeling of trepidation.

A brisk wind from the south kept the weather warm, and every day after J.C. walked her home, Annie would put her books up, get Robbie and Jo-Jo, and go over to Miss Mercer's.

They roamed the woods with her until dark. Annie, happy now at school with J.C.'s attentions and Ruthie Lynn her friend again, delighted in the treks, seeing the spice bushes in full bloom, the abundant spring beauties, trout lilies, and bloodroot blooming, and the woods were filled with the sounds of sparrows, warblers, and the ruffled grouse that sounded like a motor starting in the distance, gathering strength, and then the bright flush of the red birds out of the brush, a whir of pinkish orange fantails. It was startling every time to see.

Miss Mercer carried a long stick with a fork on the end. Snakes, she said, would be coming out now, and there was no telling what you might run across. Annie didn't particularly want to come across any snakes, but everything seemed to her to be coming alive, waking up, exploding in color.

After starting back to school, Annie didn't see much of anybody in the family, usually fixing supper for herself and Robbie after the others had eaten. Neal was working almost every day now at the store, staying over a lot, sleeping in the back storeroom. Her daddy and Claude were spending a lot of time in the field, and when they weren't planting, they were hunting wild turkey, so Annie managed to avoid Claude. At night she kept her door locked and didn't leave the room until the next morning when everyone was up.

Friday night Annie was thinking about going to spend the next day at Miss Mercer's. She was going to help dye some cloth. Robbie was asleep and she was in her night-gown, sitting on the bed and brushing her hair, when she realized that Jo-Jo wasn't in the room. She shook Robbie awake.

"Robbie, where's Jo-Jo?"

Robbie roused himself, leaned over, and looked under his bed where the dog usually slept. He looked up confused.

Annie put her brush down. "Never mind. You go back to sleep. I'll go find her."

Annie looked all over the house, everywhere except in the room with her father and brothers. They were sleeping, and Annie knew that the dog never went around any of them. She checked to see if their door was closed in case Jo-Jo had got shut in the room by accident and couldn't get out. It was open.

Annie opened the front door and looked out. The night was clear and bright, and as soon as her eyes adjusted, she could see out into the yard. She moved onto the steps to call the dog. A sound behind her made her twirl around.

It was Claude. He had been on the porch and had now stepped between her and the door.

"You looking for that mangy dog?"

"Where is she?"

"I got her. Locked in the smokehouse."

"Why?"

"I kind of wondered what a dog would look like with a missing front and *back* leg."

"You wouldn't—"

"You want the dog back or not?"

Annie didn't say anything.

"I see you got a tongue problem again."

The sound of running feet on the hard dirt of the yard drew their attention. Robbie crossed the front yard and headed toward the smokehouse. The dark swallowed him.

Claude glowered at his retreating form. "The door is locked. He can't get in."

"Give me the dog or I'll tell Daddy."

"Little Miss Tattletale again. Who cares what you tell him? He won't do nothing. Maybe gripe a little, but that's all. He ain't got the balls. You want the dog? Come to the smokehouse and get her."

Claude walked past her, reaching out and pinching her breast. "You got about a minute to get there before she loses a leg," he said.

Annie froze when he touched her, every part of her drawing up so tightly that she felt the slightest movement would splinter her. She didn't know what to do. Her mind flopped about like a frantic bird in the still cage of her body. If she tried to go for her daddy, Claude would hurt Jo-Jo before she could get help. If she went with him, there was no telling what he would do to her.

Then she saw Robbie, Jo-Jo in his arms, run by the side of the porch and around the back of the house. She was back to her room by the time he got there. She shut and locked the door behind him.

Robbie's face was flushed with the effort of carrying the puppy and running and he was breathing hard. He had a wild, alarmed look about his bulging eyes, and he held onto Jo-Jo like any minute someone would try to snatch her away.

Annie knelt down next to him. "It's okay now." She gently pried the dog from his arms, petting her, and putting her in Robbie's bed. "Here, she can sleep with you tonight."

Robbie looked relieved and climbed in by the puppy, wrapping her in his arms and giving her a wet kiss on the top of her head.

"Robbie, how did you get in the smokehouse?"

Robbie was already closing his eyes. "Back door."

"Back door, what back door?" Annie didn't understand.

"Back door," Robbie mumbled, "like otter."

At first she didn't know what Robbie meant by a back door, but then she realized that he played in the smokehouse just like he played all over the yard and in the outbuildings, and she guessed that somehow he had made himself a back door like the otter's.

The thought of Claude's face when he got there and the dog was gone momentarily replaced the fear that had filled Annie with a jolt of pleasure.

Then a noise, something at the window, drew her up sharply, and she jumped before she realized that it was probably Claude, trying to scare her. She blew the lantern out so that he couldn't see into the room, not even a shadow.

He persisted for a while, scraping and fumbling at the window, and Annie couldn't make herself ignore the noise, every sound scraping against her flesh like the point of a needle, and after he finally left, it was a long time before she went to sleep, Miss Mercer's words about him, *bad heart* and *evil*, echoing through her mind over and over.

The next morning at breakfast she waited until everyone was served, then she took a deep breath and said, "Claude locked Jo-Jo in the smokehouse and was going to hurt her."

Claude, who had been staring at her as if to warn her

not to mention it, slammed his cup down, the coffee splashing out. "She's a liar!" He got himself under control. "Daddy, I put the dog up because it's a chicken killer. We need to get rid of it."

Annie glared at him. "Jo-Jo has never killed a chicken."

Claude glared back. "Daddy, ask Lacey."

Lacey looked surprised for just a moment, then a sly look came over her face. "Yes sir, that mutt sure did. Just yesterday. I wasn't going to say nothing about it, but that dog's a chicken killer for sure, just tore that chicken to pieces, all over the yard." She looked at Annie. "And I don't like having that dirty mongrel in the house either."

Annie's daddy picked up his fork and started eating again. "Get rid of the dog, Annie, or Claude'll do it for you."

The smile that spread on Claude's face was almost too much for Annie to bear, but she wouldn't leave the table, wouldn't give him the pleasure of her leaving. She ate the rest of her breakfast looking down at her plate and making herself swallow the mouthfuls of food that tasted like cardboard.

Saturday afternoon, Annie sat on the top porch step. Robbie was on the step below her, his head in her lap. He was crying, while Annie absently stroked his hair. She stared off into space, her mind replaying over and over her visit to Miss Mercer that morning after breakfast.

leave the dog here girl he won't bother it here
i hate him
don't waste your time on hate
he won't leave me alone
hating him ain't going to make him leave you alone
i'm scared of him, i need to tell daddy
you won't get no help from your daddy
if momma was here she'd fix him she'd make him leave me alone
what would she do
something i don't know what but she would just fix it just like she did before

would that help if you could talk to your momma
what difference does it make i can't she's
you can talk to her in a way i can tell you how would
that relieve your mind
yes yes but
here's what you do you can write a letter to the dead if
you do it this way use a sow's milk and water that a
glowworm's been in and put it in the fire then use it like
ink to write the letter and you don't dot no i's or cross no
t's none if you do even one it won't work you can only
see the writing at night so write it after dark so you can
see what you're writing make sure you don't dot no i's or
cross no t's take it to the cemetery on the night of the full
moon at midnight bury it at the head of the grave you'll
sure get an answer believe me yes siree you'll get an
answer
   how will i get an answer
   sometimes dreams sometimes a sign different each
time but you'll get an answer all right

Leaving, Annie looked back at Miss Mercer holding Jo-Jo, who had tried to follow Robbie, in her arms. The dog was whining and staring mournfully at Robbie, who was walking backward and waving at her. Annie held onto Robbie's hand like it was anchoring her to the earth. "Don't cry. I'll think of something. Jo-Jo will be all right. Come on, let's get back."

letters to the dead, miss mercer said, we all write them
don't dot no i's don't cross no t's pages of black and
white hindsight fare for worms a scribble of unspoken
pleas buried apologies. . . .

"Are you sure you want to do this? It sounds kind of weird to me." J.C. leaned against the tree trunk.

He and Annie were in a stand of trees behind the school. Through the branches she could see the afternoon sky split open, bleeding red and yellow streams across the sinking sun. The tallest trees clutched the remaining sheer skin of light in their long leaf-fingers, and the soft sinuous spring air seemed to Annie hollow, waiting to soak up whatever she said. She felt her mind moving like rain-scented wind moves, pregnant and heavy with anticipation, and she thought she could count her measured bloodbeats, so strong was the rhythm in her pulses.

"I already thought about it for a week now. I want to do it."

Annie, lying fully clothed under the cover, in a shirt and overalls, had her eyes open in the dark room, her straining ears filled with the regular sounds of Robbie's breathing. She waited until the clock struck eleven. Then she got up, and after checking on Robbie, who was sleeping on his side with his mouth hanging slack and snoring softly, she got the ink that she had prepared earlier just as Miss Mercer had told her, slipped on a sweater against the night chill and went quietly past the other bedroom, into the kitchen, and out the back door. In just a half-hour, she was at the new school, knocking on the door.

J.C. opened it and put out his hand to take her bundle. Annie was so wound up with expectation and uneasiness that she practically leaped through the door.

They spread a paper out on the desk, and Annie, with her glasses perched on her nose and the tip of her tongue stuck out between her lips as she concentrated, dipped her pen and wrote. The letters made a liquid glow as they followed the pen, and without any dots or crosses the script was one continuous fluid line of brightness. J.C. moved away from her and busied himself on the other side of the room.

"I'm ready," she said, and despite her resolve, her voice shook like the letter she was waving back and forth to dry the ink.

J.C. didn't hesitate. "Let's go."

The woods were dark and rich and still held the mellow heat of the spring sun, and Annie felt herself sweating slightly as they climbed the steep trail to the cemetery. It seemed to her as if everything—the bushes, the trees, the flowers, all the small things hidden around them—

breathed in the dark, filling the air with an aliveness that permeated her skin and flowed along her nerves like quicksilver. She was filled with an awareness of herself, the rhythm of her blood, the quickened beat of her pulse, her own warm moist breath on the air, and her eyes felt chafed, burning with the intensity of constantly moving around, always seeing, looking.

The air got thinner and colder the farther up they climbed and the sweat drying under Annie's sweater sent rivers of chills up and down her spine. J.C.'s lantern bobbed ahead of her, the light playing on leaves and stones and creating loose shadows that slipped and darted with an antic grace.

J.C. looked back once, when she stumbled and let out a small sound, her boot tripping on an exposed root.

"You okay?"

"I'm all right. I just tripped."

The cemetery was filled with a feeling like that curious thick contemplation that covers a congregation after a moving sermon, broken only by an occasional owl hooting, a litany of whippoorwills, and the strident screech of crickets.

J.C. stopped at her mother's grave and Annie came up beside him.

"Annie, what do you expect to get from doing this?"

"I don't know." She didn't want to talk. She wanted to do what she had come here to do, and he seemed to sense it.

"What do you want me to do?"

"Dig a hole right there." She pointed to the head of her mother's grave. "Deep enough for the letter, so nothing won't dig it up."

J.C. had no trouble digging the dirt since the soil was still soft from planting the tree. Annie took the folded letter and placed it flat, facedown in the hole and pushed the dirt over it, covering it and patting the dirt down. It made a hump over the spot like there was more dirt to go back than had been taken out.

She stood up, a feeling of immense relief flooding her,

and when she turned around, she found herself right in front of J.C., who reached out and held both of her arms next to her side.

"So, what's wrong?"

Annie wanted to tell him but she didn't know how. What if he knew about Claude, what he had done, how would he think of her, as dirty, used?

But then she knew, as sure as if the words had been inscribed by an invisible hand on her mind, *tell him, tell him,* that she should tell him, tell him everything—

"It's my brother, Claude. He's always bothering me—"

J.C's hands tightened on her arm.

"I'm scared of him—" She told him about Claude and his threats the night of the service, then about Jo-Jo.

J.C. listened without comment, but his face twitched as if the words were being pressed against his skin, like they were burning it, and then she told him about her momma's death, the baby, and the mix-up about the medicine. When she finished, he let go of her and paced around like her words had caused too much turmoil in him to be still.

"You don't need to be scared of him." He turned back to her. "I'll take care of him. Don't you worry. He won't bother you no more."

"How? What can you do? I—"

"Let me think on it. Don't you worry. It'll be all right. Let's forget it now."

Annie nodded. She knew that he meant it, that he would take care of it.

He cocked his head to one side, regarded her carefully. "You know you sure look good in those overalls. I ain't never seen *nobody* look good in overalls until now."

Annie laughed at his pleased expression, her eyes following the movement of his lips, feeling them moving on her skin, causing a melting, a secretion of her senses, and he moved closer, wrapped her in his arms. . . .

And in the church, the window pane J.C. pushed out lying broken in a pool of moonlight on the floor, the night was thinner than outside, and it seemed to wrap around her heart in tender tendrils, the airy fingers of a ghost, as J.C. unbuckled the straps to her overalls letting them fall, and she stepped out of them, boldly and without shame, her long, coltish legs tingling in the cool air, and the smooth way he pulled the shirt over her head, letting it drop soundlessly in the circle of light from the lantern, brushing her rumpled hair back with his hands, his fingers moving back to caress her face, the floor under her hard and cold through the spread-out clothes, his body eager and warm, her need to get her hands inside his shirt, the wonderful smooth tight skin of his chest, the deepening of the night. . . .

Annie's blood thrummed in her ears like the plucked strings of a guitar, her body filled with energy, the mark on her hand on fire, then the sweet stab of pain radiating outward from a core deep within her, changing, softening to rich waves of pleasure. Afterward, behind her closed moist lids, she had a glimmer of something like a vision, and she saw how it was the night she was conceived *the man, my daddy, turns to you in the deepest part of that summer night, any guilty thought of your sons drowns in the dark Cherokee blood filling his eyes, and you come together as beautiful and dangerous as a flash-fire on the mountainside. . . .*

18

J.C. walked Annie to and from school every day the next week, even staying for a while to talk with her on the porch and play with Robbie. To Annie's protests that there might be trouble if he hung around, he answered that he would handle any problem. He wanted her family, he said, to know that they were together.

Strangely, Annie's father, although he had come up several times when J.C. was in the yard with her and Robbie, hadn't said anything. He nodded at J.C. and went on in the house. Annie had felt J.C. stiffen slightly at his approach, and she was relieved when her daddy walked on by. Even Claude didn't approach them, but would glare at them whenever he passed by. J.C. would instinctively move closer to Annie, returning Claude's stare. Annie worried some. She thought she could feel Claude's eyes always on them, even when she couldn't see him, like a prickling at the back of her neck.

On Friday afternoon, a fierce downpour sent Annie and J.C. running through the clearing for the porch. Huge drops of rain fell without warning, sudden and swift. Darkening the cloudy day to evening in minutes, the pounding water filled the gray air with a noise like the unrelenting beat of insect wings. Annie and J.C., laughing and holding one another up, were both drenched by the time they reached her house.

"Jesus, the bottom fell out!" J.C. shook the rain out of his hair and wrung his shirttail with his hands while Annie, out of breath after the run, collapsed on the porch swing. Neither one saw Claude standing in the front-room window, watching them, his eyes drawn to sharp slits as his breath fogged up the pane.

"Is anyone here?" J.C. sat down by her and put his arm across the back of the swing.

"Just Lacey and Robbie. Neal works every day at the store now. He even stays overnight several times a week, and Daddy and Claude are probably sitting out the storm in the field."

"Well, then, come on over here." He guided her over into his lap.

The door flew open, and Claude rushed out. He snatched Annie up, slung her against the wall, and J.C. wasn't ready for the blow, the hammer-fist to his chin that knocked him out of the swing, then a second blow that sent him back out into the rain, knocking him sideways into the yard that had turned to mud. Suddenly he was on his back, the rain filling his face and stinging his eyes as he struggled to get up.

J.C. saw a darker gray blur coming out of the lighter grayness of the rain. Claude stood over him, then bent down, his face looming out of the mist, glowering down, a screwed-up red mass of ferocity. "You goddamn sonov-abitch. You been porking my sister. I'll kill your ass!" He kicked J.C. in the side of the chest.

The breath flew out of J.C. leaving him strangled. He tried to see up through the rain, through the red haze that covered his eyes, frantically looking for the next attack. A bright flash lit up the murky sky, and thunder, close and heavy, cracked in his ears.

Then Annie was there, yelling, her words lost in the rain. A hand came out of the rain, knocked her back, her head twisting sideways from the blow. She disappeared like a doll that had been tossed off to the side, and then the boot came at him again, in slow motion it seemed, as it parted the silver streams of rain, emerging huge and black. J.C. reached out, grabbed the foot, and twisted, raising his body off the ground with a savage thrust.

Claude grunted, a thick, raucous gut sound. J.C. pushed harder, wrenching the foot around again until he felt Claude slip in the mud. Then Claude was down, flat on his back, right next to him. J.C. got up by using Claude's trapped foot as leverage. He pushed Claude, using the foot to slide him through the mud.

"You crazy bastard! Get out of here!"

J.C. turned his back to Claude, wanted to see about Annie, but Claude jerked forward, grabbed him, snatched his shirt, and pulled him back. J.C. caught his balance and swung around with his fist raised, bringing it full down into Claude's face. The flesh and bone imploded under the blow, making a soft thud, and he felt Claude's nose give way under his hand as blood spurted out on each side of his fist. He raised his hand high and brought it down again on the same spot.

J.C.'s head was filled with the roar from the onslaught of rain and wind, and he seemed to be whipped into a frenzy by the fight. He could hear Annie screaming, begging him to stop, but he couldn't see her through the solid rain, and her voice seemed scattered, coming from everywhere at once.

Claude, his face a mess, collapsed back into the mud. J.C. turned away and started toward the porch. Annie was standing at the foot of the steps, her hand over her mouth. Blood ran from the corner of her eye and her nose. He was almost to her, reaching for her, saying that it was over, when he felt a sharp burning pain shoot through his knee. His left leg gave way under him like it had suddenly melted.

J.C. was down and rolling in the mud, holding his leg. Something awful was wrong. His leg was full of liquid fire and limp, hanging like a noodle. He could feel blood, warm and sticky, seeping through his fingers.

Then Claude was leaning over him again. He had a large knife in his hand, and he was smiling. J.C. could see a large gap in his mouth where a tooth had been knocked loose.

"Hamstrung like a pig." Claude's voice was mushy, wheezing through his busted-up nose and mouth. "Now, asshole, I'm going to cut your damn balls off just like I do a pig."

J.C. tried to get up, but all he could do was crawl toward the porch, dragging the useless leg behind him, making a trail through the slime of the yard like a giant slug.

Claude, who was limping on his ankle, walked after him, taunting him, "Crawl, you sonovabitch, crawl!" He hissed at J.C., snot and blood dripping from his nose as he leaned over and prodded J.C. with the knife, sticking the point in his back, squealing "Oink, oink." He kept sticking as J.C. crawled, the spasms of pain spreading like rain on his back and leg.

The last thing J.C. saw clearly was Annie. She turned and ran into the house. Then he collapsed, everything a watery blur of pain in his eyes.

Annie ran back out of the house, hoisting the rifle on her shoulder. Robbie stood right next to her, holding onto her skirt. Lacey was screaming and hollering behind her. "You put that gun down! You hear me. Put it down!"

"Get away from him!" Annie heard her own serrated voice cut through the sodden air, a blade of sound, thin and hard.

Claude stopped, looked surprised for a moment. "Put that gun down, you little pussy."

"I'll shoot you! So help me God, I'll shoot you! I will!"

Lacey was still yelling, almost crying, "She's crazy. I told you. Crazy—"

Annie stepped back so that she could see Lacey too. "Get out there with Claude," she said, and when Lacey hesitated, still blubbering and mumbling, she pointed the gun right at her. "Now!"

Lacey scampered down the steps, out into the rain, next to Claude. "Crazy. Like that witch-woman—"

Claude started toward the porch. Annie leveled the gun

at him. She pulled the trigger. The gun jumped. The bullet flew through the air right next to Claude's head. The sound of the shot was lost in a roll of thunder.

"Jesus Christ!" Both Claude and Lacey jumped flat on the ground. The mud splattered up in an arc around them.

Annie came down the stairs, awkwardly holding the gun still on her shoulder, and stood in front of J.C. "Get up! Get to the smokehouse!

Robbie stood on the porch, watching it all, quiet and intent, his eyes shifting from Annie to Claude and Lacey.

Claude stood up, still holding the knife, the rain pouring off him in dirty streams, the front of his overalls a solid sheet of mud. "I'll get you for this, you stupid little slut, you and that piece of shit—" He spit toward J.C.

"Shut up! Drop the knife!" She shot into the dirt next to him, the recoil knocking her back. Claude jumped again, to the side and down in the mud. Lacey started crying in earnest, "Lord, Oh Lord—"

Annie glanced at J.C., who was lying against the steps. "Stay here. I'll be right back."

She pointed the gun right at Claude's head. "Both of you. Go on."

Claude gave Lacey a push, then lumbered off behind her. Annie followed, Robbie right behind her. She herded them into the smokehouse and then, using the hammer and nails that she sent Robbie for, she nailed it shut.

In just a minute Annie was back. "Can you get up?"

She put the gun down and got J.C. on his feet, but he couldn't put any weight on his leg. She eased him down again. "Robbie, get your wagon. Hurry!"

J.C. was having trouble focusing, the whole scene like something behind a smeared windowpane. His head reeled. "Annie. . . ." He tried to say something to her, but couldn't.

"I nailed Claude and Lacey in the smokehouse. We got to hurry." Annie talked as much to herself as to him.

When Robbie brought his wagon around, Annie helped J.C. sit in it, and with him helping by pushing with his good leg and Robbie guiding while she pushed behind, they started to Miss Mercer's house.

The going was almost impossible. The mud bogged the wagon down, and soon J.C. was falling to the side and would have fallen from the wagon completely if Annie hadn't finally stopped and held him up. He felt cold to Annie's touch and wouldn't respond to her questions. She could see that the leg was bleeding bad.

"Robbie, you run ahead and get Miss Mercer. We need a wagon. Have her drive her wagon here. Do you hear?"

Robbie nodded and took off running through the rain while Annie tried to conceal J.C. and the little wagon in a stand of fir pines off the trail. She pulled J.C. out of the wagon, dragging him deep under the trees where there was some protection from the rain. She took off her blouse and tore it into strips and bound up his leg, putting a big pad over the ugly slash that gaped wide and deep. She tried to stem the flow of blood by knotting the ends of the bandage holding the pad in place around a stick and twisting the stick.

The rain chilled her through her undershirt and J.C.'s body felt heavy and lifeless in her lap. At the edges of her mind, panic gnawed, the fear that Claude would be after them, every sound coming through the rain evoking images of his fury-filled face. She stared off in the direction from which Miss Mercer would come, *Hurry, Robbie, please, hurry. . . .*

The rain had not surprised Miss Mercer, who, all morning, had seen the low-flying birds and heard the chorus of metallic clicking from the tree frogs. She knew that rain was soon to follow, so when the onslaught came, beating against her house with a frenzy of clattering drops, she built a fire, lit the lanterns, put on a fresh pot of coffee, and settled down in the front room at the small table where she liked to read her cards.

She shuffled the deck over and over, feeling it take on the rhythm of her manipulations, absorb the warmth of her skin, and when the cards felt like part of her own hands, merely an extension of the sensitive ends of her probing fingers, she shuffled the question into the pack, *What's in store for Annie?*

Miss Mercer chose the Page of Swords to stand for Annie. The sword to represent her turmoil and fears of harm. On the card, storm clouds move across the sky, and the ground is uneven, rough, treacherous, but the sky is filled with birds, a sign of action, and of things changing, moving.

She laid out the ten cards in the Celtic Cross: the first on the top of the Page of Swords for general influences; next, crossing it, the opposing forces; below, the foundation; then, passing influences; above, future possibility; then facing it, future happening; then, in a line to the right, fears; others' opinions; the seeker's hopes; and finally, the outcome.

The cards spoke to her. The VIII of Swords told a story grounded in fear, indecision, illness, threats to loved ones, and the opposition, the V of Cups, disclosed despair and agony over a loss, a despair obscuring the possibility of happiness contained in the card's depiction of the full cups behind the seeker. The foundation, the Hierophant, revealed an acceptance of conventions, static roles, and a disposition, according to the Queen of Wands, that is fond of nature, fond of home. Both cards bespoke a domestic inclination that could ignore the possibility of happiness, the happiness contained in the pictures of the X of Cups, the happy family. Immediate strife, misfortune, and a fear of the loss of a home were contained in the fears revealed by the III of Swords and the IX of Coins. The III of Coins disclosed that others wanted to reward the seeker's work and ability. The Death card pleased Miss Mercer, a sure indication of renewal and change, a new beginning for Annie.

Miss Mercer was leaning back in the chair, smoking and pondering, letting what she knew of Annie's life and how it related to the story told by the cards float through her mind, seeing moving pictures like the wisps of smoke from her cigarette, full and porous one minute and then evaporating the next minute, always shape-shifting.

Jo-Jo's whining took a while to penetrate through her concentration. The dog was at the door, clawing at the baseboard. There was a rapping, not hard but steady.

Miss Mercer pulled Robbie, dripping wet, through the door. "Boy, you'll get your death of cold. What're you doing out in this weather?" She grabbed a shawl off a chair and wrapped it around his shoulders. Jo-Jo was all over her feet, rubbing against her and yelping.

"What's wrong?"

Robbie, his gaze flying every which way, kept trying to say something, but only a few unintelligible syllables came out. She took his round little head in her hands, peered into his excited eyes. "Robbie, what's wrong? Is it Annie? Something wrong with Annie? Tell me."

Robbie stared back, and gradually his face composed itself from a contortion of confusion and consternation to an understanding of why he was there. "Annie. J.C. hurt. You bring wagon." He pointed off toward the road to his house.

Miss Mercer needed to hear no more. She grabbed her cloak from the peg on the wall. "Come on, show me where they are."

It took both of them to get J.C. in the house. He was incoherent, moaning and mumbling, his head rolling from side to side. They had to lift him out of the wagon and drag him through the wet yard, up the porch stairs, his legs bumping against each step as they hauled him, by pulling him under the arms, into the front room, and lay him face down on the couch.

Miss Mercer, winded, leaned against the table, looking first at Robbie, who stood off to the side, sucking his thumb, and then at Annie, who was trying to pull off J.C.'s wet clothes.

Miss Mercer walked over to the sewing machine and took scissors out of the drawer. "Here, cut 'em off. I'll get some blankets."

While Annie cut, Miss Mercer went to one of the large chests in the corner of the room and took out several light wool blankets and a large swatch of white cotton cloth.

Annie had cut off J.C.'s pants, leaving the blood-encrusted bandage and was working on his shirt when Miss Mercer began to dry him with the cotton cloth. "We got to get him warm," she said. "That's the first thing."

She looked at Annie, who was shivering, drenched to the skin, her clothes sodden. "You too. Go change yourself. Robbie too. Go on. In my bedroom. Get anything."

Miss Mercer folded away some of the bandage to look at J.C.'s leg. The blood wasn't clotted, so the cloth pulled away easily and didn't stick to the wound, but the easing of the pressure was followed by a fresh stream of blood. Miss Mercer dabbed at it, trying to see how bad it was. She didn't know what had happened yet. Getting J.C. in the wagon, the brutal rain, Robbie going into a crying jag, had taken up any talk they might have done, and she had concentrated on getting here, driving, cursing the slow pull of the wagon through the resistant mud and Annie in the back with J.C.

Miss Mercer blotted the wound. It looked bad. The tendon was cut clean in two. She could see it coiled like a baby snake, down in his calf.

She checked his pulse—steady but faint. His color was coming back a little, two red spots starting to show on his cheeks that had been fish-belly white when they brought him in.

Annie appeared at her side, dressed in a cotton smock. "Claude did it," she said. "There was a fight."

Miss Mercer snorted, a kind of consent, an affirmation of *yes, that's what had to happen,* and said, "Okay, later, you can tell me about it later. Right now, pour yourself and Robbie a cup of coffee. It'll warm you up. Me too. Get me one. We got to think what's best to do for J.C."

They sat next to the couch, Miss Mercer and Annie on chairs and Robbie on the floor with Jo-Jo in his lap licking every part of his body. Annie, who hadn't shed a tear throughout the entire incident, felt her insides melting as she warmed up. She tried to tell herself that it could be worse, that at least no one was dead, but the tears still accumulated behind her eyes and in the pit of her throat, swelling her heart, replacing the panic and adrenalin of earlier.

"Go ahead, girl, let it out. Cry, if you want. Get over it. We got work to do." Miss Mercer got up and busied herself, going between the kitchen and front room, setting out something on the table, putting on the kettle, and glancing every so often over her shoulder at Annie.

Annie cried as she drank her coffee, sobbed unashamedly, then, after a while, feeling drained, hollow and dry, she stopped. Then she got up, patting Robbie on the head as she walked by, and went over to Miss Mercer. "What do we need to do?"

On the small table Miss Mercer had laid out knives, tongs, needles, and what looked like some kind of thick thread. She went in the kitchen and came back with a basin of boiling water and dropped everything into it.

"What're you doing?" Annie's mind tumbled back, remembering *a basin filled with water a knife bloody water gnarled roots hands ugly twisted hands. . . .*

"We got to sew that tendon back together or that boy won't ever walk on that leg again. He might not anyway. But we got to give it a try."

Miss Mercer walked over to the couch. "Look here," she pulled up the blanket and pointed to the coiled snake curled down in J.C.'s calf. "That's got to be pulled up and sewed back."

Annie felt like the room split apart, like the air parted into a thousand sharp slivers, each one rubbing against her skin, and a swath of hot panic cut its way to her bone, invaded the marrow *her momma the way she had died nothing helped no matter what she did it didn't help. . . .*

"Is he going to die?" Annie stared at his profile, the fluttering eyes, his wonderful hands now clutching sporadically the edge of the couch *did she say that did she ask such a question. . . .*

Miss Mercer covered his leg back. "I don't know. The moon is passing on to full, and it's going to draw that wound, suck it out. He'll be a bleeder for sure. We got to staunch the bleeding as much as we can. Then if he lives through the shock, he ought to be all right."

She paused and looked at Annie, touched her on the arm. "Annie, I can't help but think that he won't ever walk again if we don't sew that tendon, you understand? There's death and there's *living death*. You understand? We need to try and fix his leg."

Annie nodded. She understood.

Miss Mercer walked over to the big table, started shoving everything off onto the floor. "We can tie him down here."

Annie swallowed, took a deep breath. "Can't we give him something to keep him asleep?" She remembered the drink Miss Mercer had given her and how it had put her right to sleep.

"You can't pour liquids down an unconscious man unless you want to strangle him. But we're going to try and wake him. Then I'll give him some liquor and a potion. It'll knock him out, but whether or not he stays knocked out is not sure. He might just wake up in the middle of it. That's why we need him tied down. Come on, let's get him moved."

"Here, J.C., lift your head a little."

He felt pressed down, something holding him down, pressing on his back—

Suddenly, hot, fiery hot, sharp pain tossing up from somewhere in his lower body, into his mouth, his nose—

"Right here, throw up here." He felt his head turned to the side, a bowl pushed next to his mouth. He retched, his body heaving against the restraints on his wrists and legs. A cool rag passed over his face and mouth.

He collapsed. His face fell back to the table and his mind went briefly blank, before he tried to rise up again and found that he was tied down, his arms and legs stretched over a table and tied. Before he could react, another pitch of pain washed over him, liquid fire, and a wave of vomit followed it, rolling up, the bowl, the hands, falling back, trying to focus, the room tilted on edge—

"Should I stop?" *Annie's voice?* Low, urgent, familiar. *Annie?*

"No, you got to finish. Go on. The quicker, the better." *Miss Mercer?* Someone was right by his head, holding his head in her hands, her fingers felt like soft clamps over his ears. It must be her, Miss Mercer. He wanted to say something to her, thought he was talking, *what happened, what's wrong,* but nothing was coming out and without wanting to he kept pulling against the restraints, his eyes seemed to be loose in his head, rolling back, everything in front of him suddenly going red, like when you try to look through your closed eyelids at the sun *Annie, Annie.*

The old voice, Miss Mercer's voice, came through the redness, real close, forcing itself into his mind. "J.C., do you hear me? Be still. You got to be still for a minute longer. Just hold on." And the soft clamps moved to his forehead, stroking, while his heart flipped around in his still body, the torrid fire centered in his leg roasting it, frantic irregular beats against his chest wall, making his stomach knot up again *Annie? Where's Annie?* then blackness *the school blackened and falling down in ruins Jo-Jo trying to swim in dark water with one front leg and sinking snakes cut in pieces wiggling in fire—*

"Hurry, Annie. I don't know long he'll be out this time. Those ties ain't going to hold him if he decides to get up. He's starting to feel cold too; his temperature's dropping."

Annie was shaken by his waking up, the reserve of calm she had pulled on earlier dissipating under the feel of his body moving. "I can't! It's gaped too wide. The skin won't come together!" She snatched off her glasses and rubbed her eyes with the back of her hands, oblivious to the blood she was spreading on her face.

Earlier, she had been just the opposite, working with her mind numb, mechanically following Miss Mercer's instructions.

After the initial shock when Miss Mercer had said she had to do it, Annie's vehemence, "No, no, I can't, no," and the old woman's insistent hands on the sides of her face as she held Annie's shaking head, "Annie, I'm too old, I can't see that well, my hands shake, you got to do it," Annie had put on her glasses, washed her hands, let Miss Mercer tie an apron around her waist. Miss Mercer had cut off the flow of blood to the leg with a tourniquet tied around a stick that she twisted right above J.C.'s knee, the knot resting on the big artery on the inside of his thigh, and Annie used a small, sharp knife to make the first long cut at a right angle to the knife wound, peeling back layer after layer, Miss Mercer mopping the blood, to get to the tendon coiled almost down to the ankle.

The tendon felt like a small wet eel, round, slippery, a fat springy worm in her fingers. She pulled it gently, and it followed her hand up to where the other end waited.

When she first touched the tendon, she had felt a wave of sickness, the reality of what she was doing breaking out of the back of her mind where she had pushed the awful knowledge to concentrate instead on the small area of leg, on making the long cut, on the layers of skin, the sharp parting of skin like slicing into a pulpy fruit, on the needles, on the catgut, on the rags *just a sewing job, nothing but a sewing job, mend it up, a stitch in time saves nine—*

Miss Mercer sighed when Annie brought the tendons together. "Good, now, make small stitches. You understand? They got to be small or they won't stand up to the movement of the leg. Sew inside to outside. Tie each one off. A knot. Just like when you sew material."

Annie took the threaded needle from her and saw Robbie standing at the head of the table petting J.C.'s head like he petted Jo-Jo, his wide protruding eyes following her every movement.

Annie held the tendon together with one hand and put the needle in with the other, carefully knotting each stitch as if it were the last one she would ever make. Miss Mercer constantly pinched together places with one hand and mopped blood with the other, and under her guidance, Annie placed the stitches close and straight, even, listening to Miss Mercer's cadence as the old woman's voice led her hand, "Put the needle in, pull it through, loop the thread, bring it under, tie it off," then the old woman would clip it and they would do it again. . . .

> *You do it like this, Annie. Her momma held up*
> *the skirt she was working on, showing her the*
> *small, even stitches going up the side seam.*
> *Yours are too big, she pointed to the small*
> *squares of material that Annie was sewing*
> *together to make a pin cushion. They'll just pull*
> *out and you'll have to do it again, you want to*
> *sew so that the seams will hold under stress,*
> *like this, and she reached over and guided*
> *Annie's hand, the needle going in and out, in*
> *and out. . . .*

"There's no way to close that gap!" Annie's heart that
had lain a quiet, still, clenched fist in her chest opened up,
came awake, recoiled from the way he had moved, how it
must hurt—

Miss Mercer left the head of the table, came up beside
Annie. "You put your glasses back on now and wash your
hands again." Then she put her hands on each side of the
wound and pushed until the edges puckered together.
Holding it shut that way, she looked at Annie. "Okay,
now sew. Close together and tie off each one again."

Annie counted them. Thirty-two. She put in thirty-two
stitches across the ugly livid gaping mouth that Claude
had cut, feeling the leg start to move again under her fingers.

MENDING

19

J.C. woke up right as Annie was finishing, and he was able to help a little as the two of them half carried, half dragged him to the big high bed in Miss Mercer's bedroom, where she removed the tourniquet. Annie, now that it was done, felt weak and had to prop herself against the dresser as she watched Miss Mercer work on J.C.'s leg.

"Shock from blood loss and infection," Miss Mercer said, "that's what we got to worry about now."

Annie's mind registered that Miss Mercer was sending Robbie to the porch and she heard the words *spider web*.

"He lives in the corner behind the rocker, gather the web, but don't bother the spider now, you leave him be, he'll have another web ready for us tomorrow when we need it."

Annie wanted to ask why a web, but she didn't have the energy.

Robbie came back with a handful of the web, and Miss Mercer took it and mixed it with salt, packing the mixture into the wound.

"Web is good and clean and has the power of restraint," she said to Annie. She kept up a constant flow of words as if she knew that Annie needed words to fasten her to the earth, words to bind her now unfastened mind that wanted to scatter and break into pieces, words to control and shape the formless, words to hold onto—

While dressing the wound with cloth, Miss Mercer told Annie that soot and green persimmons were good to stop blood too, not as good as a web though, and then she asked, "What's J.C.'s full name?"

Annie told her, "John Clark Freemon."

Miss Mercer pressed on the bandage, her hands in the shape of a cross, and said, "And when I passed by John Clark Freemon, and saw John Clark Freemon polluted in John Clark Freemon's own blood, I said unto John Clark Freemon when John Clark Freemon was in John Clark Freemon's blood, live, yes, I said unto John Clark Freemon when John Clark Freemon was in John Clark Freemon's blood, live."

She said it three times, her hand pressing on the bandage.

"You got to say the words just right, miss just one or mess up at all and it won't work."

Then she called to Robbie again. "Okay, now boy, give me your madstone." She held out her hand.

Annie watched passively, feeling a melting in her bones, a slow harsh heat that seeped through her. Robbie didn't hesitate at all, but pulled out the stone he always carried with him, the one she had given him at the falls that day, and put it in Miss Mercer's hand.

"Look here." She motioned to Annie, who moved next to the bed and, not sure she could stand up any longer, leaned on the headboard. Miss Mercer put the stone right next to the wound where it stuck to the skin. "Now, look. You see how white the stone is? In a while, it'll be green, the sickliest most putrid color of green you ever seen. That's the infection—it's pulling it out. When that happens, you take it off and soak it in milk until it's white again and keep putting it on until it don't turn green no more, understand?"

Then she told Annie. "You watch him, keep him warm, make sure his color stays good, if the wound starts bleeding a lot, press on it till it stops. I'm going to see your daddy."

Annie didn't ask why, or react in any way. Her whole system had been drained of any feeling except for a great weariness that filled her, soaking deep into her skin, leaving no room for any other emotion or response.

Miss Mercer peered at her, the old eyes alive and quick in a nest of wrinkles. "Go on, girl, splash your face with cold water. You look like you been rode hard and put up wet. Fix yourself some of the tea in the blue tin. Go on now, do that while I get ready."

Outside, the storm had slackened for a while earlier, only to pick up again with the wind blowing against the cabin making a loud rattling from some of the roof shingles being loose, the rain pounding like thimble-covered fingers at the dark windows.

Annie, sipping on a cup of tea, came back into the front room, and saw that Miss Mercer had put on a big rain cape and hood and had her ever-present sack. Then Miss Mercer seemed to remember the fire and sent Robbie for more wood from the porch and then stoked it up.

Annie watched from the porch as Miss Mercer disappeared into the torrent, the old dark figure melting into the sheet of gray rain, becoming part of the downpour.

Annie closed the door and locked it, *you lock every door*, the old woman had said, *and check all the windows, don't you let nobody in, you hear me, nobody, even if you think you know them, even if it sounds like me, i can get in, i got my own way to get in, lock everything, don't you open that door to nobody*, and she had reached out and shook Annie until Annie nodded and said, *yes, ma'am, i understand, nobody*.

Several hours passed. Annie made Robbie a sandwich of bread and meat, and she drank several cups of the tea while cleaning up the front room and kitchen. The familiar motions of wiping, washing, dusting eased her.

Robbie had fallen asleep on the couch, Jo-Jo on the floor. Annie sat in a chair pulled next to the bed, studying J.C.'s face, her mind magnetized by the calmness in his features, circling, noticing the tiny blue vein that throbbed on his temple like a small heart, and the way his eyelashes, long and silky like a child's, lay on his cheeks, making feathery shadows in the lamplight. When she reached over to wipe the sweat off of his forehead, her eyes strayed to the long exact line of his neck curving into his shoulder, and, compelled, she ran her hand down the curve, savoring the soothing rush through her fingers that the feel of his skin evoked, and she sat now holding his hand, fondling it, feeling each crest and valley, memorizing the contours, the ridges, the lines.

Gradually, she felt herself coming back, the numbness dissolving, giving way to a welter of emotions—fear, love, a wash of mixed memories—all rising in her, and impulsively she reached out and put her hand on J.C.'s heart, into the hollow on the side of his chest, nestled her hand there so that she could feel the beat. And it seemed to her that it was erratic—slow and hard one minute and fast and shallow the next. She placed her other hand on her own heart and stayed that way, trying somehow to conduct the sure beat of hers into his through the conduit of her arms.

We use so many sayings about the heart, Miss Mercer had said, *heartache, heart sore, to eat your heart out, to have your heart in the right place, to take to heart, to wear your heart on your sleeve*, and her momma's heart had just faded out like a clock winding down, getting fainter and fainter; the baby's heart had stopped like it had been dropped; Claude's heart when he had hurt her had been in his face, a red, hungry, mean, loud thing; J.C.'s heart when he had loved her had been in his eyes, beating tender and earnest and full.

Annie's mind picked at these thoughts. Willful, it poked at the painful as well as the pleasant, stringing associations like converging streams of water running from the roof into the rainwater tub. Soon, Annie felt like she couldn't bear the persistent images anymore, so she blew out the lamp, undressed, and crawled in the bed next to J.C., pulling the covers over herself and him and putting her body close to his. In the mirror on the door of the wardrobe, she could see the lantern still burning across the hall in the front room and the light-filled circle on the dark heavy-curtained window behind it.

Even though Annie tried to empty her mind, refusing to think about anything, she was unable, lying there so close to J.C., to stop her hand from constantly moving to check his forehead, to lie on his chest, to trace his arm. But soon her hand stilled, and she fell into a fitful sleep.

A knock. A voice. "Open up! Let me in!" Startled awake, she sat up in bed, listened, but she didn't hear anything, only J.C.'s breathing and the noise from the storm outside, drumming, rattling, night sounds echoing and dying away.

Startled, uneasy, she tried to stay awake, to listen, but before long, exhaustion overtook her, everything about her giving in, and she fell into a deep, dreamless sleep until again she was wrenched awake by the voice. This time, she thought, it was coming from the front window, the raspy words like fist blows against the window panes. "Open up!"

Annie got out of bed. The room and furnishings wavered indistinct and insubstantial before her sleep-fogged eyes. She felt her way into the front room, the cold, misty air of the room resistant to her entry as if she were pushing through an invisible membrane.

Although she knew the house was closed up tight and the curtains all drawn, she couldn't shake the feeling that she was being watched, and she held her arms across her chest and stepped as lightly as she stepped on new ice on the stream.

Robbie was sound asleep, Jo-Jo quiet, the fire burned down to embers. Annie wanted to check the window but was afraid to go next to it. She could not bring herself to go to where she thought she had heard the voice. Perched on the edge of a chair, she tried to think what to do. Instinctively, she started to light the lantern that had burned down; then she stopped *don't make a light, he'll know where i am*, felt paralyzed, exposed.

She waited. Nothing. It was quiet *maybe i imagined it, maybe i was dreaming* but then from the kitchen, the back door seemed to move, like somebody was testing it, pushing on it, then a noise like knocking, maybe calling, the words melting into the rain. Circling, she could feel it, him circling, testing each opening, each way in, trying each one. . . .

Annie couldn't think. Her mind had choked to a stop, congested with fear, fear for J.C., fear for Robbie. She knew someone was there, *he*, the *he* who had taken her momma away from her, the *he* who was going to take everything else away from her, the *he* who wanted in, *he*, the unnameable terror that she now felt for everything in her life. . . .

Help *miss mercer she would be back* Annie felt her whole body constrict, jerk, stabbed by the sudden thought—there must be a way into the house. The way that Miss Mercer was going to use.

Claude's matches were all gone. He thought that he could not bear it— the invading darkness, the close meaty smell of the viscous blood-soaked air, being penned up, the need to get out, to get back at them—and the rage inside him was laced with something else, something close to panic, something hidden and raw, something not quite remembered, like the sound of wing beats at the edge of his mind, like the rising, threatening wind from a thousand wings beating. . . .

> *the inside of the cave, an abrupt shift from light to dark, and he is always blinded at first, the sound of the waterfall stopping up his ears, and he panics, reaching for his momma's skirt, but she always rushes in, leaving him behind, and even as he begins to see shadowy outlines, the figure of his momma spreading the blanket right inside the entrance to the cave, she is telling Neal to stay, watch Claude, don't come any further into the cave, call if you need something, don't you dare come in, then she leaves him again. . . .*

He was filled with a thrumming ache that had no root, was not caused by his injuries, yet the pain was constant and tenacious. He had to get out. His ankle had long since swollen up, cutting off any feeling as long as he didn't put too much weight on it, and his nose had stopped bleeding, although he was having trouble breathing and had to hang his mouth open to draw in the air, making a loud, raspy noise and having to taste the smoky cure with each breath.

He had watched the day die and the smokehouse gradually fill with the darkness from outside as the rain beat on the roof like a thousand relentless hammers. Since the small shack was made of logs chinked with mud, no light from moon or stars penetrated it, and whenever Claude struck a match, the room was filled with sparkles from the salt coating on the huge shapes of ham, shoulders, hocks, and middling meat, stacked on shelves.

Lacey, worn out from cussing and whining, was asleep on the dirt floor. Pulled into a fetal position, she had moaned herself to sleep and now was making small fitful, crying noises that made her body jerk in spastic movements.

His mind moved frantically among the possibilities, picking up one after another, sniffing it, gnawing on it, only to discard it, the churning anger in his belly growing more hungry with each idea he tossed away.

The walls were solid, the door heavy and locked with a crossbar, and he had heard her, the little bitch, she had nailed it shut, the sounds of the hammer metal-sharp in the soft rain, and he had already beaten his hands raw against the door, despite knowing that there was no one to hear him, Neal in town, his daddy gone somewhere, but he couldn't stop, couldn't make himself quit smashing his hands on the wood, first his fists, then his palms, screaming, tearing the blood clots away from his nose and mouth, making the blood flow fresh down his face. Once he thought that he heard someone right outside the door. He pounded and yelled, but no one answered.

That was before dark, before the walls closed in. Now he couldn't see, nothing but dim shapes and shadows. He had to think. *The dog. That little flat-faced idiot got the dog out somehow, somewhere. . . .*

Claude dropped to his knees and crawled to the side wall of the smokehouse. Reaching under the shelves, squeezing his body in as far as it would go, he methodically, carefully, examined every square inch of wall, looking for a crack, a loose log, a hole. When he didn't find anything at all, not one crevice, he began again, this time on the dirt floor, feeling of the dirt next to the wall, circling again, and when he got to the back wall, his hand moved from hard-packed dirt to loose dirt—a square foot of loose dirt. He stuck his hand in it. It was loose as far as he could feel.

Claude's gut lurched in excitement. He began digging, tossing handfuls to the side, some of it falling on the sleeping Lacey. He uncovered a hole to the outside, a small hole, big enough for a small dog or even a boy. He needed to make the hole bigger, but the surrounding dirt was too hard to dig with his hands, so he lay on his back and, using his good foot, kicked the shelf over the hole loose. The noise woke Lacey who wanted to know what he was doing. He ignored her. Using the shelf for a shovel, he made the hole big enough for his body to pass through. Lacey followed, got stuck in the hole, called to him. He left her without a thought. His mind was already moving towards Miss Mercer's house.

Miss Mercer had been waiting in the dark Williams house for over two hours. The rain had slackened off then stopped altogether as she sat in the front room, smoking and looking out the window, waiting for Henry. She couldn't help thinking that maybe she could have stopped all this, done something, removed one link in the chain of events, maybe just one would have done it, sent it all twisting off in another direction. But since Julian, she had always been an observer, never a participant, watching human behavior, and she knew now that she had not followed her heart, had not intervened with Henry about Evelyn, had not tried to do something about Claude herself. Now she had to remedy it.

Coming into the yard earlier, she had heard Claude in the smokehouse, banging and yelling, feeling his ominous presence even through the heavy door, and she had stopped only long enough to find a footprint, a large man's footprint followed by a smaller one, fresh under the eave of the smokehouse. Looking in her bag, she had pulled out a nail and had used a rock to drive it into the ground in the center of the footprint, repeating the words under her breath, *Cause evil to....*

She had come through the front door of the house and hearing noises coming from the back she had walked in that direction and found Neal in the bedroom. He was packing his clothes into a sack.

He saw her in the doorway and looked confused for a moment. "I'm leaving—"

"Where's Henry?"

"I don't know. Off somewhere. Probably drinking. When he stays off this late, he's usually drinking." Neal got the bird cage and tied a cover over it.

Miss Mercer felt a rush of pity for him. He looked so frail, his hands, slender and pale, shaking as he gathered his things and his worried eyes, constantly moving around the room, trembling like hands also. He opened a drawer and got out a book to put it in the bag.

"What're you reading?"

He seemed to relax a little at the question. "A book Grady, uh, Mr. Grady, gave me. *The Bridge of San Luis Rey*, by Thornton Wilder. Mr. Grady said it won a prize."

Miss Mercer moved into the room, sat on the edge of the bed. "Grady's good to you, ain't he?"

Neal blushed as if what she said had embarrassed him, but nodded.

Miss Mercer reached out and took his hands and he backed away a little. "I ain't going to hurt you."

She looked at them, felt their softness, the cool, clammy skin. The left hand had clear distinct lines, a long line of the sun. The life line and head line didn't meet but had a large space between them at the beginning. The right hand looked as if it belonged to a different person, the lines muddled, a faint sun line, the head and life lines meeting. *The hands*, she thought, *of a person who fights against his own nature, the right battles with the left, the outer man with the inner.*

She looked up at Neal. "You go on. Get out of here. Best that you do. Another place."

Neal's eyes widened. "Grady keeps talking about going to a city, the place where he used to live—"

Miss Mercer let go of his hands. "Go," she said and walked out of the room into the front room and sat down to wait.

Not long after he left, Lacey came in, covered with dirt and talking to herself. She was shocked to see Miss Mercer and let out a gasp.

"Where's Henry?" Miss Mercer asked as she rolled a cigarette.

Lacey started into the kitchen. "I don't know nothing about nothing," she came back out, a bundle tucked under her arm, "and you can tell these crazy white folks they won't be seeing me no more." She went out the door still going on about "crazy white folks."

Henry came in soon after. He was walking unsteadily through the door. He drew up sharply when he saw Miss Mercer's cigarette.

"What's wrong? Where's everybody at?"

She got up and lit a lantern. "Gone."

Henry fell down sloppily in a chair. "What's that mean? Gone?"

"Well, Evelyn's dead, the new baby's dead, four other kids dead—"

"Huh? What're you talking about—"

"—and when I got here around dark, Neal was packing a bag. He said to tell you he's moving in with Grady—"

"The stupid little queer." Henry lay his head back on the sofa for a minute before straightening up and rolling his own cigarette. "No good for anything anyway. Never was. Good riddance."

"Ain't you got a lick of sense?" It was a statement not a question, as she settled back down into the chair, contemplated him, studied his big cruel face, his shifting eyes.

He looked away.

"There's been a fight. J.C. and Claude. Claude cut J.C. pretty bad. Annie's with me. Her and Robbie. They ain't coming back. Not as long as you got that animal Claude here. He's locked in the smokehouse now—"

Henry looked confused. "A fight? What're you talking about? There ain't nobody in the smokehouse. I just put my horse up. I would of heard something—"

Miss Mercer didn't wait for more. As fast as her old body could take her, she went out to the smokehouse. The door was still nailed, but there wasn't no life inside. She knew it, could feel it. She looked around the back, found the hole, saw where he had dragged himself out of the hole. "Annie—" she said out loud.

Annie, searching for the way in, too scared not to find it, found a small crawl space that ran from the cellar to inside the pantry, and she blocked it, pushing shelves of canned goods against it, ignoring the jars that tumbled off and splattered on the floor, puddles of stewed tomatoes, fruits, pickled pigs' feet. But she knew it wasn't enough. It wouldn't hold long.

The rain stopped, and through the enveloping silence, Annie clearly heard the picking at the back door, a constant metal sound. If it had been a dream earlier, this was no dream. He was using tools. Jo-Jo, hearing it too, got up and went over and crouched down, growling, at the back door.

Annie tried to think, tried to focus, but felt her mind unraveling, spinning around and around until the only thread of thought left was that she had to get him away from Robbie and J.C., had to lead him off, get him away from the house.

After dressing quickly, she shook Robbie awake. "Robbie, I'm going out. You come lock the door behind me, and you keep it locked. Don't open it for nobody. Nobody! Miss Mercer will be back soon."

Robbie, half-asleep, followed Annie to the door. He waited while she slipped through, and then she stood on the outside until she heard the latch fall and Robbie's shuffling steps going away.

She could see clearly. The night was bleached by a bright, bloated moon lighting up the freshly washed sky with a silver radiance that dripped in streams from the trees. She didn't think about what she was going to do beyond get Claude away from the house, the thought of facing him so horrible that it completely absorbed her mind, soaking up her fear into a thoughtless determination to get him away from Robbie and J.C.

From the corner of the back of the house, she saw him working, his dark figure bent over doing something to the edge of the door. He must have got tools from the cellar where the door was standing open. She stepped out so that the light from the moon caught her in its web.

"You looking for me?" She didn't decide what to say. It just came out.

He looked up, sharply, and when he saw her outline, he stood up, started toward her, led by his shadow, huge and misshapen, thrown against the house by the moon, the screwdriver that he still clutched a sharp extension of his hand. Annie could hear his breath grating the soft air and see the impatience in his limping walk, his left leg dragging behind him.

She turned and ran. She ran through the woods, dodging trees, ignoring bushes, the branches pulling at her. She ran, hearing the crashing behind her, knowing that he was keeping up, coming right through the path that she was clearing with her body. The night was saturated with bird cries, night calls, the loon's eerie laugh rising high and strident in her ears. And the thought of her home, that hated house, where everything she had loved had died or been hurt, drove her in the opposite direction. Without planning to, as if pulled along by an invisible force, she climbed up to the ridge, heading for the falls, the cave, the underground lake.

Annie realized that he would have to slow up to climb down to the pool on the steep path, so after she ran into the cave, everything going black suddenly, she leaned against a rock, panting, waiting for her eyes to adjust, listening for sounds behind her that didn't blend with the falling water, with the hollow rush of the cavern . . . *the boat get the boat.*

It comes to him in a flood, the memory falling over his mind with a force like the sheer drop of the curtain of water behind him, the violent roar familiar in his ears, just like it was then, always the deafening noise, then the suffocated light. . . .

> *tired of playing, tired of Neal, his whining, he goes to find his momma, he hears the voices, his momma's light and murmuring and the man's deep, making funny sounds, he is going to call out, ask to go home, call out to his momma, but instead he keeps going closer until he sees them, the man leaning against a rock with his pants down and holding his momma up in the air, and she has her legs wrapped around his waist, scared at the sight, he turns around to run back out and steps on Neal's hand who is crouched right behind him, Neal yelps, and his momma comes, looking distracted and irritated, and picks him up, takes him back to the blanket, rocks him, offers him a breast, and he greedily seizes it but it's dry, he starts crying, he wants his milk, he hates them all, the mean man, crybaby Neal, his dry momma. . . .*

Claude can't make himself go any farther, the dark folding around him sullen and relentless, like the suffocating presence of a malicious ghost, and his body instinctively pulls back.

He calls out. "Annie! Come on, quit fucking around

now. Get out here!"

Nothing but silence and the thickening dark.

"You're just going to make it worse on yourself if you don't come on out like I say."

It is hard to breathe in the closeness, his swollen nose sucking asthmatically at air, the smell of cave and water filling his nostrils with odors of nightmares, and his mind reels like a top *the top the man gave Neal, red and white and blue, a blur of spinning colors, the sound of the slicing air like the sound of hateful whispers.* He needs to get out, to breathe.

He calls again, claustrophobic panic in his voice. "God damn you! Annie! I said get out here!"

Claude strangles on his shouted words, feels the night air crack into pieces and then something breaks loose in him, something uncontrollable, wanting to get at her, make her pay for how he feels, her fault, all her fault, the slut, laying down for that sonovabitch, leaving him alone—

He starts in.

Annie won't let herself breathe. It's not difficult because the sound of Claude's voice, rising and echoing in the dark vault, snatches her breath away like a high wind.

Afraid that he can see her shape against the blackness, she makes herself as small as she can and pushes the boat off, the cold water parting around her legs, then rising to her thighs, as she wades out as far as she can, making no noise, before getting in and using the oars to push herself out to the middle. Then she gets down into the bottom of the boat and huddles there, feeling the motion below her, the rock of the small boat on the water, and tries not to think of the ebony water filled with deep shapes and forms, all moving toward the disturbance. She closes her eyes, turns her mind inward, nursing inside her a small, intractable, cold, curled core of waiting *love from the grave is cold, girl.* . . .

"What the hell do you think you're doing?" The sudden flare of light from Henry's lantern blinds Claude as he turns toward the voice.

"Daddy? Is that you? It's Annie, Daddy . . . that carpenter fellow, the sonovabitch. He's been messing around with Annie. We got in a fight and she run off with him. I was trying to get her back. It's her fault. It's all her fault—"

Henry, with Miss Mercer standing right behind him, holds the lantern high. He looks at Claude, sees his ruined face, hears his repeated accusations, and recognizes a vision of himself, the way the boy's eyes are filled with haunted landscapes, like this cave, a thick darkness that chokes all light out, and Henry can feel the violence in Claude, smell it seeping through every pore, feel the fear and anger crouching like hulks in dark corners, and his own mind drops back, falling down into that cobweb-lined hole in himself where he stores memories that he refuses to have *Evelyn rocking and nursing Claude, his tiny baby fist clutched on the breast to prevent it from being taken away, her hand rubbing the dark down on his head, playing with each finger of his hand, each toe of his foot, Evelyn, hanging out clothes, Claude running stumbling through the sheets, laughing, Evelyn deeper, falling back, tumbling down Frannie, the sharp sound of the ax chopping wood, the chicken feathers floating through the air like falling snow, the soft sound of the ax on flesh.* . . .

Henry feels something drain from him, like marrow sucked out of a bone, leaving him empty. "Let's go."

He hands Miss Mercer the lantern. "You take the girl with you."

20

Since the trouble at the cave the night before last, his daddy had become remote and withdrawn, ignoring Claude most of the time like it was all his fault. This morning the old man had sat quiet chewing his cold bacon and bread, and last night, he had sat on the porch until almost morning and then he had gone to bed without saying a word.

Claude tried to stay out of his way, give him time to cool off, but he hated the silence in the house, the air was so still he could feel it resting on his skin like something moldy and clammy. He wanted to get away from the house, get away from his daddy for a while.

Almost a week ago, the cow had sat down in the pasture, refusing to get up despite everything his daddy had tried. The "goddamn sitting-down" disease, his daddy called it, and if they didn't get her out of the pasture pretty soon all the cows would be down. He had seen it happen once when he was a kid. The whole goddamn herd just sat down and died.

He said, "I'll go see if the cow's up. If she ain't, I'll rig up a winch and hoist her up in the wagon and take her to the slaughterhouse, maybe stay the night in town."

Claude hooked up a boom and sling on the flatbed and went out to the pasture. He got the sling under the cow by

digging under her with a hand hoe to make a place to slip
the sling through. She paid no more attention to him than
she did to the blue bottle-nosed flies that buzzed all
around them, stinging Claude all over as he cursed and hit
the cow while he hitched the harness to the cable.

He lifted her about four feet off the ground and was
guiding the loaded-down sling toward the back of the
wagon when it happened. There was a loud crack and a
painful noise of wood being split, and the boom shifted
suddenly, swinging the cow into him and knocking him to
the ground. He hit his head on the hard ground.

It was the yellow-brown smell clogging his throat and
nose, thick and foul, coating his tongue, that brought
Claude around the first time. Raising his head off the
ground, he tried but couldn't see anything because of a
dark blob in front of his eyes. He felt a crushing weight
on his chest, and a white-hot pain shooting up his leg. The
huge cow, placid and calm-eyed, lay across his chest as if
he were some kind of fleshly pillow. He could move only
his head and one arm because his body and the other arm
were trapped under the cow. *The cow! Jesus Christ! The
cow had fallen on him.*

He threw up once, turning his head so that the vomit
could roll out the side of his mouth, making a thick yellow puddle on the dead grass. Earlier the cool dew from
the morning mist had seeped into his back, but now as the
afternoon wore on, the warmth from the cow's body
seemed to flow through him like sunshine, and he even
thought he could hear the coursing of the cow's blood all
mixed up with the flies' buzzing in his ears. Someone had
to come—

*come on Lacey, hurry, before somebody comes . . .
muddy eyes rolling back teeth big strong white . . . you
go on, Mr. Claude. i ain't got no time for your foolishness
and this be your momma's wake too . . . ah, come on, you
know you want to herelooklook at this . . . oooh put that
thing back in your pants now you go on . . . you is bad . .
. smoky mouth filled with shadows flashes of pink . . .
skin so black it shines purple . . . i'll slip you some home-*

brew to take home   come on   here . . . yea oh yea that's good . . . hair in his hand kinky greasy little mats . . . neal come on in lacey can't talk her mouth's full that's right run you little runt oh yes yes swallow, damn you, nigger, swallow. . . .

He beat at the cow with his arm. She had her back to him and didn't respond at all. He beat for hours, yelling until he lost his voice, the sound breaking like glass against the hard sky, beat with his fist, with the flat of his hand, beat until he couldn't raise his arm anymore, beat until he passed out then woke up to beat again, and now no matter how tightly he closed his eyes, the yellow sun sitting at the top of a lemon yellow sky burned through his pale eyelids, coating them like melted butter, and even if he turned his head, the yellow oozed in the corners of his eyes, and the buzzing of the flies filled his ears with a sound like frying—

frying Annie would be frying dinner pork chops grease smell heavy yellow smell stupid little idiot hanging on her dresstail yellow snot hanging from his nose Neal shoveling shit in the chicken house cheesy little bastard wouldn't wipe my ass with him. . . .

He had felt almost comfortable for a while, but that was before the snapping started, a snapping in his chest, like frozen twigs being stepped on, sharp puncture-like snaps, jabs, the sudden liquid loosening of marrow, and the snapping sounds pooled in the bright place right at the base of his neck where a fire had been set, a hot yellow flame searing the backs of his eyes. He was thirsty, so thirsty—

milk, the dry breast, his milk, gone, momma, momma, i'm hungry, hungry, hungry. . . .

At sundown they came. Attracted by the smell of blood trickling in a steady stream from the split skin of his leg bent back like a broken matchstick, the bone sticking out through the gap.

Rangy, dirty, they approached in twos and threes, then milled about, closing the circle tighter and tighter, their eyes tawny, long timid red tongues flicking at the air, tasting his fear, and constant noises, filling his ears and head, excited whines and yelps, snarls, as some, then more and more, darted in at the curious animal that looked like a hurt cow.

They were a dream he once had as a kid, a dream of Indians, fiery circles of them, red-orange shapes, blazing dark against a slateboard sky with hellish sounds rolling from the dark holes where their mouths should have been, circling tighter and tighter *bloodstreaked sky the blood ruby running between his mother's legs blood on his fingers when he took them out of Annie red teethredhunger bloodredsun sinking blazing into his chest.* . . .

His daddy found him by following the vultures circling overhead. From the road he saw them in the pasture, next to the wagon, landing in packs, pulling off pieces of something in a heap and flying off, coming back again and again.

The cow and Claude were mixed together. Most of his face was gone, one eye hanging out on an exposed cheekbone, and one hand was completely detached from the body, lying on the ground about three feet away, bone with a few shreds of meat.

Claude must have been easier to tear apart than the cow because there was more of the cow still intact, and Henry had to cut the cow up to get to what was left of Claude.

He didn't think he would tell anyone, just bury what was left. Throw him in a hole. No one would care.

Annie woke to a room splintered with glass-strained light, the heavy curtains drawn back from the bedroom window letting in the sun high in the sky.

J.C. was awake too. He lay quietly with his head on his arm, gazing at her, his face expressionless, open, calm.

Annie drew herself up in the bed.

"You been asleep around the clock. Miss Mercer gave you something to make you sleep. She's over at your house."

Annie let it all come back to her, the onslaught of memory *the voices coming over the water, getting up looking at the shore, the light, her name being called, momma, momma, she answered, here i am, miss mercer, the slow walk home wrapped inside the old woman's cape, the warm bath, a soft white gown, sleep* and then she said, "It's not my house."

Annie settled down in the curve of J.C.'s arm, turned her face toward the window, closed her eyes again, savoring the warm light, feeling a dream of tenderness growing under her lids, beginning to bud in the sun's eye. . . .

The Williams house was empty, the doors unlocked, the air dense with dust as if it had been shut up for a long time, and as Miss Mercer looked around, touching this, rubbing that, giving in to a need to feel the house, to experience it, everything seemed to her to be covered with invisible palmprints and fingerprints, all telling stories, speaking with the dead voices of the past, *blood will tell*, she thought, *it always comes back around.*

She filled her sack with Annie's and Robbie's clothes. When she put the items from the dresser into the chest to load in the wagon, she saw the doily-wrapped hair and the carefully folded handkerchief. The sight saddened her, brought to her a sense of a presence in the room, an image of Evelyn rising in her eye, and she was suddenly tired, filled with the weight of the dead, feeling, like a strong, dragging current, the passing of all things. All gone now, but the young, Annie and J.C. *Annie, your Annie, Evelyn, now mine too, i'll take care of her, you rest now, i'll take care of everything* she smiled, moved to the window. She could see Robbie playing in the yard, dragging a long stick in the dirt as he turned in circles, turning around and around, his round head titled back to look up at the sky, reeling in spirals, while Jo-Jo yelped and tried to bite the stick.

Her eyes shifted to the yellow jasmine vine blooming next to the window where she watched a long bluish black caterpillar crawl off a large glossy leaf, avoiding the yellow trumpet-shaped flower, and pull itself across the window ledge. From where she stood, she could see its home, a silky nest of threads spiraled in the crouch of a willow oak shot through with sun, and she thought how the tent caterpillar always leaves its home to feed, refusing to eat the leaves in its own web, and how this one had passed unwaveringly by the poisonous lure of the jasmine, to make its sure way to the apple tree in the corner of the yard.

EPILOGUE

. . . and what you show me, mother, is a haunted land-scape, a place where even the sky is unreliable, a moon the color of clotted cream, stars cold as pearls. I walk through frosty moonlight, palpable as gauze against my skin, moving aside silver-webbed foliage, white moles and snowy foxes scampering from beneath my feet, while overhead immaculate ivory night birds float every which way, forward, backward, sideways. I'm surrounded by luminous forms that slip in and out of the milky mist, evaporating and materializing again and again, like dou-ble-faced wavery visions in a frosted mirror, and my ears are filled with whispers, echoes, bursts of pure maniacal laughter. Everything here, it seems, is flowing inward toward some common source, and I know that in such a place, secrets curl like thin white worms in the hearts of pale flowers and refuse to lie quietly for long.